# The Heart Is Witness

# The Heart Is Witness

*Stories From the Life of a Colombian Woman*

PENNY VILLEGAS

Copyright © Penny Villegas.

All rights reserved. No part of this book may be reproduced in any form or by any electronic or mechanical means, including information storage and retrieval systems, without permission in writing from the publisher, except by reviewers, who may quote brief passages in a review.

ISBN: 978-1-64826-514-3 (Paperback Edition)
ISBN: 978-1-64826-515-0 (Hardcover Edition)
ISBN: 978-1-64826-513-6 (E-book Edition)

Some characters and events in this book are fictitious. Any similarity to real persons, living or dead, is coincidental and not intended by the author.

**Book Ordering Information**

Phone Number: 347-901-4929 or 347-901-4920
Email: info@globalsummithouse.com
Global Summit House
www.globalsummithouse.com

Printed in the United States of America

# ACKNOWLEDGMENTS

"The Villa" appeared in <u>Revista/Review Interamericana</u> from the Universidad Interamericana de Puerto Rico in 1987.

"Pecoralia" was published in <u>The Fiddlehead: Atlantic Canada's International Literary Journal</u> from the University of New Brunswick in 1990.

"Matrimonio" appeared in <u>The Orlando Group: A Collection of Writings and Art</u> in 2000.

"Services" won an award in the Florida Writers Contest in 2001.

# The Heart Is Witness:
# A Colombian Woman's Life

By Penny Villegas

# CHARACTERS

The Bernal family from Manizales: Luisa, Maruja, Ines, Sola, Jose

The Gomez family from Medellin: Armando (El Mago), Pablo, Teresa, one of two Theresas

Chapter 1: **Jesus Saw It Happen.** The story begins in Medellín in the Gomez house as Teresa, known ever after as Teresa-who-died-so-easily, dies in childbirth. Her new-born daughter, named Teresa after her mother, is carried on the back of an Indian porter across the Andes to Manizales while her father, Jose Bernal, and older sister, Adiela go on horseback to the grandparents' house.

Chapter 2: **Orphans of Mother Only.** The two little girls are raised by the sisters of their dead mother and her parents at the family home in Manizales. Papa Jose Bernal, grandfather, and Mama Luisa and her grief, make lasting impressions on the little girls. While in Medellin, their father, Armando, comes more and more often to visit his daughters and thus comes to know and love aunt Luisa; they marry, move back to Medellín, a new house, a new nanny and a new life.

Chapter 3: **The Snake in the Garden.** Luisa is the storyteller. Her servant, the nanny, is her confidante and her life is almost perfect. She loves her husband, but she hates his fascination with gold mining. He is called *mago*, the magician, as his fame and wealth spread.

Chapter 4: **Some Advance and Some Fall Down.** We meet a new character: Faustino, a Maestro de obra. He has worked with Armando for most of his life and he has learned all all the expertise of his *patron*. His knowledge cannot help him when he falls. Armando helps and his son.

Chapter 5: **How the Virgin Came to the Plaza Zea.** Luisa's sisters and brother carry the *Virgen del Rosario,* Mama Teresa's companion in grief, to Medellín when the man they loved, called *Mago,* dies unexpectedly. Luisa retreats into her grief, leaving her children in the hands of the older daughter, Teresa.

Chapter 6: **Everyone Came Home**. Flashbacks into the life of Mama Luisa and her grief. Teresa struggles with rebellious teenagers and flea-bitten dogs. Time passes, and the oldest son miraculously graduates and goes to the United States on a trip. Nine years later, he returns with a university degree and an American wife. Luisa suddenly finds her life and her house full of people. The same woman who helped her raise her children comes with her daughter to help again.

Chapter 7: **The Nuns of the House.** Adiela, the oldest sister, recalls her years in the cloister as she takes a bus to the Social Security Hospital. Released from the confines of the cloister, she travels all over town. Flashback into how the young girls at the beginning of the story become nuns. Luisa recalls their childhood and rails at the convents and the pope who let the nuns out.

Chapter 8: **Luisa Comes Back.** Flashback to Luisa's married life and to the death of her husband. The youngest son recalls his father. Luisa returns from her years of sorrow.

Chapter 9: **Everyone Came Home**: Sisters and cousins appear. Problems with the youngest daughter and Teresa's opinion from the convent is needed. The newlyweds come home.

Chapter 10: **The House is Full of Happiness.** Armando returns to the villa, the palm trees sway in welcome, and he brings his wife, the gringa. Soon the house is filled with smiles and happiness as Ines and Teresa come to help with the babies. Luisa is delighted.

Chapter 11: **Naming the Names.** Suddenly Luisa is alone again in her big house. For many good reasons, Armando his wife, Penny and all the grandchildren leave. Luisa paces the halls with the old dog and calls out the names of the people she loves.

Chapter 12: **The Villa**. Family comes to visit Luisa and finds the old house that was built for Luisa, and her family is falling down. The family decides to move Luisa to another house, though she rebels and calls her old servant to help her.

Chapter 13: **The Second Floor.** The family moves into a new property. Teresa is returned from the convent to help Luisa. She lives on the second floor, and one night she hears a war in the streets.

Chapter 14: **Turnabout.** The world is turned upside down. Luisa has only one word to her vocabulary. Teresa turns her broom to a new use.

xi

**Chapter 15: Years Do Not Come Alone**. The American wife returns to the house. Luisa is in a wheelchair and Teresa lives in another world. Still, they pray together and the birds come to sing there in the patio.

**Glossary**

**The Years Do Not Come Alone**

# TABLE OF CONTENTS

Acknowledgments ................................................................. v
Characters ........................................................................... ix

Chapter 1:   Jesus Saw It Happen ........................................... 1
Chapter 2:   Orphans of Mother Only .................................. 17
Chapter 3:   The Snake in the Garden ................................. 27
Chapter 4:   Some Advance and Some Fall Down ............... 39
Chapter 5:   How the Virgin Maria Came to the Plaza Zea ... 45
Chapter 6:   Called to Holiness ........................................... 55
Chapter 7:   The Years Do Not Come Alone ...................... 62
Chapter 8:   Luisa Is Called Back ........................................ 70
Chapter 9:   Out of a Dark Place ........................................ 79
Chapter 10:  The Family Is Complete .................................. 85
Chapter 11:  The Sisters ........................................................ 95
Chapter 12:  What's in a Name? ......................................... 103
Chapter 13:  Calling Their Names ..................................... 112
Chapter 14:  The Villa ........................................................ 117
Chapter 15:  Turnabout ..................................................... 126
Chapter 16:  The Second Floor .......................................... 132
Chapter 17:  The Years Do Not Come Alone .................... 138

**Short Stories**

Story 1: Ines Seeks her Mother ........................................ 153
Story 2: On The Street ..................................................... 158
Story 3: Don Samuel and His Science ............................. 164
Story 4: La Pecoralia ........................................................ 172

| | | |
|---|---|---|
| Story 5: | Services | 180 |
| Story 6: | A New Order | 183 |
| Story 7: | Secrets | 194 |
| Story 8: | The Specialists | 205 |
| Story 9: | Matrimonio | 216 |

Glossary .................................................................................. 223

# CHAPTER 1

## Jesus Saw It Happen

### Medellín Colombia 1980

An old woman leans out the balcony of the large old house overlooking the Plaza Zea. She spends much time there in the window, looking out at the world and talking to herself, waiting for the people in her life to come home. In its time the Plaza Zea was clean and stately with a fountain and swept sidewalks. It had flower gardens and thick grass and sixteen royal palms along the curve of the avenue. Her husband, *Don* Armando, had planted them sixty years earlier. Could it be so long? Yes, sixty years and despite everything they haven't changed. There they are, stately and graceful, and there she is too. She leans far over the railing to search the crowds below. Finally, her face eases as she spies the short dark woman clutching a plastic bag to her chest, elbowing those who crowd her. This is Cornelia. Sixty years earlier, it was Cornelia who stood on the balcony waiting impatiently for Luisa. Now both raise a hand and smile.

Luisa, the old woman turning away from the balcony, walks through all the bedrooms and the little family sala, to unlock the door for Cornelia. Luisa's name has as many forms as she has had roles in her life: *Luisita*, the second of five sisters; Luisa, the young woman who had won the love of Armando and raised his daughters; Bisa, the childish name given her by the two little girls she raised before she raised four children of her own; *Doña* Luisa to Cornelia. Sixty years earlier, it was Cornelia who rushed to open the door, that same door, that same Cornelia who now comes thumping up the stairs, then a raw young girl brought from the *pueblo* by Armando to carry his girls as they said in those days. That was to say that she would play with the children, carry them around on her hip, fetch things and follow the lady mother's instructions. That mother was not Luisa but her sister, Teresa-who-died-so easily. Cornelia, then only twelve, had been handed over by her father to *Don* Armando to be fed and cared for. As an old woman Cornelia has the same qualities she had then; she is good natured and honest, she can read a few words and gripping a pencil, sign her name.

There were smiles on that first meeting followed by consternation as Cornelia, in her excitement, jumped up and down and squealed, calling attention to herself. Caught again. She would never learn to stay behind the scenes. Bubbling with pride and childish energy, she jumped forward to announce herself as the nanny. She squeezed a little girl in each arm and they squealed in delight. Luisa put her hands on her hips, grimaced and scolded, "No Cornelia, *por Dios*! You're just a child yourself!" Years later Cornelia's daughter Regina and then her granddaughter Esmeralda Ana would come into this same house to talk too much and to stand boldly in the balcony just as Cornelia had.

So many decades earlier when the two women first met, Luisa came as the bride, though with two little girls already, while Cornelia came to carry those same little girls and serve Luisa.

So many years since that first meeting! Luisa, hurrying to open the door, nods to the Sacred Heart of Jesus as she passes through the room. A life-sized painting with large pale hands that beat, yes, she has seen them moving, pendulums signaling the heart, the heart, the heart, the same heart that witnessed the birth of little Teresa and the death of her mother Teresa sixty years earlier. Luisa nods and continues to the door. She turns the three brass locks and swinging open the door, sees Cornelia. Though fifteen years younger, she looks as old as Luisa herself. She clutches a package wrapped in brown paper and tied carefully with twine. They turn together toward the kitchen, talking about the hot sun of the winter season and the curse of the crowds in the city, the unbelievable price of yucca, and again, for the thousandth time, the dangers of an open door in such a world.

The world was different when Luisa first came to live in the house, came expectantly up the stairs and found both wings of the door standing open while her new husband Armando, arms crossed, hugging himself with delight, watched Luisa's response to the house he had fixed for her. Cornelia had hopped squealing on one foot and then the other. She clapped and wriggled in anticipation of a new life, a grand and happy life with *Doña* Luisa and the little girls in this house totally remodeled and refurnished expressly for the lady and *Don* Armando's new family where she Cornelia would be official nanny.

The house was rescued from mourning and grief. It was the house where Teresa, first wife of Armando, oldest sister of Luisa, mother of the child Teresa, had died. When he decided to remarry, Armando determined to rebuild the house, adding sunny colors on the walls, lace curtains from Belgian, a marble table from Italy; it would be a grand new house for his new wife, his new life. From that old house of sorrow only the painting of the Sacred Heart and the dining room set, hand carved in Brazilian mahogany, remain. Only those material witnesses to that day when the midwife had come for a birth and stayed for a funeral. Cornelia too had been there, a big girl holding the frantically weeping three-year-old Adiela, while the midwife held the newborn and drenched her soft pink blanket with her tears. So many tears. After that terrible day when *Doña* Teresa was buried and the little girls taken to Manizales to be with the grandparents there, Cornelia was sent back to her mother and father in the pueblo, back to being one too many mouths in the house, hungry in a town so small and forsaken that bony cows grazed in the dusty park and only the *plaza principal* had rough stone paving. Cornelia had told Luisa a dozen times about those terrible years, that terrible day.

* * *

"Stop, for God's sake, Cornelia," Don Armando had hissed at the stocky girl clutching his daughter. But what did men know? If he had known at that moment how the day would end, he would have urged her to weep, he would have joined her as he did later, after the doctor left and he was there alone with babies and servants, a widower. Yes, a widower, the one he loved, his beautiful Teresa dead. But really no one can tell how things will turn out, so no one blamed him, not then or ever.

Both whimpered, the child Adiela in the arms of her nanny, just a child herself, Cornelia. Both shrank from the man. He was frightening, his face running sweat and dark with repressed fear and anger. He motioned them out, out of the room, furiously! God keep him from these hysterical women! And where were her sisters? Ines, Sofia, Maruja, Luisa? They should have come. Now the birth was upon them; he was alone in a house of women!

There lay his wife, Teresa, pale and tearful. All the life in her seemed centered in the huge, visibly quaking belly she clutched. Why was he here in the middle of this woman's business? Where were her sisters? Where was the nurse-midwife he was paying? Yes, he had called a medical doctor too because he was rich enough and educated enough to have both, but still he was a man alone with all these tears.

The nurse who would take care of the new mother, stewing fat hens for the rich yellow broth every new mother needed, the nurse would cook special treats to coax her appetite and swell her milk and bring the baby to nurse in the middle of the night. The nurse, she who had all the mysteries in her large breasts and ten fingers with which she entered all those secret women's places, she was in the kitchen fixing herself a cup of tea. She held the mysteries of her trade; she smelled of herbs and milk and soap. She was both nurse and midwife and had delivered dozens, oh hundreds, of babies by herself. But in some houses, in these modern days, they also called a man in, a *doctor*. She clucked, carrying her cup of tea back into the room.

Suddenly there was an urgent rapping at the door. *Don* Armando sprang to open the double doors to the calm slight grey man who stood with his small leather satchel. He was used to such profuse welcomes by husbands and kept his cool demeanor, nodding graciously. He followed, repeating the soothing litany, "Calm yourself, *Don* Armando, calm yourself and leave everything to me!" Even as he shook hands and smiled, the doctor, for he was a good doctor, the best in the city, was listening to the women's voices in the other room. Armando knocked gently on the bedroom door and waited hesitantly for the midwife to call them in. The two men stepped into the darkened room. Without a pause they walked to the bed; the husband took one of the laboring woman's hands, while the doctor took the other. His professional eye studied her face, crumpled now with tears to see him, while his hand traveled over the globe of her belly. Then, a moment later, catching Don Armando's eye and patting the woman's hand he turned and the two men walked out of the room.

"Everything is as it should be. Relax yourself." He took off his jacket and handed it to the other man. After rolling up his sleeves carefully, methodically folding in the starched cuffs, he began to wash his hands in the sink there in the patio. The two men stood there, one clutching the jacket and calling for a clean towel, the other soaping his fingers, hands and arms dripping. In the distance they could hear the maid Cornelia and the nurse chattering, while the child Adiela whimpered.

"Cornelia!" *Don* Armando bellowed, ignoring the doctor's half smile. Then in a softer voice, "A clean towel for the doctor!" Cornelia came in, her hands outstretched with a folded towel while a little girl, her face tear streaked, her black hair in sweat curls around her face, clung to the big girl's apron. They all stood, the two men, the child and Cornelia, and they listened for a moment to the voices, punctuated with yelps of prayer and stifled sobs from the bedroom. All the outside noises of the world, horses' hooves on the street, birds, voices were gone. The men stood deliberately, an island of manly strength in an ocean of female emotion.

Now, the two men walked solemnly back to the *sala*, the formal parlor where the doctor's good grey suit jacket would be hung on the back of one of the chairs. *Don* Armando couldn't help noticing that it was good British wool as soft as the baby's sweaters the blasted nurse was wringing in her hands instead of helping!

"What are these tears, *Doña Teresa*? We've been through this before. Just relax and soon we'll have a new baby. Perhaps the little man to complete your family."

The doctor brought a calm understanding that all was well; all was as it should be. The midwife wiped the pregnant woman's brow and retreated stiffly to the corner to watch them. Cornelia wept and squeezed the child who, panting and hiccupping her distress, stretched her arms out to her mother. Her father's voice interrupted her.

"Cornelia." The father's voice was cold and even in response to the servant's outbursts. "Control yourself, you're frightening Adielita," and he held out his arms to the child.

Cornelia, sobbing, exploded out the side door as the child settled in her father's arms. The bedroom, a large room with two man-sized windows, shuttered now against the day's light that was thought to be too strong for the new baby, would stay shuttered against the night air. It had been six hours since the nurse and the pregnant woman had gone into the darkened familiar space overseen by the large painting of the Sacred Heart of Jesus, six hours since Teresa took to the marriage bed spread first with oil cloth and then with soft flannel sheets, six hours since Cornelia had first called the little girl away to go for a walk to the park, to play outside, to nap.

Now the father wanted the distraction of the child and he called to her, "Come, Adiela, come keep *Papá* company. Come help me read these books." With relief he slipped into the next room. There, in his office, he lifted his daughter onto his lap and picked up a shiny magazine, a *National Geographic* which he, a world traveler, subscribed to at great expense. Someone in the post office had been stealing them, but he went to the post office and made a complaint, a COMPLAINT! He had reported the scene in detail to his family, and his eyes surveyed the table for the calm and the admiration that reigned there. Sure enough, it was made right, and the lost copy appeared, minus its brown mailing wrapper and some rag-eared but a sign of what might be done if a person wanted it so. It was not for nothing that he was called by many in the valley, *mago*, a magician, a man who could do anything. The thought comforted him as he opened the slick pages and settled the fidgety three year on his knee.

"I want my *Mamá!*" Her voice started as a whimper but quickly escalated to a squall, and Cornelia came running in. She had been standing in the room between where the labor proceeded and where the father and child were, moving from one closed door to the other.

"Come, *mi amor,*" she snatched up the wailing child who screamed and stretched toward the closed door behind which her mother wrestled with another life.

"Take her out! Cornelia! Out, out, out! It's too frightening for her. She doesn't understand!"

He was almost bowled over by her lunge out of the room. Cornelia's square muscular body was packed into a clean white uniform, but her broad feet were bare. The disheveled weeping child was flung over her shoulder like a bag of grain. If *Doña* Teresa had been well, it would have been different. She would have supervised Cornelia's combing of her daughter's hair and made sure the servant slipped on her own canvas shoes and tied the laces in bow knots and then put the patent leather shoes with little lace topped socks turned just so on the child. Then and only then would the lady and mother have blessed them as the two sallied forth to parade in the Plaza Zea. Today they were fleeing from chaos.

The child, sensing her father's nerves, stretched to go back into his arms, but he refused. "No, no, take her. Here!" He scooped a handful of change from his pocket, "take her for a soda, for ice cream. But remember, no candy!"

When the door to the street slammed, and voices began to hum inside the bedroom, Armando tried to bury himself in his books. He clutched his head, read the same page over and over; he paced the room. He leaped up at a knock at the door, answering it before the echoes in the hallway died. The messenger boy from his business, a skinny boy with clips on his pants' cuffs, had been sent with letters to sign.

He glanced at the papers, scrawled his signature and turned to the boy. "No, no, of course not. *Imposible*! I can't possibly come in this afternoon...." Briefly he might have thought of the peace in the office with contracts and generators and electrical wires, with the work of taking light to the little towns perched on the sides of the Andes. "No, no, no. I can't. I'm alone here. My sisters-in-law aren't coming today. They say they can't make it: landslides on the road! Still, my own sister will arrive this afternoon. Elisa, the oldest. Well, of course she will be a big help to me."

The baby's cry, that particular cry of a new baby, made him turn away from the door, leaving the boy to return to the office with the signatures and the message of a new baby's cry. Armando did not hear the boy's call of congratulations as he stood at the door of the bedroom, smiling. See, he thought to himself. All was well. All would be well. He bent forward eagerly, eavesdropping for good news. Looking down at the floor, he heard the soothing noises the doctor and the nurse were making.

"It's a baby girl, Mother, you have another little woman and she is beautiful. See her...! Don't cry now, it's all over, and look, here's your baby."

He could hear the nurse shushing the baby while the doctor soothed the now silent mother. He waited for the moment when everything would be back to normal, when his house would be his house again. After what seemed like a long time, the door opened. He stepped away from it as the doctor headed toward the sink to wash up.

"Well? Well, Doctor? How was it? Teresa, how is she? And the baby? Is everything...?"

"Of course, man. An easy birth. No problem whatsoever. The baby, a girl, is small. Perhaps a week early but I guess not as early as we had feared. Oh well, women often get their dates mixed up!"

The two men exchanged smiles of understanding and marched down the hallway to the sink in the patio. The sun was setting, the evening stars beginning to appear. There was a scrambling at the street door. Cornelia was returning with Adiela.

"*Gracias a Dios. Gracias!*" Armando breathed as he heard the child running up the stairs calling him.

"Come here, little sister," he scooped her up as she came running into his arms.

"Yes? Little sister? Is my new baby here?"

"Yes, you have a new baby sister."

"Oh Corna!" She scrambled down to run to her nanny who was just entering the door, "I have a new baby sister. Let's go see her.... *Sí, sí, sí!* Can we see her, *Papá*?"

All eyes turned to the doctor who took his time answering. He accepted the towel held out by *Don* Armando. He took it and dried each finger and rubbed at the nails and then up his forearms. As he rolled his shirt sleeve down, he glanced slyly at the little girl.

"Well, *Señorita*. First come here and say hello to me. Then we'll send Corna to ask Nurse if your *Mamá* is ready for visitors."

Cornelia pushed the little girl toward the doctor who bent over, his hands on his knees. Armando stepped in and motioned her forward. The child extended her right hand while she slipped her left around her father's knee. Her head ducked shyly and her voice was a whisper.

"What's that?" He teased her. "I can't hear! You were louder a while ago," he brushed her hair back from her face.

Adiela smiled shyly, looking up through the dark curls in her eyes, while the two men coaxed her.

"The lady mother is sleeping but we can go in to see the baby if we're quiet," Cornelia announced softly.

The child ran to Cornelia who picked her up, and hushing her ran down the hallway. The two men were shaking hands. The doctor picked up his bag. *Don* Armando thanked, thanked him as he said, a thousand times. He felt home settling in around him as the baby made soft whimpering noises and the nurse and Corna murmured, suddenly warm comfortable sounds.

"Good night, Doctor. And thank you again." He called down the stairs after the retreating figure.

He entered the room. He glanced at his new daughter, a swaddled worm whose red face twisted and turned from side to side. Adiela tugged at his knees; she clambered into his arms and he bounced her. Teresa began to stir.

"Hello, little mother." His voice was tender. "Look what we have here." He motioned with his head and the woman carried the tiny baby to the bed.

"Here, *Doña* Teresa." The midwife's voice was loud and confident; she was coming into her own. Nudging the mother, she laid the little pink bundle on her breast, "Here's your new little woman. And she's hungry! Let's sit up a little so she can have her first milk."

"*Doctor! Doctor! Doctor*, help me!"

The baby was squirming, lips searching. The midwife looked at *Don* Armando. He was perplexed and thrust Adiela out of his arms so he could bend over into the range of his wife's eyes.

"What are you saying Teresa? The doctor is gone. Here is your new daughter and Adiela too! Two daughters."

"Call him, Armando. Don't let him go. I'm dying."

"*Imposible!*" He blustered and clenched his hands. He looked at the midwife, at Cornelia, at the shuttered windows, at the Sacred Heart of Jesus tapping with pale fingers his beating heart.

Teresa lay back moaning, tears glistening on her face.

"You better call him, *Don* Armando," the midwife ventured. "It's better, even if it's for nothing." She felt a sudden uneasiness.

"Oh please, *Don* Armando." Cornelia began to blubber again.

He pivoted and spilling prayers like lava, he flung open the door to the street and thundered down the stairs. He began running after the figure of the doctor he could see at some distance. Shouting, he ran until he finally caught up with him.

"Please. Excuse me, Doctor." Panting from exertion and fear, "Please. She says she's dying. Could it be?"

The doctor's face clouded. He turned his horse's head and with the new father running at his stirrup, returned to the house. The two men rushed up the stairs through the open doors to a din of voices. The new baby bawled, the mother moaned softly. The maid sniffled and Adiela wailed.

"Here he is! Oh thanks to God, here he is!" The midwife breathed a prayer.

The doctor, his eyes riveted on the woman in the bed, waved everyone out of the room. In five minutes he called them all back in. Teresa was pale but quiet. In they came, Cornelia stony faced, Adiela tear streaked, the midwife tense, eyes darting, *Don* Armando pale and still.

The doctor speaks, She's fine. She's tired, that's all. Nothing that a good night's rest won't take care of. But look, my lady! Here are all these people who love you and want to take care of you." He went back out the door and pulled down his mouth at the other man in the room. They walked out together. "Nerves. She's a very nervous lady, but everything is normal."

Armando walked down the stairs with the doctor. Thanking him and apologizing, he walked to the corner with his hand on the doctor's stirrup, and then, like a sleepwalker he returned up the stairs and into his house.

"Teresita," he put his hand to the forehead of his wife. "My dear Teresita. You're tired out. It's been hard on you. Rest now, and we will take care of the little ones..."

"Bring me my babies."

The nurse brought the whimpering new bundle. Adiela wriggled out of Cornelia's arms and threw herself on her mother's bed. The father sighed at the sweet picture.

Armando went with the midwife and Cornelia to the kitchen where he went over the doctor's orders. They nodded eagerly, yes, of course, they would do everything. Adiela's cries alerted them.

Cornelia ran into the room where Adiela sobbed, her face hidden in the blankets. After only a glance, Cornelia snatched up the child and ran to the kitchen, "It's as she said! It happened just as she said."

Armando was again running down the street calling the doctor's name.

"She's gone." He clutched the stirrup, his voice only a whisper. "She slipped away. How can it be?"

The doctor turned the horse's head for the second time that night.

"What are you talking about?" He was tired and ready now to go home. "She just said goodbye and she's gone."

They were still crying hours later when his brothers arrived, bringing Elisa, his oldest sister who came to help him with the new baby and found herself preparing for the wake. The sound of their *llanto,* weeping that is voiced and public, their lament was so loud that they did not hear the arrival of the visitors. Passers by crossed themselves and exchanged looks of pity. The two brothers and the sister who had spent the day on horseback to come for the birth, sat frozen at the unmistakable sound. They exchanged uneasy glances until Enrique, the brother, leaped off his horse and pounded furiously on the door.

Listening carefully, the other brother swung down from the horse to help his sister down, when from among the other sounds, they heard the noise of the baby. Ah, all smiled, a new baby, and strong from the sound of its cries! They were still smiling when Armando thundered down the stairs and out the door. Seeing his family, he emptied all his confusion and sorrow.

"What," they kept asking, all at once, "killed her? How could anyone die so easily?"

"I don't understand it," he kept repeating. "I didn't know anyone could die so easily. She said she was going and no matter what the doctor said, she did."

When they stumbled up the stairs, stopping at each step to groan a prayer, they found the double doors standing open; Adiela ran from the doorway to her dead mother's side. She stood in silent dark confusion. The midwife and Corna stood sentinels, red faced from crying, at each side of the bed. These two had bathed and dressed *Doña* Teresa, combed her hair and settled her hands on her breast, in exactly the same attitude as the painting over the bed. Her hands pointed to her heart, the heart, yes, just so, approved the Sacred Heart of Jesus.

"Oh," Armando, threw his grief at them. "How could it be? She died so easily! She said she was going and she did. Just like that she slipped away."

Elisa, the sister who came to help with the new baby, wandered in confusion in the room, empty but for a corpse, incomplete with an empty crib, frightening with silence and the votive candle flickering on the painting and the crucifix. She wished for the company of the child or even the servants. They were in the kitchen. She prayed that her brothers would return soon. They had gone to the *Central* where they would place the telephone call to Manizales. They would sit and wait in the large busy building in Medellín while an operator called the *Central* in Manizales. Then a messenger would race across the city to pound on the large heavy doors of the big house fourth from the Cathedral. Someone from the family would come. Then, after all that waiting, after rehearsing the words, Armando would tell that other person. Oh, the pain, he kept repeating, the pain, the pain. Facing the impatient operator, he decided it should be Luisa to hear the bad news. Yes, Luisa was the one. Unthinkable the mother, and the old man's health was delicate. He sat with his brothers on the long, crowded benches until his name was called. After almost an hour, he heard Luisa's voice on the telephone, Luisa's voice expecting happy news of the child, heard the sad and impossible news that her oldest sister was gone. Slipped away, just like that she slipped away. Oh, the pain, *Qué dolor*! Armando intoned as he rode with his brothers back through the streets of the city, stopping briefly at the priest's house.

They all stood helplessly around the bed. They prayed and the priest came and prayed and the candles by the Sacred Heart flickered and the crucifix too stood watch in the dim room, still closed off from the day to protect the eyes of the newborn. Then Teresa the mother was carried off to the church for a day and then to the cemetery to be buried and when they returned from the cemetery with its rows and towers of dead, with flowers and friends, then the shutters were thrown open and light came into the room. The priest baptized the new baby who wore the delicate white dress and cap her mother had readied for her. And, although the sun shone and there was a healthy new baby and a little girl, they were not turned from their grief.

In only one day it was decided. Though his family was nearer and his brothers and sister were at his side, Armando decided to take the two little girls to live in Manizales.

"You're going to Manizales to live in a very big house with the aunts and *Papa* Jose and *Mama* Teresa." This name, the name of the dead mother, the name the priest had pronounced over the new baby, the name of the grandmother who waited in that faraway city brought a storm of tears to the little girl. "It's your grandmother! Grandmother Teresa! Remember?" Then he shoved her toward Cornelia while Elisa received the baby from the arms of the midwife. Elisa smiled, a flicker as brief as the baby's smile, and they went down the stairs to the horses and mules that waited. Cornelia blubbered and choked as she helped to carry the trunks full of clothes for the two little girls who were leaving their home.

Enrique and Manuel paced back and forth smoking furiously, uncomfortable with their brother's tragedy. Their brother Armando, he who had done everything, who had studied engineering when no one thought he could, had traveled and made money, had married a rich girl from Manizales, he who was called *mago* for his magical touch, seemed a broken man. They watched for a few minutes as their sister Elisa was seated sidesaddle on the mule, as Armando mounted the large grey horse and took Adiela in front of him. The *arriero*, he whose mules carried the trunks, checked all the ropes and knots, doubled checked the *silleta*. The *arriero* was a simple man, he knew how to pack and carry anything; it was his business--but a newborn! An orphan! The woman who clung nervously to the saddle of the mule was not able to hold both herself and a baby. So he rigged up a little wire cage on the *silleta*, the board frame that stretched from the top of the porter's head and extended the length of his back. On this he had lashed many things, china dishes from France, cabbages from Sonson, books bound in leather, but never before a newborn baby girl. It was the same cage for all. Yes, it was a cage but it would keep her safe. It was the best thing he could think of in these sad circumstances, he kept repeating. The porter kept his back at this precise angle, a bow of reverence, as he began to walk and his steady pace eventually silenced the baby's cries. Enrique and Manuel shouted blessings to the small group and rode gratefully away in the opposite direction towards their home.

The *arriero* moved to the front with *Don* Armando. Then came the porter carrying the *silleta*. His bare feet were splayed and roughly calloused. He was as surefooted and almost as fast as a mule. What a picture: the pale pink blanket, the tiny soft face of the newborn on the back of this sooty ragged man. Occasionally the baby startled, screaming, face and body contorted; the porter continued, stolid and silent. The aunt, clinging fearfully to her saddle, kept her eyes on the baby. Behind her, two donkeys with trunks followed. There was nothing anyone could do.

All the while, Cornelia waved from the window on the second floor and called out, "*Adiós, mi amor!*" The sight of the horses and mules stomping and turning to go with the little girl she had carried every day of her young life, brought a new outburst from Cornelia and an echo from little Adiela on her father's saddle. Armando frowned and kicked the horse forward with a great leap. "*Vamos!*"

It was a long journey. In an hour the bricks gave way to a gravel road and then the road narrowed and began to wind up the mountain. On the one side a variegated red wall of rock and stunted plants, on the other, a drop off and the tops of trees. Don Armando kept reaching in his pocket to pull out the gold watch on its gold chain; when three hours had passed, he held up a hand and the procession stopped. Armando leaped down from the saddle and lifted the child to the ground. He helped his sister Elisa down. The porter stood rock still while the *arriero* opened the cage and Elisa lifted the baby out, changed her damp clothes, tried to tempt her with bottles prepared by the midwife. It was no good. Again, the porter stood as the crying bundle was secured to the *silleta* he carried.

They would spend the first night in La Ceja, and there, on the high lands with crisp cool air, in a *fonda*, an inn, there was a good mother, an old woman who had raised many orphans. Nodding and smiling, she took baby Teresa into her arms and told her story. "*Si, cristianos y criaturas*," both humans and creatures she had mothered. "*O pobrecita la criatura*," with this linking the baby with all of creation, and she had fixed the bottle with the magic proportion of sugar and water and cow's milk all boiled together and she warmed the little blue faced baby against her enormous breasts and coaxed her to drink. There finally, filled and flushed, she slept like a baby. The next morning when they left, the woman coaxed Elisa and Armando to smile. "If you feed the baby sorrow, she will not live."

So that day, they started, just as the baby did, with tiny hesitant sips, with many stops and starts, to live again. By the time they reached Manizales where the family waited, there had been some laughter, and whatever grief the adults carried, they carried in their hearts.

# CHAPTER 2

# Orphans of Mother Only

### Manizales, Colombia 1925

When she was an old woman with white curls and a perpetual look of patience stretched to its limit, Adiela would remember how she arrived to Manizales, to the big old house fourth from the Cathedral. How she rode on the big horse with her father and how just behind them, *Tía* Elisa came riding a mule across the mountains. She recalled clearly her new baby sister, a poor little red crying thing in a cage on an old Indian man's back. And she never forgot how she and her little sister were left, abandoned it seemed in those early days, in the big old house fourth from the Cathedral in Manizales. Those few years seemed to them many years, a whole lifetime. Her earliest memory: every morning, awake, but with her eyes still closed, she would hear the sounds of mule's hooves on the stones of the street: clop, clop, clop with the enormous shush of their loads of sugar cane dragging on the ground and men's voices calling roughly to the donkeys. Every morning at the time the church bells were calling the faithful to mass, the men called *arrieros* brought hundreds and hundreds of bamboos, their large hollow green trunks, some of them as big around as the child herself, lashed to donkeys; they pulled their cargo, feathery green leaves still attached, rustling down the main street. That was the first sound she heard. Then the bells at the cathedral. She counted them, curling back finger after finger into her palm, *seis, siete, ocho* when she was still a baby.

Then she heard the tupial, Papa José's black and yellow bird start to trill. The tupial was the third sound of the morning. That was the only one in the world, the only bird and the only grandfather to own such a bird, one that was not tamed like a parrot or a canary but wild and it lived free in the patio and stayed there out of pure love for Papa José. It swooped down to eat crumbs from his hand and to perch on his shoulder with its wicked black beak right up to his eye and he was not afraid. It swooped down over the little girls who ran squealing across the patio between the dining room and the kitchen.

After those sounds, Adiela would open her eyes to the high ceiling, down to the crucifix on the wall. Though a child she would cross herself and mumble a prayer, not saying the words though she knew them but mumbling as she heard her aunts do. Then, over to the big wardrobe with two big doors where she hid sometimes, enjoying the voices of the aunts calling her, their voices growing louder and shriller. She liked that, and giggling she would dig under the dresses and wrap herself in the skirts, waiting for the door to open and all the aunts to poke their heads inside and exclaim, "Here she is!" All frowning and laughing at the same time.

Adiela did not like it when she woke and found herself alone in the bed, alone in the high-ceilinged room. She would begin to call her aunt Ines, the one whose bed she shared, and her voice wakened her sister Teresa in the next room who also began to call. From their bedrooms, the girls competed for first attention by screaming or kicking the wall.

"*Tía* Ines! Ines, come!"

And from the next room, "Bisa!"

"Ines!" Louder.

"Bisa-eeeh!" The name with a shrill scream attached to it. Teresa was three years younger but she always had to out-do.

They could add to the urgency by calling, "Pee-pee! *Tía*, pee-pee!"

The two sisters, the aunts who had taken over the raising of the orphans of their sister Teresa-who-died-so-easily, would then attend. Running, Luisa would call for someone to fix the egg, remember, scrambled soft for the baby Teresa, and Ines would shout even louder for

Adielita's hot chocolate made with pure milk. Confusion sounded with pans being dropped and dishes broken in the kitchen in the servants' indignant rush. The other aunts might run to the little girls: Maruja and Sofia home from the *colegio* run by the nuns of *La Enseñanza* in Bogotá.

"Come, my little queen!"

"Adielita, precious angel!"

Sometimes the girls accepted the services of the other aunts, receiving their embraces and taking in secret the candy they were forbidden, and as they unwrapped it, promising seriously in baby voices *nunca, nunca, nunca*-- never to tell. Their father had always thought candy was bad for children, more than just bad, look at Teresa's teeth, her baby teeth, were full of decay. There was talk of having a special set of little dentures made for her.

"Why are her teeth so bad?" he asked, examining the sharp brown stumps.

"Who knows? Maybe it comes from your side, Armando, since even my grandmother, Mama Pepa has all her own teeth and strong too!"

Any talk of ancestors was sure to stop the conversation and Teresa breathed a sigh of relief and went back secretly to wheedle candy from one aunt or another, especially from Maruja and Sofia when they were home from the *colegio*. Despite the distance, Bogotá, which was five days on horseback, Maruja and Sofía went to *La Enseñanza* because it was the strictest convent school in the country. *Don* José had chosen it for its reputation for a good education and the strict order of the nuns who ran it.

Later, eleven years later, Adiela would join that same group of nuns and sleep on a hard cot in a narrow cell. Her cell, narrow, high whitewashed walls with a damp brick floor, held a narrow cot, a crucifix, a *prie-dieu* and her coffin. How different from the room full of furniture and mirrors and a large featherbed where she slept with her dolls and her aunt and sometimes her sister too! *Don* José, or Papa José as the little girls called him to claim their bond and to distinguish him from their own *Papá,* escorted his two youngest daughters, Sofia and Maruja, on horseback to the convent and back again for vacations. When they were at home, the little girls got even more attention as Sofia and Maruja (and Solita who already had a serious boyfriend, a word they quickly understood the importance of, a *novio)* would vie for the favor of the little girls, calling to them in adoring tones, showering toys and hand knit sweaters and charming little dresses of velvet on their glossy black heads. Of course, it had to be so.

Their father visited regularly, and on these days, Ines would snatch up Adiela and Luisa would spring on Teresa and they would carry them squirming and squealing to the large tiled bathroom where Adiela would perch on the toilet while her hair was combed and parted and brushed around *Tía's* finger until it fell in long sausage curls. Meantime, Teresa's teeth were brushed until her spit ran red. Sewing machine humming, Solita, who was a grand seamstress, finished yet another little dress, pleated and tucked and decorated with lace. Over it all, lectures on manners, emphasized with pinches and long fingered pokes. Protesting all the while, Adiela and Teresa grew into meticulous and demanding young women. Fifty years later they were both nuns and they would recall these early attentions.

Also large in her memory, Grandmother's statue of the Blessed Mother. Adiela remembered the statue of the virgin, a figure as large as she was. It lived in the bedroom of Mama Teresa, her grandmother, a stern and sorrowful old woman who had never given up her grief at her oldest son's suicide. *"Ay,"* she punctuated her every hour as she had since that tragic day, *"Qué dolór!"* With the same intensity every day as though the death had been that very hour not twelve years earlier. Not just death which was hard enough for a mother, but mortal sin! She could not erase images of him as a sweet chubby baby, her firstborn! He had grown to be a bright student, fiercely proud of his gold stars and awards. She could not forget how, on that black day when they found him dead in his room, how, when the priest came and she pushed her question on the priest, he had turned his head away from her in silence.

"To hell with *him*! And the whole church full of priests all the way to Rome!" Her husband had stormed. She wanted to agree, but she could not. She kept it all in her heart, silent witness to her pain and her anger. She lit endless candles and prayed. Whoever happened by, her daughters, the servants, her sons and now the little girls, was required to answer the *Ave María*.

"*Lleno eres de gracias....*" Yes, full of grace, she who also lost a son, Holy Mother would understand. "*El Señor es contigo.*" The Lord is with you and me. And him.

And now her oldest daughter, her namesake Teresa was also gone. She did not dwell on it, but sometimes the question with which Armando had posed the news to them: *How can a person die so easily?* Slipped into her prayers and the words joined the litany to the saints and the Holy Mother. *Ave María, lleno eres de gracia*, how can a person die so easily? *Madre de Dios. Ay*, the pain, the pain, *amen*!

There were little girls, here in her house. Whose girls were they? Sometimes she knew and sometimes she did not. Mama Teresa prayed almost continuously in a dark clotted voice and prayers mixed with cautions about the ways the girls were being raised. The girls were always quiet in that room where Mama Teresa and the virgin lived. A three-foot tall statue of *La Virgen del Rosario* with a real lace mantilla, real pearls in the rosary that dangled from her hands. The thick candles burning in front of her reflected in the blue glass eyes set into her wooden head, sweeter in their expression than those in the Italian and German and American dolls the aunts bought for the little orphans.

"I want a doll like Mama Teresa's."

Shocked silence.

"You are ruining those girls," Mama Teresa would say in a voice even more doleful than usual.

At this, everyone, aunts and servants and children would leave the room, hurrying and praying she was wrong and what else could a person do with little angels like these orphaned of mother so early in life.

As for Jose Bernal, Papa Jose, *Don* Jose, he was a busy and an important man who left early every morning to ride around the fincas he owned. He was idolized by his daughters and the little girls who saw him as a magical man in a different way from their very own *Papá* but still one to whom the ordinary rules of life did not apply. For one thing, there was the tupial that flew over them squawking shrilly if they chanced to have temper tantrums in the kitchen patio. That squawk, the outstretched wings over their heads, those long black claws stopped their mouths immediately. The little lips turned up into sweet silence and blood faded from their purple faces.

Papa José had the same effect on them, but he spent little time in the house. Even when he was at home, the house he had built was so enormous with its two floors and four patios that he could lose himself. One patio was for entertaining with a rattan settee and rocker placed among the large pots of anthuriams, black and red tongues and heart shaped leaves, and pots of pink and yellow and red hibiscus, and what every visitor would admire so, hanging baskets of orchids. Butterflies fluttered in and out of the patio. When a plant stopped flowering or got brown leaves or the girls knocked the pot over leaving chunks of terra cotta and dirt everywhere, then it was all moved to the family patio where things got repotted, fixed, where the bird cages dangled from the wall and canaries sang and messed, and where the girls could play with real tea in their china tea pots.

There was another patio where the maids could hang out the laundry and sit in the sun with a cup of hot chocolate and rest for a few minutes. The little girls chased each other down the stretches of tiled hallways, through all the patios with voices calling after them: "What is this *Señoritas*? Do young ladies run around and scream like *locas*?" This delighted the girls who would run into the nearest bedroom--no, not Papa Jose's-- that was unthinkable, or the place where the Virgin lived--but any of the others, even the servants' rooms where the girls would jump on beds and hide behind chairs or in wardrobes until someone came looking for them. The fourth patio was given over to men and horses and there were buckets and bags of feed and an old bench for the workers to sit and drink coffee sweetened with *panela*.

There were eight bedrooms in a row around the edge of the house and doors that locked them off from the outside and doors that connected them from the inside and thus many more circles for children to run in. Don Jose took over a small bedroom for himself, without any discussion or the idea that it would be forever. It happened when their first son had passed and terrible to say, by his own hand. Death was a word not said casually and suicide never. Don Jose watched his wife give herself over to mourning, and after a long time of patient watching, he took to his own bed in a small bedroom. No one ever discussed that part of the marriage. Certainly he did not. So the large bedroom was his wife's bedroom and she lived there with the Virgin and did not ask about any of her husband's arrangements.

Then there were the rooms for the five sisters, large rooms with windows that opened on to the street and doors that led from one room to another. Each room had several enormous beds, often shared by two and three sisters. And one bedroom for guests or for the son who remained, the only remaining son and the one who had not remained in the house or even in the city but who appeared on rare and unpredictable occasions and such was his life that no one, not even his father, dared to ask where he had been and what he had been doing. Finally, there was the family *sala* with comfortable furniture and the radio and the formal *sala* with beautiful bent wood rockers and carved tables and chandeliers. It was a large long airy room with heavy brocade drapes and china statues of French ballerinas and Spanish *caballeros* and it led into the dining room, which because of its daily use had a more ordinary look. The other rooms: kitchen and ironing room and the three rooms for servants were off limits except to the little girls who went wherever their feet carried them.

This was the house that Jose Soto had built, a house famous inside and out of the family and the city, a house that would later burn to the ground while the family watched and even neighbors cried, sharing their hardship. His life was not what he had thought and though Jose would not have said it so, he was lonely. Thus Arcadio, a worker, whose loyalty and intelligence Jose had seen in him when Arcadio was a barefoot and dirty faced boy, had become his confidante and companion. For years he had gone everywhere with his *patron, Don* Jose and now he also listened to his stories. His intelligent brown eyes followed his master's actions and words and moods. He lived by his side, at call at all times.

He was small and brown and ageless. Arcadio's teeth were very bad, many of them altogether gone, the others sharp brown stumps. He slept in a room in the stable so as to be close to his master and he slipped into the kitchen every day at dawn to sit on the bench and wait for his food and his orders for the day. His daily good-natured greeting gave the little girl Teresa cause for alarm. In that smile she did not see his creased brown face or sparkling black eyes; she saw only his rotten teeth. What if what everyone said was true? What if she ended up like Arcadio? This thought brought tears and squalls which someone would soothe with kisses and more sweets. Every morning Arcadio brought the special mule of Papa José, the grey one who was so intelligent that, in those later days when the old man's arthritis bothered him, the mule knelt so that José could mount. And everyday the little girls went out to the back patio to wave goodbye to Papa Jose and everyday Arcadio's broad toothless grin drew tears from Teresa.

Yes, *Don* Jose was famous and his mule was famous even in Bogotá at the convent where the hundreds of girls in long pleated skirts and long sleeved white blouses, tiny girls of five years up to young women of twenty would crowd out the wrought iron gate, blocking the sidewalk and even the street, to see the arrival of the Soto girls and their father with his intelligent mule. Everyone in Manizales and everyone in Bogotá too even if it was a large city and the capital of the republic knew their Papa José, and the girls would add quickly, their *Papá* Armando too. The girls, Adiela and Teresa, basked in the reflected light of these two large men. For themselves, their fame was that they were orphans, and a particular expression fixed their faces when anyone mentioned it.

"Are these the daughters of.?"

"Armando and Teresa-who...."

And then the girls stood, lips trembling, under the rain of pats and kisses.

"Orphans!" the word would sooner or later come out.

"Of mother only, *Gracias a Dios*!"

"Poor babies. God bless them!"

Their father came to Manizales to visit them regularly. They came to know when he was coming by the special preparations made. Teresa's brown stubs of teeth were scrubbed with gritty powder to whiten them. Special care was given to their finger nails and reminders of manners.

"And don't scream. *Señoritas* don't scream."

Black looks. Muted squeals.

"Remember who you are!"

This brought frowns that lasted until the door rattled under his knock and the little girls raced each other to the door. After a brief and silent scuffle one would triumphantly and reverentially carry his carefully brushed hat to a table.

After a few years, Armando began coming more frequently. Finally he arranged some work in the area and brought his right hand man Faustino to oversee local workers. Faustino and the machinery and several mules were boarded at the *Fonda* down by the marketplace where workers would be hired. Every evening Armando would come knocking at the big double door that opened out on the street. Dressed in his suit and tie, he would sit in the visitors' *sala* talking to Papa José or perhaps writing in careful blue script in his little book with words and drawings of the plans for his next installation. His little girls would sit, one on each knee, and tell him stories about the famous mule or the tupial. They leaned, one on each knee to study his note book with spidery blue lines that meant electricity and boxes called generators while upstairs Luisa combed her long dark hair and changed her dress. Soon everyone in the house noticed, even Mama Teresa, who never left her room, that Armando was looking at Luisa with love as well as with respect and friendship. So it was settled.

Armando rebuilt the big house in the Plaza Zea for his family, his two little girls and his new wife Luisa. The Plaza Zea was the newest and most elegant neighborhood in Medellín with a park and a convent whose doors opened out onto the plaza. With his own hands, he planted sixteen royal palms along the curve of the sidewalk to celebrate his new family and he called on the mayor to plant hibiscus and azaleas and to assign workmen to keep the Plaza clean and in order. The house was prepared, filled with ornate heavy furniture; servants were hired, Cornelia was again called away from her father's pinched house in the pueblo. As the last touch, the large painting of the Sacred Heart of Jesus was hung in its place over the marriage bed. When all was ready, Armando went to Manizales to marry Luisa. It was a small and simple ceremony, out of respect for the defunct Teresa and the despondent mother Teresa. There were two bridesmaids, Maruja and Ines, dressed simply in street clothes, and two flower girls, Adiela and Teresa, dressed like princesses. There was a priest and a few family friends; there was prayer and solemnity but little *fiesta*.

When Armando left Manizales, going first on his big grey horse, first in a long train of horses and mules, he took Luisa as his bride and his two daughters Adiela and Teresa. There were ten steamer trunks balanced on the backs of five donkeys. The Soto sisters, all of them along with their brother who had come back for the occasion and the old mother and father, wept bitterly to see Luisa leave with the little girls. None wept more intensely than Ines who waved and sobbed and choked as Adielita faded from sight. Then that big house, fourth from the cathedral, fell back into the dusty shadow of melancholy

# CHAPTER 3

## The Snake in the Garden

### Medellín Colombia 1930

Cornelia, a teenager though with the thick body of a matron, waits on the balcony of the beautiful new house. Yesterday she followed Faustino as he went through the house with his paintbrush touching up what was already perfect. She and the other servant, Elena, had mopped the floors to a high sheen. Elisa, the sister of Armando who came to make sure everything was ready for the newlyweds, dusted and worried out loud and scolded. Now they all wait. Never content with peering out the little shuttered windows, Cornelia has thrown both doors open so she can lean far over the railing and see all the way down the street. She is not supposed to be seen in the window, but her curiosity and her excitement can not be contained. She hangs over the balcony stretching her neck to see up the street where *su gente,* meaning simply people but spoken in a tone of love and possessiveness, *her people*, will come. The other servant stands in the background and clucks at her, looking to Elisa for approval, and Elisa, the quiet sister of Don Armando who is there to see that everything is in order, suggests that Cornelia should go back to the kitchen.

"*Sí, Señora,*" she mumbles. Red faced, Cornelia shuffles back to the kitchen to wash a dish, clanking many in protest, or to sweep the corner of the canaries' cages, sending clouds of tiny feathers and seeds into the air and silencing their trills. Soon however, she hears a car in the street, a car, and since Don Armando always has the latest, the newest and best, if it is a car, it can only be him. Then without thought or dignity, she charges back to the window. Well, she explains, stamping a foot, shod in honor of the special day, and twisting her red face into a child's pout, she is waiting for *Doña* Luisa, her new *patrona and* the two little girls. They are orphans, God bless them; the oldest, Adiela, Cornelia considers her own girl. Now her chin trembling, she explains how she carried her and calmed her on that awful day when Teresita was born and the mother, Teresa-who-died-so-easily, had slipped away from them all no matter what anyone did.

Finally it is a car, the car, and it stops in front of the door and Cornelia begins to jump up and down like the child she is, a moon faced fourteen year old in a starched white uniform. Punctuating her excitement with a little tremor, she points: "There they are there they are! *Mi gente!*" They, her people, are coming; they are out of the car and coming! Yes, in through the double doors at street level flung open for them, up the stairs and surely life is going to be grand, splendid, very happy, since she will be in the house of rich people eating what she wants and getting paid too and not taking food out of her little brothers' and sisters' mouths who will also be happy to share her portion and her glory. She is the official nanny for *Don* Armando and *Doña* Luisa.

The little girls swarm to Cornelia who scoops them both up at once and presses them to her bosom. She turns first one ear to Teresita and then the other to Adielita, she listens and laughs and squeezes them as she carries them around the house. Luisa walks from room to room. The light in Armando's eyes follows her as she admires the design of the carpet in the sala, the sunny patio with canaries, the painting of the Sacred Heart of Jesus. Yes, and she taps her own heart in confidence that that calm smile and radiant heart will protect them and keep them in this state of carefree exuberance.

Truly those are happy days. Luisa slips easily into her role as *Señora de casa*, house-wife of a fine new house. Not as big or as grand as the one she came from but more modern, designed by her electrical engineer husband with an outlet in every room. Aunt Elisa stays for a few days to help Luisa settle in but the little girls prefer the fat red cheeks of Cornelia (which they pinch in good natured play, much as they do the dog at the *finca)* to their aunt's lean lined face. Truthfully, even in those early days, Luisa already shies away from her husband's family.

Armando sets up an office in a building downtown and settles in to his business that brings both money and admiration. So far seeing is he that he has earned a degree by correspondence in electricity, a modern invention whose magic many of his compatriots have not seen, and now he is ready for the business of carrying electricity to the small villages that dot the sides of the mountains. Since he is first and since the fad of electricity is running like wild fire through the world and Colombia too, his business grows fast. Though he is tireless, business is so good that soon he takes a partner and a secretary. He calls his brothers and puts them on the payroll. He hires a messenger boy and buys him a shiny new bicycle, black. Everything he touches prospers. In recognition of his ability to move people and places to bright light, he is called *el mago*, the magician. It's the magic of hard work and personality and luck too. A farseeing man, Armando Gomez buys several properties in good locations. On three of them he builds houses and on two others stores and all with the help of a man named Faustino, a *maestro de obra*.

Faustino is a man who can build anything, an honest and loyal man who loves his *patron*. Faustino rides in the front seat in one of the first automobiles seen in Medellín. There at the right hand of his *patron*, Faustino rides from one site to another, where he takes charge of his own magic, that of raising a building from the ground, from air almost. And he works in the material his patron desires, bricks or *tapia*.

All the building and activity, the business and the charities were proofs of Armando Gomez's excellence as a man, all the wealth and success proof of the goodness of God. But there's always a snake in the garden and she, Luisa, saw the serpent in her perfect garden: the mines. When, early in the morning, the children still in bed, the couple sat at table, she with *café con leche* and a little white roll with guava jelly and he with strong black coffee and Kellogg's Corn Flakes, conversing and smiling, and the door thundered under a certain kind of bold hand, Luisa would choke and sputter. That knock meant a sample of ore from the countryside. Only the men from the *flota* knocked just so and at that time. The *flota* consisted of hundreds and hundreds of large busses painted the brightest colors with open sides and bench seats. Travelers packed into the benches and their bags or baskets or stalks of plantains were piled on top. This system ran the country, carrying not just passengers as any bus system would, but written letters and spoken messages, sick people and packages of all sizes from the villages to the city.

Yes, the *flota* brought letters with good news and bad, air mail letters from New York, blue with stamps and filled perhaps with greenbacks, but they also delivered canvas bags of sand, samples from the creek of some Andean village. Both were carried to the door by a special messenger from the *flota* in his *cariel*, a large shoulder bag made of leather with patent leather trim around the flap of natural cow skin. This bag was typical to the men of the mountains with its large pocket where a revolver might fit and smaller ones for money. Samples arrived regularly and after joking good naturedly with the man, after slipping him a good tip, Armando would turn back into the house, weighing the bag pensively; he would patiently untie its knots, open it and smell its earthy breath, shake some grains into his hand and study them under a magnifying glass. He had forgotten the familial breakfast conversation, and unknowing or uncaring that Luisa ranted in the kitchen; he immediately took the sample to the assayer's office to be analyzed.

If the reading was high enough, that is to say the proportion of gold to earth and rock high enough, for every sample that came from the mountains had some gold, and if the area was historically known for its gold, worked earlier by the Indians, then Armando would call his friends for an evening at cards at the country club, the club he and his friends started and staffed, and he would tell them the story. He would take the new deck from the hands of the *maitre d'* and break the stamp. Deliberately he would put the jokers aside and weigh the cards in his hand. As he shuffled and sipped from a small crystal glass of aged rum, he would tell the story, the history, the location, the weight and color of the grains of gold. Thus were the companies formed that developed the big mines.

Since he had so many businesses, and since Luisa resented any time or money spent on mining, he called on his brothers. Mining was better suited to them than the business world of offices and letters. Enrique was a jolly man, good natured and expansive. He had two daughters, whom he adored, by a woman he also loved but had never married. He didn't care and she didn't care, and if his brother's stuck up wives from Manizales thought that was reason enough not to know him or them, well, that was their way of being and not his. Enrique had a little store in a village where he and his woman, for nobody dignified her with the title of *Señora,* sold beans and rice and coffee and laundry soap; they had no ambition for money or position. He had his store, a little store but a business with income and a place in the village where he lived. He had his family and he could not leave them, as willing as he was, he would say with an embrace to his brother. Nor did the hard work of chasing after gold appeal to him.

Manuel, on the other hand, was crazy about mining. *Loco,* everyone said so.

Manuel had no money and Armando had no time; it was a perfect arrangement. Everyone trusted Armando Gomez for his honesty and his good luck. They called him *mago* and the mines were one more proof of his magic. "Look," he held out his hand, and gold, tiny grains glittered in his palm. His eyes gleamed and his voice beckoned, "Look!" It was not just for the gold, but the adventure thrilled him and his children. For these same reasons Luisa disapproved. "Don't call them mines! Call them holes to throw money in! And full of dangers too!" Over and over she would ask him what he thought would become of his family if he spent all the money on mines and then died. Or, she would pursue him, pulling at his sleeve, what if he was hurt and died up there in one of those holes? What would become of them, what! Later she would remember how often she brought that up to him, how often he laughed at her.

"Remember!" She would shake her finger, "you can say that a fool told you this would happen!"

It was Cornelia who listened to most of Luisa's rants and she too ignored her. Cornelia thought Luisa's life was perfect: Luisa had a house where she was boss, where there was always plenty of food, where there was a bed for every person in the house, even the children. Luisa was the center of her universe with children and a husband whereas she Cornelia lived in the corners of other people's houses. About once a month Cornelia took the day off to travel by *flota* to her father and mother's house in the mountains. There in the tiny house where she had grown up, she entered with shopping bags of food, some bought at the *plaza Mercado* with her wages and some pinched from *Doña* Luisa's plenty. At night, Cornelia slept on a mattress in a corner with her two sisters; during the day she sat outside in the shade of the overhang of the roof to mend her father's work shirts. There from her spot overlooking the road, she renewed acquaintance with Felix, a neighbor she had known in her childhood, now a widower with three children who found Cornelia's red cheeks and irrepressible manner charming. At least he said so gruffly. The attentions of a man were so unexpected and so new to her that she became entranced.

Soon Cornelia was spending every Saturday away from Luisa's call, and arriving later and later on Sunday, hours past the time when she was supposed to arrive to help with the breakfast and the new baby, with the two little boys as well as Adiela and Teresa. "*Desagradecida!*" Luisa would scold her openly, reminding her of how she had begged to come to work for her. Cornelia would open her mouth to protest, to defend herself, "Ah, Aah," in a tone that promised defense but ended in a giggle.

When Cornelia confessed the truth of it, expecting perhaps some admiration for her feat of finding a husband, Luisa began to look into her future. "He's an old man. He only wants a servant, someone to take care of him and his brats, and that's you. He won't treat you right. Wait and see! Then he'll die and leave you with kids and debts. Does he even own his own house? Well, get it in your name. His kids will kick you out! Listen! I can tell you about marriage." At this point Luisa would bustle around and deny that she knew this from her own experience. Her marriage was perfect. Her husband was perfect, but she always continued, "Matrimony is the hardest road in life." Then shaking her finger in the girl's face, "You, you who have everything here, want to throw it all away to get married. *Desagradecida!* Remember me! You can say that a fool told you this!"

Despite all the good advice, soon enough Cornelia left, embracing all the little ones and blubbering. Luisa gave her an extra month's salary and cautioned her to hide it where he would never find it. Several years later Cornelia again climbed the stairs and knocked at the big double doors. She had her own daughter Regina, a sturdy red-faced child of three tugging at her skirts, and her worldly goods tied up in a small parcel. She came to tell Luisa that everything had come true, just as she said. Now she was alone with this one little creature, the only thing that was her own in the world.

Luisa, in those four years had gone from one servant to another to another: some of them *dañinas* who broke plates, others were lazy, some dirty and one memorable one stole a gold brooch. Cornelia's simple flaws looked almost like virtues at that time. So she was welcomed back and for years Cornelia lived with her daughter in the little room behind the kitchen, sleeping together in the one narrow bed. Luisa offered to get another bed but Cornelia, after studying the child's worried face, said no, they would share a bed as they always had. Regina played in the patio of the laundry room. She peeked down the hallway where the other children played and ran and laughed and sometimes came running down the hallway to study her, barefoot and sturdy and self possessed in her realm of the kitchen and patio. She never went out of that space unless her mother had her by the hand. Regina would go through life saying that she had been raised in the house of rich people and that *Doña* Luisa had been a mother to her. Regina dressed in the hand-me-downs of the little girls, she played with their discarded toys, and she ate the food from their table. Through this year, Armando's angina bothered him more and more. His response was to push himself even harder. He bought more properties; he helped found a country club, the new modern one on the outskirts of the city with tennis courts and swimming pool and a gambling room. He didn't care about tennis or swimming; the old club had those activities, but he loved to gamble. In these days too, more samples of ore were delivered to his door, bags heavy with gold; he bought the mining rights, determined to bring the gold to light. Luisa didn't share any of these enthusiasms. She hated travel and clubs and gambling and most of all she hated gold mines. She prayed, she preached, she pleaded. She scolded and ranted. He would tease her, kiss her cheek trying to win a smile, buy her jewelry, and ignore her protests.

He combined his engineering with gold mining; in one trip he could do both and only report on one. When he was called to set up the electricity in a town, he would tell his wife, he would bring the papers and spread them on his desk while he planned, out loud and on the telephone with Faustino the project. At the office he directed his brother Manuel to enquire about the history and minerals of the area and if it was promising. Manuel was a man on fire for gold. He took the earliest flota to the village and with his wallet in his hand set out to find rumors of gold. If there were rumors backed by nuggets, by old Indian excavations, he wrote his report and packed his bag. He would be waiting with his hat already on his head for his brother to walk in the door of the office. The two of them would close themselves in a conspiratorial and brotherly meeting to look into the report and each other's eyes and see the prospect of gold.

When it was decided, and it was usually decided, Manuel went ahead to establish the gold search. It was his job to look for the water, to talk to the *cateos,* the hounds of gold, men, usually poor and uneducated whose only talent was for sniffing out the veins of precious metal in the mountainside and for tracking down the glitter in the creek bed. After this meeting, if the signs were promising, Manuel would call Armando. He would pay for a nice room at the best inn and wait for his brother's arrival. Heads close, they would confer most of the night and early the next morning the two of them would set up a table in the plaza. Quickly the word would be spread so that dozens of poor men would come and stand in line and take off their hats at the end of the line, at the table where *El Mago* sat writing down names with his gold fountain pen in precise blue flourishes. Most of them had never seen their name in letters nor shaken hands with a doctor, and as everyone said, a *mago* who could make amazing things happen. Manuel always stood at his right hand in these meetings, watching everyone, examining the stories and the faces of men. Armando would turn to him and with a few words- -they always agreed-- they would chose one man, someone brave and honest to carry the gold once it was found. To him they would give a large blue steel gun, a shooter they called it. Those who had been to the city to see a movie knew that gun was just like the guns in the movies; the gun was the badge. The other men, the many, were *burros*, mules to move rock, to risk fingers and arms, to dig the rivers out of their own channels and bring them where the *Mago* wanted them. He could move the river out of its bed and make rollers out of tree trunks and wheels that would turn the waters and crush the rocks. Then followed baths of the poison called cyanide, so toxic that magically the waters for many days down stream would be stricken and everything: fish and turtle and caiman, would die and float belly up and stink in the sun, and people would say, the miners are upstream.

So the mining grew and the children grew. Adiela grew to a *señorita* and after working in her father's office for a few months followed her heart into the convent, back to the place where she grew up, back to the smiling encouragement of *Madre* Juana. There was a terrible hour at the convent when the two most important people in her life met face to face. Her father and the *Madre* sat, and she in the middle felt herself being torn in two. Armando tried everything to delay her entry for just a year. For once he had no power. The minute he stepped through the massive doors, doors he helped pay for, he was powerless. While he sat at one end of a room and waited, listening to his heart pound, listening for the step of the Mother Superior, he studied the things he had admired. Order. Thick walls. Subdued sound and light. They seemed impervious to human intention. He shifted in his chair and the scraping noise echoed in the grey anteroom. A crucifix hung on the wall and a tiny holy water font shaped like a sea shell. He wished now he had used some when he entered the room, touched his fingers to it and used its blessing. Now it seemed too late.

The curtain of dark gray gauze swayed as a door somewhere opened. He heard swishing of skirts and a chair move on the floor. Then a soft voice started, and though it paused politely for his words, it never changed, no matter what he said or how he said it. He exhausted his tactics and sat empty. When she stood, almost an hour later, he looked at his watch and bitter tears sprang to his eyes. None of his weapons could stand against her. Neither temper or money or diplomacy moved the Mother Superior from her position. Adiela was hers.

Luisa gave Adiela the gold rings that had been the wedding rings of Armando and Teresa. She curled her fingers over them and the two heads met and tears fell on their hands. These would be melted down and made into one ring, the ring Adiela took when she made her vows.

Armando stayed at home this day. He heard the unnatural quiet of the women bathing and dressing. Instead the conversations and laughter, silence. They did not come to stand before him to show him their finery. He did not walk out into the hallway to joke with them. When there was a knock at the door, and he heard the voice of his best friend, Santiago, also quiet, quiet as for a wake. Armando Gomez, *el mago*, he who could do anything, was powerless.

Finally he swiveled in his chair to see them all standing in the door of his office. Santiago, his eyes serious and pained, stood with the women of Armando's life, his wife, and his two daughters. They were dressed for ceremony and they stood silently at the door waiting for him to join them. He turned away to open a book, studying it with furious intensity and blurred vision. Those four turned and with a funeral solemnity marched down the stairs and into the street. The man Armando was frozen. His little children who played around the house were not heard, his mines, his constructions were forgotten. All day he shut himself up in the room that held his samples of ore and diagrams of generators. The things he knew, predictable diagrams, manageable connections stood dumb before him. He was trying to erase from his mind the picture of Adiela, slim and elegant in her first grownup dress.

He did not see, and no one ever told him, how the families, twelve families with their young brides, entered the convent doors. They were led into the room used for gatherings where old fashioned uncomfortable furniture massed at one end and at the other nothing, only double doors under a crucifix. The door loomed large in the empty wall. Santiago, Luisa and Teresa did not hear the words or see who spoke. At some signal they all missed, Adiela left them and she did not look back. Awkwardly, in her first high heels, she crossed the room to join the other girls, none of them over sixteen. There were twelve in this class who walked out of ordinary life and into extraordinary life.

The families turned away to the street. Three walked in terrible silence, aching for the one they had left behind, toward the Plaza Zea. Santiago sighed heavily as he thought of his friend Armando. Luisa and Teresa mumbled prayers and groaned, looking right and left. Their grief was constrained by the man's presence and they left him gladly at the bottom of the stairs. When they pushed open the door, the little boys came running to catch at Luisa's skirt with their dirty hands. The girl who had been left in charge of the kitchen and the children, handed over the baby and left. All the little ones began to cry. Luisa and Teresa swallowed their grief and tried, without success to comfort the sobbing children. Mute, choking, they walked around with a lump of unspoken pain in their throats. After a while, Armando came out asking for coffee. They picked up their lives and it was a long time before Adiela's name was mentioned.

Luisa wrote a letter to send to the pueblo to call Cornelia to come back and help her. She offered to pay anything. Alone in the house, Luisa struggled. It was only a week, a black week when the children cried for everyone else and fought for all the angers that could not be expressed. It changed though, slowly and simply. Cornelia came back up the stairs with her daughter. It took Luisa a few minutes to decide, but Cornelia was already in the door, already cooing over the baby and greeting the little boys, no longer little or eager for her embraces. No matter. She bustled to the kitchen as Regina, holding on to her skirt and watching everything with big eyes, tottered behind. Before Luisa knew it, Cornelia was washing the dishes stacked there with her little one silent, but clearly experienced in keeping up with her mother, clinging to her sturdy leg.

"And *Doña* Luisa," she pauses in her bustle. She is in her element. She is with Luisa and her daughter is by her side, "everything you said came true!"

# CHAPTER 4

# Some Advance and Some Fall Down

### Medellín Colombia 1930

A farseeing man, generous and expansive with the pesos that pour in from his businesses and his mines, Armando Gomez buys many properties all over the valley of Aburá. The largest property, best in every way, he gives away to the convent that will rob him of his daughter. On others he builds houses and then store fronts, offices, and finally the country house for his family and all with the help of a man named Faustino, a *maestro de obra*.

Faustino is a man who can build anything, as he will tell you solemnly. He is a family man, an honest and loyal man, and he loves his *patron*. Faustino rides in the front seat in one of the first automobiles seen in Medellín. There at the right hand of his *patron*, Faustino rides from one site to another up into the steep hills and down into the low valleys of Aburá.

After so many weeks, months, years, call it years and tell the truth of it, it is a kind of school he has been in. For fifteen years he stood by and listened to his *patron*, observing with sharp eyes how things go. Now he knows. He could almost do it himself, the building and even the plans. He has walked over all the properties. As he paces he envisions the little *casita* up, up he gestures, higher with his head, at the end of the bus run, the casita will be made of *tapia,* but not too big. Two little patios for laundry and maybe a garden. But, and he will stop and consider the other property, close his eyes as though surveying the place, the large lot near the park must be built with adobe with special tile floors and three patios, a nice big patio to receive guests. He plans. On the day when Don Armando, the man they call *mago*, speaks the words, the very words, "a little *casita* of *tapia*," Faustino turns his face away to hide his pleasure. When Don Armando unrolls the plans drawn just as Faustino imagined them, he almost whoops with pleasure.

This is his life and his school. He is the right hand of Don Armando Gomez, *el mago*. He, Faustino, is a *maestro*, who can take charge of any project, can raise the building whether in adobe bricks or *tapia*, can finish it inside and out. From the time he was five years old he worked alongside his father, doing the work he could as a child. At first when he was five or so, he carried the lunch of rice and cold coffee, then after a few years, he fetched the tools or carried one adobe at a time. That was how he learned, passing the trowel to his father, studying the art of the cement mixed just so, the plumb bob, the level with its yellow eye had to center.

But though he knew about this hard work, *burro*'s work that broke a man's back and his spirit too sometimes, he didn't continue it all his life. No, he was advanced, advanced by Don Armando till he became a *maestro de obra* which is to a say an artist almost. He didn't start there, but he arrived there! Now he wears shoes every day and a long-sleeved white shirt ironed by his wife that he changes every day not every week.

Before he wore white shirts every day, before he rode in the front seat of the car, before he had his own horse to ride, before he had an old donkey to haul the red clay, then he did *tapia* like his father before him. Before all those marvels, marvels that no one could have imagined, he was a poor boy like so many others. In those far off days Faustino, from the time he was very small, four or five, had helped his father pick up the horse manure that was necessary to *tapia*. Yes, two simple materials were necessary to raise a wall of *tapia*: horse manure with its strings of grass needed to bond the red clay that was part of every mountain. These were his early life: dragging a burlap bag through the fields gathering horse manure and then, struggling to lift the bag and dump it into the cart. Digging the red clay out of the side of the mountain, lifting it into the cart. Through work, he learned to be a man as his father was a man. Not like most of the lazy no-goods he met these days.

His early life with so much work so early made him a hard master, though not to his only son or his wife. With his wife and son and of course with his patron he wore a serious and attentive look and spoke with a soft voice. But once he got out of the front seat of the Ford and waved good-bye to Don Armando, he was a different man. Faced with the men who came looking to work, he saw only faults. The man who leaned against the wall to smoke a cigarette between loads of mud was useless, the adobe bricks that did not align perfectly were signs of sloth and worse. "There," he would say, pointing at the offending lump, "you are. That is a picture of you." Frowning, grimacing, stomping the dirt under his feet, he would repeat, "*Ahí está pintado.*" Most apologized and promised to do better, scratching their heads, running rough hands over the error that they had not even seen. Some did not bow their heads, and Faustino counted these men, as *mala clase*, bad ones to his boss. They were paid off and told not to return.

*Tapia,* that old science that was falling out of favor, was exacting but in many ways it made a better house. None of the young men who came looking for work knew *tapia* in the way Faustino did. He knew it in all its stages, recalling exactly the big wooden box with handles where his father would dump the red mud, and then just the right measure of horse manure and then, with the artist's eye, the water. His father, when the largest clods of clay were broken, when the stirring stick thicker than a man's arm could move no more, would roll up his pant legs and step into red mixture in the box to tread it all into a smooth pink mush. Faustino as a boy watched his father; that was his first school. His father called himself a *maestro de obra* but not because he knew only *tapia* which was *burro* work. Brute strength, no more. It took two strong men to carry the box full of mud and then the hundreds and hundreds of hods of mud from the box to the wall, box to the wall, clapping the trowel full onto the bamboo uprights. Smoothing and adding more, smoothing, holding what was mud and manure and water, elements of earth resistant to man's will, holding it against the wall until it became a wall, layer after pink layer. Well, Faustino thought when he watched the others moving their bare feet in the mud like pigs in the pen, that was work for *burros* and he was not a *burro*, he was a *maestro*. He knew how it had to be done though, knew from his own walls, *muchos, pero muchos,* raised by his hand alone. Speed and perfection he had learned from the belt of his father. And so he had advanced and hoped for his son, whose back had never felt the belt, advancement. Just ask him about his son and his face will soften. His son, only son, Faustino Segundo, had taught him, the father Faustino to read and write. By day, he raised walls and his son went to the local school. By night, by the light of a candle with mother sleeping, Faustino learned first letters and then words and finally his signature.

Now he can keep records of projects, he can sign for deliveries. He can write and read and keep records of costs. He, Faustino can do the finest inside work too, supervising the doors and frames and the iron grilles over the windows. Painting he loved, painting and mixing paint to achieve the color his patron wanted, applying it evenly, meticulously, as a true *maestro*. He also reads well enough, thanks to his son, and with hands calloused and rough from concrete and paint and splinters, he writes meticulous notes to his *patron*, recording the addresses and dates and listing how many bags of cement, how many loads of gravel, how many nails, the names and hours of the workers.

When Armando starts the *finca* for his family, a project dear to him, Faustino does most of the work himself. He finds most workers lazy or sloppy, indifferent to the high standards of the *patron*. He prides himself on understanding *el mago*, who shared many of his ideas with him. There in the mountains overlooking the city, on a large property complete with a creek and meadows and orange trees, guava trees and a large stand of sugar cane, Armando will stand with Faustino at the top of the slope.

Waving his hand in the air, he paints the image of the large open house looking onto the green jutting Andes mountains, of the stables below near the creek and a *casita* for the *mayordomo*. The big house, the house for his family, would have thick *tapia* walls, whitewashed inside and out. It would have a pink tile roof and a courtyard with roses. Wide shady corridors on the outside invite the family to sit and admire the mountains, wide shady corridors on the inside hold the soft chairs where the family can lounge in the fragrance of roses, can look up to the stars and hear only the soft sounds of night.

Before the first wall went up, Armando had dreamed of his country house which he called *La Suecia*, after the mountainous country Switzerland he had visited and loved. For years he looked for the right property, a place outside the city, but not too far, rolling hills and a view of the mountains, good water and fruit trees. Finally he found it. It was at this time and place that Faustino had his accident. It was an *accidente bobo*--this is to say foolish and impossible. But it happened, *bendito sea Dios*!

Faustino fell from the scaffolding. The other workers swore no one pushed him. He picked himself up and walked alone to the *pueblo* where he got on the bus while blood soaked the shirt and burlap sack he had wrapped around his right arm, nerves severed by a broken bottle. The doctor called Armando who left a meeting with important clients to rush immediately to the hospital. Later Armando interviewed the workers who had been on the job. One called it *suerte perra*. The other stoically called it *accidente bobo*, as they searched for words for their boss. Whatever name it had, the tendon in Faustino's right arm was severed. He had fallen on a glass bottle which came up to meet him, shattered, and here is where the *suerte*, luck, became *perra*, bitch; the bottle was an ordinary aguardiente bottle washed and filled with lemonade sweetened with *panela*. Every workman carried one and that homely constant had become weapon. It left him, a *maestro de obra*, with only one hand to do the work he knew how to do. Forever after his left arm was stiff as a rooster's leg, useless to him.

That was how his boy became *doctor*, a real doctor, the same as all doctors, for the *patron*, after talking to the doctors in the hospital about Faustino's arm, went directly to his house to talk to his wife and then to the public school where sixty students scuffled their feet, elbow to elbow in a tight dusty classroom. What silence fell over the room when he knocked and opened the door. Even the *profesora* was struck dumb at the sight of him. Don Armando only nodded at her. Quickly he picked out Faustino Segundo's face. "Pick up your things. You won't be coming back here." Frightened, proud, confused, the boy called Segundo stumbled after the great man.

The boy's heart leaped when he saw the car and the door opened for him. But when the patron called him Faustino, Faustino that was his father's name and not his yet, not for a long time he thought, he was only Segundo which is to say, the second, he froze and could not move. Armando threw the boy's books into the back seat and nudged the boy into the front seat. Then he stopped and studied the boy.

"It's your father," he said slowly. Then sorry for his clumsiness, he put a hand on the boy's shoulder as he sat in the front seat of the Ford, in his father's place, and he huddled tight against the door, "but he's alive. *Gracias a Dios*, he's alive." Armando drove directly to the Jesuit high school, and took him to the office. He wrote a check to the priest in the office, and with his own hand entered the boy's name on the rolls. Armando paid for everything: tuition, books and lunch, and even on the way home, new shoes. And so the boy advanced. Every year he studied and learned while his father Faustino continued on the Gomez payroll. He pottered about, overseeing projects and giving some orders, though not with the same command as before. The boy graduated from high school high in his class. His mother and father and Don Armando sat in the audience and smiled. Armando did not stop there; the boy's tuition was paid to the university where he excelled too. And when, thirty years later he met at a meeting the son of the man responsible for his title and education, he was *Doctor* Pineda and not Segundo, son of the *maestro*. And both men knew this so only bowed stiffly to each other and went about their business.

# CHAPTER 5

# How the Virgin Maria Came to the Plaza Zea

### Medellín Colombia 1965

Luisa turns from the balcony and rushes to pull the latches and bolts that protect her from the street. Thanks to God, here is Cornelia at last! "*Por Dios*, Corna!" Luisa says and the tone falls somewhere between thanks and complaint. "*Gracias a Dios*! Cornelia! Cornelia! It's time you came. What took so long? You know no one else can help the way you can!" Pausing at the top of the stairs, Cornelia grunts to acknowledge this truth. And then the two old women, elbows jostling, step matching step, exchange companionable murmurs as they walk down the long hallway toward the kitchen.

They stop, by long habit, at the patio where the birds live. How many tupiales have lived in the shadow of that first who knew his master Papa Jose? These, along with canary newcomers, are flying at their bars in hopes of a fat caterpillar at the hand of Cornelia. The floors of their cages are littered with birdseed and chunks of oranges, all put there by Pablo. Every day at dawn, the cages are uncovered by Pablo, in his pajamas, his graying hair standing on end.

If it is winter, days of long gray rains and cold winds, the cages and the birds stay in the breeze way of the kitchen, but in summer, he moves them out into the sunny patio. Two small shiny cages hold the canaries, Luisa's latest fancy. Six tall rusty cages hold tupiales. Each of these brilliant gold and black birds looks exactly like the special one owned by Papa José, but these are not special; they will gladly peck out their owner's eyes or fly away into the trees. "*Desagradecidos!*" Luisa scolds them for their ingratitude. She bends her head close to the cage and, in a low voice, reminds them how lucky they are to be safe from boys with slingshots and corn poisoned by DDT.

Roused by the entrance of Cornelia, the birds start jumping on long thin black legs from the perch to the floor of the cage up to the bars. Without pausing in their conversation, the two women stop at the cages. Luisa takes the package of yucca in her arms while Cornelia opens another smaller packet of newspaper; she takes first one and then another fat green worm, still dewy and squirming, from the cabbage plant where she found them. Luisa throws her head back to watch through her bifocals the birds she has loved and feared all her life. One by one, they cock their bright black heads, sight the squirming green worm, impale it and gulp. One for each cage and the tupiales whose turn has past, rotate their heads to watch from first one yellow eye and then the other. The two women move on at the same pace into the large tiled kitchen that is so much a picture of Luisa's life.

This kitchen has, as many Colombian kitchens do, white ceramic tiles from the fourteen-foot ceiling all the way to the tiled floor; a relentless face. The sink is recently remodeled to receive hot water declared *necessario* by her professor son. Now he is *el Doctor* Diego Gomez Soto, she declares in a matter of fact voice and gives him his way with the old house. But she has insisted that the kitchen keep its *piedra*, a large flat stone embedded into the counter beside the sink. All the hard work is done there, breaking *panela* with the smaller round rock, or tenderizing the slices of raw beef that must be pounded with the small rock until transparent. The stone is death on dishes and glasses, but it's always been so. Luisa cannot imagine a kitchen without a *piedra*.

Luisa begrudges every minute she has to spend in the kitchen. She has maintained all her life that the kitchen is ungrateful. She denounces it as seriously as though it were a person or a beast or a bird and it almost seems so. On the days when Cornelia's liver is acting up and Regina is too busy to come, the kitchen exacts from Luisa many more hours than she wants to give it, and despite the hours she spends, terrible things happen there. The smell of burnt rice in the air is a sure sign that Luisa is cooking. Once she stood at the balcony for so long while potatoes boiled that the aluminum pan melted down onto the range and the potatoes became dust.

A shiny new General Electric range, an ugly color called mustard, is now a centerpiece and as Cornelia unwraps the yucca, breaking each tuber in half and grunting in approval at the chalky white flesh, Luisa picks up a rag and cleans the drips of coffee from the stove top. It was brought by Diego and Debbie from the United States. "General, General," she croons as she cleans around the clock and timer. General Electric is a company, a famous American company, Armando worked for. Since that time thirty years earlier, Luisa and the whole family have called it affectionately by its first name, *el General*, pronouncing the G as gringos do and rolling the R just a little.

She remembers when the company came to this town and the manager came to her house, this very house. A nice enough man, the first *gringo* she ever saw or heard. The furniture was new in the sala the day Armando announced he was bringing the new manager, a *mister*, home to see the family. At exactly the hour Armando had said they heard a car door slam in the street. Armando ran down the stairs to welcome him. Luisa heard them barking strange sounds, speaking in English, all the way from the street. Of course Armando mastered the language. Luisa knew he was bragging on her and his children in all those sounds the two exchanged. She did not go out when she heard them enter the *sala*. Only when she was called did she go in to see the Mister perched with his long skinny grey knees and elbows like a spider on her new Luis Quince chairs with rose colored brocade covers. She sat while he admired the famous table that Armando had brought from Italy, running pink fingers over the carving in the stone top. Though embarrassed, she held out her hand to meet his. She took *tinto*, little demitasse cups of strong coffee on the best silver tray, and then she called each of the children to meet the Mister. Diego, even at the tender age of five, resisted and only went to see what a *gringo* looked like. He sulked then because he was stuck there looking at a man who, though uglier, taller and skinnier, looked like any other old man. Pablo's chubby face was still spotted with soup, as Luisa noticed too late, when Cornelia carried him into the room and bobbed him up and down. Only Adiela and Teresa, as teenagers studying the language, seemed interested in the man and his strange way of talking.

The family was studying the tall thin man, very tall with red hair and grey whiskers and teeth as large and yellow as piano keys. Too bad about the way he looked. *Pobrecito*, Luisa thought. That was when she learned to pronounce those English words. It was the first time and Armando had rehearsed them all: *General, G, G, G*, making the *ll* sound with which they pronounced *villa* and they all laughed when the gringo tried to say *villa*. Of course, Cornelia also tried to say the word, since she had never, not in all those years learned her place. And the two men and Luisa and the children, stopped in their smiling and turned to hear Cornelia without any shame at all, address the important man. "Mister, Mister, *es General?*" And the truth was that she pronounced it better than anyone.

*General, General*, Luisa croons as she polishes the little red raised circlet of the emblem, recalling that day. I thought a job with such an important company would be the end of mines for him. *Boba! Boba!* She sighed at how foolish she was in those early years. How was I to know? I didn't know anything about anything and certainly not about men. It was hard to refuse him on any topic but especially when he got on the topic of gold. Even my father listened to him when he talked mines. *Papá*, I begged him, just don't listen when he starts that. Do as I do, walk away. But of course, he had not. And that one little mine, which Armando discovered almost accidentally while he was out in the mountains taking electricity to Sonsón, that was the beginning. The idea that made him crazy.

She had done the wrong thing in forbidding it. She could see that now. He had stopped talking about it to her and started talking to his own family. *No, por Dios!* She clutched her head remembering the day she overheard him on the telephone speaking to his brother about going to the mine. He made a deal with his brother to manage the mines.

His brother! His whole family! She didn't want to say ignorant. Even provincial--she hated to say it. But irresponsible! They were, they were! His brothers had encouraged him in the madness of the mines without any thought of the little children he had and his wife. Soon he was spending all his time and energy and money looking for more mines. He had taken Diego and wanted to take the others too, as small as they were, to infect them with the thrill of it. It still made her cry in exasperation to think of it! What?

What? Luisa finally turns to Cornelia who, clucking in impatience, has been displaying the white faces of the broken yucca. Luisa nods and pulls her mouth down in approval. Then, the morning ritual past, Cornelia takes off her good sweater, one from the United States given her by the *Señora* Debbie. Folding it carefully she puts it in the servant's room and puts on the old ragged sweater she works in. She turns to wash the dishes, using cold water as she has always done, with a little rag and a bar of gritty soap.

Luisa wanders about the kitchen peering first through the tops of her glasses, and then through the lower half moons. She looks on counters, in cabinets, under the newspaper for the cup of coffee she fixed several hours earlier. It will be cold. No matter. She made it triple strength, plenty of caffeine to keep her awake. She finds it in the dining room and without stopping to sip, picks it up and begins to wander back into the rooms, the many enormous rooms of her life.

She shuffles in her house slippers past the statue of the blessed Virgin Mary. This image was her mother's devotion and her mother's statue; she would never call it a statue but an *image*, a holy word for something loved. At any rate, Luisa won out over her sisters to have custody of the holy image of the Blessed Mother. She kept it as her mother had, near her bed with candles, the expensive ones, yellow and thick as her arm, burning night and day. This was not the bed that had been her marriage bed but the one she took to after the terrible day when Armando felt ill at the finca and came home to die. He was the only man who ever did his own laying out but that did not surprise her or anyone who knew him. They were only surprised that death could get him, could do its final magic on him.

When he fell ill in the middle of the night on their first night of the vacation there at the finca, oh, so many years ago, a lifetime! he had not complained. He would not say how ill he felt, though she could see his ruddy face turned to a color of earth, dull and dark and his eyes sinking deep in his face. He simply sat upright studying the sensation until she woke. Luisa rushed first to Teresa, who was spending her vacation from the university at the finca with them. Then Luisa ran back to watch and pray over her husband while Teresa ran from bed to bed, shaking the children and calling their names with a low husky voice. Diego and Pablo did not want to go back to the city; they had plans for horseback riding; indeed, they did not believe in their father's illness. At least they did not believe it would ever change.

How could they think he would die after so many years of illness? They had heard stories of doctors around the world, even at the famous clinic of the Mayo in the United States. There, after he paid his bill at the office, Armando had placed in the palm of his doctor's hand a large nugget. Only rarely did he tell such stories, but the children felt sure that there were many; they held them as a sign of their father's special quality. They heard over and over in their minds, though he only said it once to the family describing that visit to that famous clinic. "Yes, gold. It came from my mine in Colombia." He had lived with angina; one day it was worse, one better, but it was always present, so on this day, this dark night, no one thought it was any different.

He knew however, though he did not say it. He simply got up and dressed. There was nothing for it; they were dangerously far from a doctor. Teresa did not yet drive, much less Luisa. There was no telephone. Armando had to drive; he sat slumped over the wheel while Luisa and Teresa loaded up the children. Then he drove down the dark driveway, the headlights making goblins of the plants in the fields. Down, down the dirt road to the lonely highway. Luisa felt a second blow when Armando drove off the main road to stop at the home of his doctor. He neared the double shuttered window and rapped there. The two men spoke at the opened dark window for a few minutes. Armando returned to drive again and only the braking, the accelerating, his fingers white on the wheel told the story. Suddenly, her voice breaking the terrible silence, Luisa insisted that he stop at the priest's house and he did. This obedience, one of the few he ever made to her, was another black sign. He went into the dark opened door of the parish house while Luisa mumbled prayers, Teresa answered them in her gruff voice and the little ones dozed. Armando, son, at fourteen as tall as he would ever be, a man, silent and sullen, unwilling to face the present darkness.

He sat planning how he would take the workers' bus at first light and escape the sorrow as tangible as heavy rain that had begun and that fell steadily pelting the car and his father's face, returning from the priest's house. Armando turned away from Teresa who scolded him to pray and from his father's dark face caught in the street light. When the car started again, Armando the son bellowed, awaking from a dream. Diana, the baby, responded with a little howl that Luisa hushed instantly. Armando, father and husband, half soaked from a few paces in the winter rains, rested his head again on the steering wheel. After a few minutes, the car went on its way. Armando looked out at the familiar streets made strange by the dark, a time of night he had only seen when the family went to midnight mass, the *misa de gallos*. No sooner had he thought this than he heard the first rooster's crow and realized why it was called *misa de gallos*. What, he wondered, did the rooster see to tell him morning was coming? Armando determined to return to the *finca* no matter what anyone said. Buses going to the factories now filled the dark streets. He would go on his own immediately; he could not bear to see his father pale, still, losing light and will.

No, they could not believe, not one of them, despite all the signs, they could not believe anyone as strong and willful as Don Armando Gomez would ever surrender to death. On this night he stepped from the car and walked slowly up the stairs. He ignored his ritual of closing the garage, of jiggling the handle to be sure, of locking up the house, his nightly round to check doors and locks. He left all that to the others.

Diego locked the garage door and then slipped across the Plaza to catch the factory bus and return to the *finca*. Teresa went around from room to room and door to door checking locks and turning out lights. Luisa sat in silent prayer while Armando showered and shaved and chose his best suit and tie, brought from Italy on his last trip. So there was no need for anyone to lay him out. He was ready.

Later they sent a taxi driver, a man they knew, to the *finca* to fetch the son with the strictest orders to say only that he was needed in his house. That message and the somber face of the driver told him everything. He came back to find his father, the man known by the magical name of *Papá* in his family and *mago* all around the country, an effigy. His body lay on the double bed in the room where the Sacred Heart of Jesus observed all. Below that painting and oblivious to it, the two men were silent, the father in death and the son in some place untouched by his mother and brothers and sisters' chorus of *llanto*, a storm of tears. But the day became lost in Diego's memory and he would never know who came for the funeral and how the day progressed from the room to the church to cemetery.

So Luisa never slept in that bed again but saved it for guests and when finally Diego married and there was a *matrimonio* again in the family and a need for a *cama de matrimonio* she had made it up with great happiness, forgetting the sorrows it had held for her. She had given birth there, three sons and a daughter, God was good! *Bendito sea Dios*! Her husband died there leaving her a widow with four children. That very bed.

She went from having a father who could do anything to having a husband who could do anything. Then she was alone, unable to do the simplest of things. He who had changed her world had left her alone except for the children. Alone. Alone.

Thank God for Teresa. A student in university, a grown woman, Teresa had been with them on that night. Teresa who managed everything on that night and for many nights after, when Luisa was lost in grief, did everything. It was Teresa who remembered her sister Adiela in the convent, Adiela who did not yet know the enormous and irrefutable change that had happened in the world. Teresa ran, yes, like a child she ran, down the broad sidewalk to the convent and rang the bell, rang and rang until the deaf door-man finally pulled it open. Teresa, her face tear stained and red insisted on seeing her sister. No, no, *imposible*, wasn't she a nun now and no longer a sister to any one person and so Teresa told with tears and gasps and silences the story to the *Madre Superiora* who listened in silent grey sympathy. Clutching at her heart, Teresa walked home alone. Somehow, someone would tell Adiela that now she was truly an orphan.

No, Adiela could not come to the funeral. Unthinkable. She would hear mass in the chapel of her convent and retreat to her cell to pray and weep, contemplating the empty coffin, her own coffin, adornment and reminder, that waited there for her. She would weep for all the deaths, and for all orphans. Now she was truly orphan of both father and mother. She closed out the voice of her father pleading with her to wait, wait a year, travel, experience life. This was life, this death.

So Teresa took charge in the large house on the second story of the Plaza Zea. She had already taken over because when Luisa saw her husband, recently bathed and shaved and combed, smelling of the same French lotion he had worn all the days she had known him, the smell that had crept to her across the room when he came to visit the little girls in the *sala* of her father's house. Here it was again so many years later and Armando dead with the Sacred Heart of Jesus over him, seeing, as He always did, everything. Luisa too was felled by shock and by grief and it lasted a long time.

That was when she got the Virgin, that was when her sisters had allowed it to be moved from the big old house in Manizales to Medellín out of pity for her and all the little ones. They had brought it from the room of her mother there on the street of the Cathedral. Mama Teresa had died at an advanced age; she died and left behind the vale of tears and all her children. Then, the sisters and her brother too, Sebastian, came bringing the holy image in a wooden box. And when the box was opened there in the patio of the big house in the Plaza Zea and the sun caught the blue eyes of *La Virgen Maria*, the one who had been witness to the pains of her mother, the one who was brought from Manizales to help her *support*, yes that was the word, it was a heavy load on one's heart, *support* the death of her husband. When her family brought the Virgen Maria, she was roused to exclaim, "*Jesus mio*! Look, how beautiful--such sad and understanding eyes." Luisa had it moved into the small room that had belonged to Adiela. Luisa moved there to that narrow bed. Huh! It was like her mother's life again. A woman suffering and the Blessed Mother who suffered so sharing a room. Luisa prayed without ceasing in those days and the habit remains though a little fallen now. When she passes through her room on the way to the balcony or to the bathroom, she prays and when she leaves her bed at morning and enters her room at night and of course when she needs a confidante.

Stepping into the room, her widow's room with a crucifix over the narrow bed and the candles burning, she mumbles a prayer, the *Ave María*. She pauses a moment for the response, "*Llena eres de gracia,*" waiting for someone, anyone who might be passing, to give the response, to complete the prayer. *Nada*. She continues through her room and the other bedrooms all in a row to the balcony and throws open the large doors for a better view. For a few minutes she leans out into the air, turning from one side to the other. She surveys the plaza, the traffic directly under her, and the two dogs in the park. Her cup tips and coffee spills onto the sidewalk, no, onto the heads of two workers who look up and shake their fists at her. "*O Jesus!*" she steps back into the room and puts the cup down on the desk. Giggling, she watches from the shadows until the two men go around the corner. Stepping back, she closes the doors to the balcony and opens only the small window. She can watch from there. She will watch and pray there until someone comes. She will doze too, standing, holding the coffee cup in her hand.

She dozes at the balcony, at the dinner table and at mass. Pondering on it, she finds the reason for this new failing, well, not entirely new but certainly worse than ever. Years, yes, it was the years, her years and she announces solemnly, "The years do not come alone." It sounds good and true and she repeats it out the window to all the people who are walking on the sidewalks and sitting on benches in the park.

# CHAPTER 6

## Called to Holiness

### MEDELLÍN COLOMBIA 1980

Adiela climbed the steps of the bus, planted herself solidly in the doorway and began to tell the bus driver, fixing him with her sharp eye, with the precise look that she used to silence the roughest boys in class, that she was a nun and a *profesora* from the famous convent and school of *la Enseñanza*. Rolling his eyes first up, then away to the rear view mirror, he pinched the ember off his cigarette butt, dropped it out the window and jabbed his dirty finger at the fare box.

"*Ah. Ah bien,*" her voice grew softer. She would turn the other cheek. She stood in the door of the bus counting out small coins, *cincuenta, cincuentycinco, sesenta*, oblivious to the impatience of four men behind her. With a smile, she dropped full fare in the box and turned to find, *gracias a la santa Madre Juana*, to whom she gave credit for all miracles, a seat for the long ride to the Social Security Hospital. She shook her head in amazement at the bus driver: so few knew these days about the convent, there was so little respect. It was a sign, one of many, of the ignorance that abounded in Colombia, its fall from grace. *Gracias a Dios*, she at least had been raised right. Though an orphan, she had had proper training. Early, early, she learned about convents and prayer.

She had learned to pray in Manizales where all the aunts gathered every night to pray the rosary with Mama Teresa, the grandmother who prayed day and night at the foot of the Blessed Mother. In that same

55

house Adiela had learned to appreciate convents and at a very early age. Twice a year she had gone with her grandfather and her sister Teresa who would not be left behind for anything to take her aunts Sofia and Maruja to Bogotá and see them safe inside the walls of *El Colegio de la Enseñanza*. There they learned the power of the nuns. Even Papa Jose bowed to them! Both little girls waited with feverish pitch for those trips. In Medellín too there was a convent they discovered when they moved there to live with their *Papá* and Bisa. The girls waited for their own entrance into the tall wrought iron gates of the *Colegio de la Enseñanza*, one near their home, built, they thought in those innocent days, for them by their own *Papá*. The brass sign with 1928, the name of the colegio and their father's name (first among many) stood sentinel and witness to that important building. It needed polish she reminded herself. She would borrow some brass polish. Tomorrow.

On Adiela's first day of school, she was scrubbed, combed, dressed in her uniform, and led by the hand by Cornelia, herself scrubbed, combed and shod for once, down the long stairs, out the street door, around the corner and to the gate of the school where many girls and their nannies waited. Though invited to accompany them on this historic day, Teresa had refused and through the long early morning ritual of Adiela's preparation, Teresa had kicked, screamed, sobbed, and begged weeping to go to school too. She was not too small. Stamping her feet, she was not too young. She could study the same as Adiela! Still the footsteps went down the stairs and happily into the street. School! Adiela was going to school!

Never had Teresa been separated from her sister, never had she been left out of the lime-light. It was also the first time that her temper got her nowhere; Luisa, preoccupied with Pablo who was cutting teeth, made only a half-hearted attempt to soothe her, and Cornelia, who always loved Adiela best, was busy. All day Teresa sulked in the room she shared with her sister, breaking Adiela's crayons and scribbling angrily over the pages of Adiela's favorite books; she sniffled and moaned for hours waiting for her father to come home to console her.

But when at noon Armando came for lunch, and she ran headlong into his arms, he tossed her in the air and asked her about Adiela and the school, so Teresa ran sobbing to her room and when the phone rang for him, an important call about the mines, he did not come after her. That afternoon, when Cornelia left the potatoes unpeeled in the sink and primped herself to go out into the street, Teresa turned her nose to the corner of her room and studied the book shelf. She restrained her curiosity when she heard Cornelia return carrying an exhausted but triumphant Adiela up the stairs. Her starched blouse a mess, her hair a tangled mass of curls, she paraded from one admiring adult to another a practice sheet of her names printed diligently over and over. All five names: Adiela Maria Consuelo and her mother's surname and her father's surname and those important names filled the lines of the whole page. She told how the *Madre Superiora* had singled her out for a smile.

From that day Adiela contrived to be in her path, to be noticed by the woman who was mother over the convent and the school too. A smile or a nod from the tall serious woman sent shivers of the promise of goodness through her. Later Adiela would explain her vocation in terms of *Madre* Juana. Wasn't it true that saints were magnets drawing ordinary people to God? She was Adiela's saint no matter what the Vatican thought. She had all the proof she needed in her heart. When *Madre* Juana died there was a long and passionate discussion in the convent. All thought it likely, no, inevitable, that Madre Juana would be declared a saint. Accordingly, four nuns were assigned to cut up her clothing and Adiela prayed to be one of them. Like all nuns, the *Madre* Juana owned only what she needed but her extra veil and white wimple were cut into pieces no bigger than the fingernail on the smallest finger. These shreds were sealed in small plastic circlets along with a tiny smudged picture, not much bigger than a finger print, of the *Madre*. One nun cut and another nun sealed the tiny packages with a hot press. All took turns attaching the brown ribbons to the scapularies, all prayed. What pain, what bliss!

That was forty years ago, but Adiela still has a supply of relics. She is small but indomitable, dressed in a carefully mended suit she has inherited from her sister-in-law, a much taller woman, and as she pushes her way through the other passengers on the bus, she fingers her scapulary. When the final word came from the Vatican, Adiela had seized an apron full of scapularies and stashed them in a box under her bed, oh so many years ago. She has worn out dozens (though she keeps their tattered remains in a cigar box whose slogan and picture of an Indian maiden she covered with prayer cards) and has given away dozens. But she has enough left to last the rest of her life. "*Bendita Madre Juana!*" She steps down off the bus and onto the crowded sidewalk. All scapularies are worn close to the heart; the brown ribbon a remnant of convent penance. This one reminds her of her early vocation and the saintliness of the *Madre* Juana. And if those old men in Rome didn't think so, well, so what? Who could say this little shred of yellowing cloth wasn't a remedy for sin? And doubt and sorrow too and so Adiela blesses herself, fingers making a tiny cross and her thumb marking her forehead and then her lips and finally her heart. Then the whole hand making a sweeping cross with her head bowed just so, just as she had been taught by Ines so many years earlier, just so.

Adiela is going to the Social Security Hospital for her weekly visit there with the doctors. And why not? Isn't that what they are for? After all those years doing *burro's* work, twenty-six years in a cloister, twenty-six years closed away from the attentions of doctors unless or until the *madres* were dying and then fully robed and behind a screen while the doctor asked questions which either had medical terms no one could understand or common words that should never be spoken to a lady much less a *Madre*--. Well, those were the days of saints and these are not. Once a week without fail since the Pope had ordered the doors of the convent opened and she had been pushed out into the streets, she has visited the Social Security.

She pauses at the street vendors outside the door. A young woman sits on a plastic sheet spread out on the sidewalk and on it are mangos, little piles of bananas, of *mamoncillos*, and a battered tin basin in which float chunks of fresh coconut. Adiela eyes the woman.

"Those bananas are too ripe. They won't last the day."

"*A la orden, Señora,*" she answers in a flat voice, looking down the street.

"*Señora* no. I am a *Madre de la Enseñanza*." Her tone solemn, her eyes searching.

The woman on the sidewalk frowns. With her finger she stirs the coconut in its milky water. The nuns are the worst.

"You could give me those extra ripe ones and earn some favor in heaven."

"You could give me ten pesos for them and earn the thanks of my children."

Sternly Adiela holds out a five peso bill. "This and my prayers."

She takes an old grocery bag out of her large battered black purse and packs the bananas. They are not too ripe but just right. She will take them over to Luisa and the family as soon as she is through with the doctor.

The crowded room smells bad. The air is heavy and dark. So many poor women clutching their bellies, and sick children coughing and blowing, whining and wheezing make Adiela fear suddenly for her health. What if she is contaminated here? She tugs her little plastic *sufragio* and finds a chair. With a sigh she settles back to squeeze the yellowed plastic and remember the blessed *Madre* Juana. Of course, she remembered the day she died; her heart went heavy inside her recalling the day. Adiela was then just eighteen years old. *Ay, que dolor, que dolor!* With the six other young nuns who had entered the convent at the same time she entered, she both rejoiced and mourned in a confusion that seemed holy. There was death, a blessing, a release, a cause for jubilation but there was the cold still fact of her body. Adiela sighs a deep sigh; finally, she can admit the pain she had felt in those days just after *Madre* Juana's death. The nuns had been so sure *Madre* Juana would be sainted, that after the formal mourning they prepared relics, many hundreds of them. They prayed and they waited, rehearsing the stories they would tell when the officials of the Vatican came collecting history, remembering details that would convince them. Oh, the convent was strong in those days! They had opened cloistered convents and schools in Cali and Medellín after Bogotá did so well.

It was her father Armando who had helped the nuns buy a whole block of good flat land bordering on the convent and conveniently close to the Plaza Zea. He had given a gift, an amount of money that would give the nuns a good start on their school in Medellín; Adiela and Teresa were the first students signed into the book. A tall brick wall was built around the whole block and inside they planted gardens with flowers and mango trees, fig trees, tangerine and lemon too. Inside the enormous brick building there were many more walls for the rooms of the boarding students and cells for the *hermanas*, sisters, who did the cleaning and cooking and larger cells for the *Madres*, mothers, who were the teachers and somehow more fully nuns. There was a chapel too that joined the old convent with the new school and the chapel featured one vividly stained-glass window that showed *Madre* Juana in ecstasy at the feet of the *Santisima Virgen Maria*. Priests came to say mass every day and the *Madres* knelt and prayed in the front and the *hermanas* knelt and prayed at the back with the girls in their uniforms ranked in between. Every morning the students came to mass, each class with its teacher and the girls learned to be still, to keep their eyes downcast, to pray, to kneel and to stand. If they did not, they were punished with rulers smacked across their palms or an hour of standing in a dark corner. Fierce scoldings and threats of calling the parents and sending the hopeless girls home to ignorance and a low life followed. After she completed her novitiate, Adiela was trained as a teacher. For many years she has taught Social Sciences. She has a large collection of postcards and calendar pages with pictures of far away places to help the girls imagine lands: Egypt and Greece and the mountains of Switzerland. She believes in them, although she has not seen. She also taught knitting, embroidery and etiquette, duties she took seriously, determined to teach the girls the fine points of being a lady. There were happy times too, basketball with friends, parades to the Blessed Virgin Mary, and the everyday pleasure of following in reverent wake of a favorite nun who would turn and with a smile and gentle hand make the girl's heart overflow with happiness. The very next year Teresa had started school. She was too young they said at the school, but she had convinced her father and between the two of them, they had their way. Fiercely Teresa made herself ready. Since the smallest of the uniforms hung like a tent on her tiny body, Ines came from Manizales to help Luisa sew uniforms to fit her. Luisa and Ines took apart Adiela's uniform seam by seam and studied the cut, then duplicated it in miniature. Sure enough, there was the uniform, doll sized! Teresa marched through the gates with great satisfaction, walking several paces in front of Cornelia and Adiela. She was determined to learn everything. Her eyebrows knit in concentration, her small feet scuffling in a dance of frustration, she soon knew all her sister Adiela knew.

On the yearly visits from the *tias* from Manizales, Ines and Sofia and Maruja, after the caresses and embraces, the adoration of the aunts, the exchange of gifts, with the two girls exchanging quick speculative glances at the other's gift, they raced for their books. Then the two little girls stood at the ready, taking careful turns since now they were *señoritas,* to read to their admiring audience. If Adiela read quickly, then Teresa whirled down the page. Then Adiela pulled down her lips and taking up the *Don Quijote* began to read with great expression. Flying away, Teresa returned with her Bible; she would choose most dramatic tones for her reading from Isaiah. Oh, Adiela smiles, remembering, the foolishness of children!

When she hears her name called, she rouses herself. "*Madre* Adiela," she corrects the nurse. Standing, she moves her hand from forehead to breast to shoulders; she makes the sign of the cross in the face of a violent attack of coughing from a dirty little boy. She tucks the *sufragio*, the relic of her revered *Madre* Juana Lestonnac back inside her blouse. It is her turn to enter the white doors. She hopes it will be Doctor Rios who always listens so attentively. He has more sense and more preparation than some of the others. He will give her a prescription, she will stand in line no matter how long it takes and get just what he orders, pills, sometimes tonics or capsules. She will squirrel them away with all the others for the one day when she needs medicine worse than she does on this day. Patiently, filled suddenly with Christian love, patting little babies and smiling at poor enormous mothers-to-be, she waits in line at the *Farmacia*. As soon as she gets her prescription, she will take the bus to Luisa's house where she is expected. The bananas will be just right for lunch.

# CHAPTER 7

# The Years Do Not Come Alone

### Medellín Colombia 1970

Luisa stands in the window of the balcony waiting for *la gente*, that is to say, the people, her people, her family. She likes to stand in the window and spy them, her people, out of so many on the sidewalks. Debbie, the wife of her son Armando, a doctor graduated from university and father of beautiful children all in school and a good husband, *Bendito sea Dios*! is in the kitchen. For most things Debbie is intelligent, but she likes the kitchen and she will help Regina, the daughter of Cornelia to prepare a nice lunch. She, Luisa, is waiting for Adiela to appear. She has to tell her about a *visita* from the nuns of the *Sagrado Corazon*. That was yesterday and it's been on her mind ever since.

Her mind is intent on the nuns, all nuns, but especially the nuns of the house: Teresa and Adiela. They who were raised like princesses are now servants to convents and the pope. That pope and his modern ideas caused a lot of harm. Just thinking about him, that smile and blessing makes her angry! She has a photo of him in a nice gold frame. It is signed by his very hand, and she has turned it to the wall. How can he call himself a pope! Vatican II indeed! Anger is boiling up in her, indignation she can make real. She can't say too much to the others but she will seek out Debbie and unburden herself. She likes talking to her daughter-in-law about many things but especially the convents and the pope. Luisa likes watching Debbie's eyes get bigger and bigger as Luisa looses all her complaints about the church. If she gets too loud or too bitter, Debbie will stop her in perplexed concern, pointing around the house, "But what about your saints? What about the Blessed Virgin Mary?"

With patient exasperation Luisa will explain again how her house has many saints and how she knows their names and the prayers they like best and so what? She will walk in her bedroom leading the younger woman to the statue, a beautiful image, the size of a child, of *La Virgen del Rosario*, see, with a real lace mantilla and pearls in the rosary draped in her hands. It had belonged to her mother. She won it from her sisters' house when her husband Armando died. Debbie nods. She knows that. She knows that thick candles burn always there, making the blue glass eyes seem alive. Also in that same room, Luisa's room since the death of Armando, all in elaborate gold frames, are elaborate parchment blessings signed by Pope Pius XII, Pope John VI and now Pope John Paul brought from the holy city by Teresa on her trips to Europe. Each has a small photo of that pope, his hand raised in blessing and his real signature done by his hand and not one of his secretaries. The first letters of the blessings are illuminated in gold letters. One of the frames, the one holding Pope John XXIII, the pope who let the nuns out, is turned to the wall. As they pass through the room, Luisa prays and Debbie has to answer, "*--y bendito es el fruto de tu vientre Jesus.*"

Gesturing at the walls, Luisa confesses, "I never thought I'd speak against the Pope, not any Pope but especially him." She points to the picture with the pope's face turned to the wall; only brown paper and the stamp of the frame shop show. "I thought he was a saint. Maybe he was a saint but he didn't know about human nature. Why did he want to go and turn the nuns out on the streets? In the old days a nun was a nun and she looked like a nun and she stayed in her place. The two women go into the small sitting room. Luisa picks up her knitting and sinks into the dark green over stuffed chair. For a moment she studies her knitting, needles crossed in their nest of yarn. She leans forward in the chair reaching for her cup of cold extra strong coffee, one of many left here and there around the house. Her dark hair, streaked with grey is pulled back in a bun. Her glasses sit low on her jutting nose unnoticed. She never looks through them.

Debbie searches for another topic. The general topic of convents and popes worries her. Luisa gets more and more upset, counting sins of commission and of omission of the convents, naming the actions and adding error to insult to crime. "Why," she asks, "does *La Madre* Josefa Maria," and her voice carries a cartload of anger, "fly to Rome twice a year while Adiela takes a bus to teach rough boys who don't want to learn anything?" There are more examples too from the other convent and when Adiela or Teresa arrive, an argument is certain to follow. Debbie opens her mouth but too late; Luisa is heating up, remembering old wounds. Debbie, nodding, listens to Luisa's voice growing with the same tone and words of all her anger, "*No. No. Nooo.*" And then freed, "*No, por Dios,*" and she is off and in a tremulous voice denouncing religious figures near and far. Debbie frowns. If Luisa's faith goes, nothing will stay.

Isn't this old house full of witnesses to faith, crowded as it is with images, saints and virgins and Jesus at all ages? All sorts of helps, relics and rosaries and remembrances of holy people. There is the ivory-colored watered silk skullcap worn by Pius XII, wrapped and hidden on a top shelf for serious headaches or problems with memory. Years later when she worries about losing her mind, about the dementia that overtakes some in her family, Luisa will sleep with it attached by bobby pins to her long grey hair. Pablo wore wore it last year for the long hours he suffered through a tutor's attentions and Luisa's prayers. None of the teachers or even the parents who spoke of learning disability overcome would imagine the boy learning to read with a papal skullcap. But as Luisa would have said had she discussed it, that was a real Pope and a saint who died before he could do the good he would have done and there would be proof: Pablo will someday attend university and succeed. The cap carries the smudged fingerprints of an eight-year old struggling with a first reader and faint rust marks of hair pins. It could never be washed.

Another secret is the bottle of water from Lourdes that has lasted for twenty years, ever since Teresa went to Lourdes and brought back two liters in a large cloudy glass bottle made in the figure of Bernadette kneeling beside the grotto. One liter was used, to no avail, for the soup of Armando the son who fell on his head and was left with a terrible temper, counted terrible in a house of bad tempers. What remains is saved for emergencies, measured out in tablespoons.

"But tell the truth, Luisa. You don't blame the church for *everything*, do you?"

"Everything? What do you mean?" raising her hand in a sweeping gesture. "Not *everything*, but the convents took her money. Then she worked hard for them for twenty years. Now that she's losing her memory, they want to send her home--to take care of me!"

She jabs herself in the chest with an accusing finger, and continues, "Not everything, just that little thing, that's all!" Now she seethes openly, "*Bobos! Bobos*! In this tone, the word nails every fool in the world. Glaring at Debbie and then at the doors around her, she dares anyone to deny it. In seconds, she giggles. She enjoys the worried look on Debbie's face and the horror Adiela and Teresa show when she argues about the convents.

"The years do not come alone!" After this solemn pronouncement she giggles again. There are advantages. Since her seventieth birthday she has resigned from the community of women; she has given up on her womanly duties. She leaves the kitchen to the maid or Debbie or whoever wants to go in, even her sons. Let them all wash dishes. And cook too and let it burn. Let them learn what she has always known, how ungrateful the kitchen is. *Desagradecidos*, all kitchens. The idea of ingratitude reminds her, "... and the convents too." She leans forward to speak earnestly.

"These girls were brought up to be ladies. They were no fools. They traveled! Both traveled to Europe with their father and later on their own. No, that's not true. Adiela went into the convent too young to make a trip alone. We protected her! We wouldn't let her walk down the street alone! For years she at least taught young ladies in the convent. She taught them how to be ladies. Now, she goes across town on a crowded bus to teach a roomful of snotnosed boys! See! She had an education, for what?"

"But Luisa, I ask you again. How can you blame all that on the convent?" The tremor in her voice is met by a giggle from the older woman.

"No. You're right. Don't worry so. No one hears us." She waves away the saints' faces on the wall. "These girls got off to a terrible start. You know they were orphans of a mother. My poor sister Teresa-who-died-so-easily left them to us. I was one to help ruin them. But I knew what was happening and my poor sisters," and here she crosses herself, "did not. I knew one Christmas it was not going well. I remember that I had bought a beautiful Italian doll for Teresa and I knit it a sweater," she poked at the pile of wool on her lap," and made it a velvet dress. Red velvet with a lace collar, matching the red velvet dress I had made for Teresa. As soon as my sister Ines saw it, she bought an even bigger doll for Adiela with eyes that opened and closed. And then Maruja went out and bought a bicycle. Our mother saw all this," and again she crosses herself, "and she told us we were making a big mistake but we wouldn't listen."

"What in the world were you thinking of?"

"We just wanted to buy them some happiness, poor little things. Teresa, poor baby, had rotten teeth from the time she had teeth. I think they came in rotten. But she loved sweets and was terrified of the dentist. What could we do?"

A fierce knocking on the door stops them. Luisa moves a hand across her lips and purses her mouth in a child's gesture of secrecy. She smiles across the room to erase the previous conversation as Regina rushes to wrestle with the locks that bar the door. A small sallow woman enters, limping and complaining that she had to knock three times before anyone answered.

"If people knew how bad my feet are," she walks gingerly on thick soled shoes, "they'd run when I knock." She collapses into a chair and bends over her feet, squealing as she takes off her shoes.

"Hello Teresa," the younger woman speaks, "What a surprise! We were expecting Adiela."

Teresa looks up from her feet and laughs apologetically.

"How do you like that? My manners are gone! I don't even say hello when I enter." She laughs and bows elaborately from her chair to both women there. "I'll owe you a proper hello until I get my energy back. And to my sister too if I'm here when she comes."

"We were talking about you."

Luisa raises her eyebrows and purses her lips. She picks up her knitting and concentrates on counting stitches.

"Luisa was telling me you had bad teeth when you were a child, but your teeth are good now, aren't they?"

"My teeth were terrible as a baby because everyone gave me candy all the time. I loved it so much. One by one my aunts would call me into their rooms, 'Come little Terre. I have a surprise for you!' What a surprise. The surprise is that I didn't have a tapeworm from so much sugar."

Luisa's mouth hangs open and her eyes are circles over her glasses.

"You mean all the others were giving you sweets too?"

"Everyday." Laughing still, Teresa takes her feet in her hands and groaning, begins to massage them.

"Was it the same with Adiela?"

"Where is she?"

"She should have been here by now."

"She's probably at the Social Security."

"Maybe that's how she got so sick, all that sugar."

"No, don't believe that," Luisa leans forward in her chair. "For one thing she's not sick. She's never been sick. Not once. She just likes to get some attention from doctors. They're sly ones. They know who the fools are." She is interrupted by Teresa.

"True. And beside that--she never liked sugar. She only ate it in front of me, when she wanted to torment me. Otherwise, she gave all of hers to me. Who knows, maybe I wouldn't like candy now if my aunts hadn't given me so much. Everyday, all different kinds."

"But coconut was your favorite."

They both hum a three note melody that is part of every family conversation. A musical "*Eso sí*," an affirmation that needs no words. Both nod happily.

"So you still like candy...."

"Yes, but not as much as I like smoking."

"In all my life I never knew nuns could smoke."

"Well. Nuns are people, you know. I tried to quit for a long time. Months after I went into the convent. Specially when I went to Rome, because just as you say, most people don't know nuns can smoke. But I just smoke a little bit, once in a while. I can't afford to smoke like I used to."

"How many times did you go to Europe?"

"Once as a nun, four times before that."

"Just what I was telling you before," Luisa lean into the words. "The girls in this house were raised to be somebody."

Teresa gingerly fits her shoes back on, moaning and wincing.

"Well those days were long ago. I can hardly remember them."

Luisa leans forward and whispers, "Look at that. That's just what I mean. She doesn't even remember she's a nun. She's going to go find a mop. Then she'll be chasing us all out of here so she can clean under the chairs."

"At least it's good she can come home now."

"When I needed them, they couldn't come. No! *Por Dios*!" She claps her forehead remembering how she suffered. "Adiela, as young as she was, chose the *Enseñanza* for its strictness and she will tell you for the *Madre* Juana. It's true she was a good woman and a real nun who stayed in the convent and prayed and gave service to the girls." She leans forward and holds up a hand to hide her mouth, "Teresa chose *Sagrado Corazon* for its habit. She wanted the fanciest habits and they had the biggest, whitest head dress, all standing up pleated. They had to have maids just to wash and iron those things. In those days, they wouldn't let the nuns out for anything. They all dressed the same. They all stayed in the convent to pray for the world and for their families. Look at them now. That's the Pope! Things might have been different in this house if he had stuck to praying."

Luisa lifts her needles and after counting the rows carefully, pokes the needles into the ball of yarn and placed it under the faded satin pillow of the Baby Jesus who rests on the shelf under the television. Debbie follows her down the hallway, past the bird cages, past the patio to the dining room. The large painting of the Sacred Heart of Jesus that has witnessed all the happenings in the family now hangs in the dining room. Debbie looks at it again; the hands painted too small, too graceful for work or life, gesture towards his heart in flames. Next to it, a recent addition, a framed verse in Gothic letters: "Christ is the invisible guest in this house." He overlooks the dining room table where the Debbie and Luisa sit.

"Join us, Terre." They call Regina to bring coffee frothy with milk and sweetened by brown sugar.

"Here, Terre, leave that mop there and come have a little *cafecito* until lunch is ready," says Debbie, pulling out a chair.

"I don't have time for lunch. And you know I never eat between meals. These customs are too much for me. Imagine eating before lunch! Besides," she swings into the dining room, mopping all the while, to examine the cups, "I don't like that coffee like that."

"Regina," and Luisa's voice thunders. "Bring the coffee for the *Madre* Teresa. Just sit here with us for a while as any Christian would." Luisa's voice is commanding.

"*Sí, Señora.*" She almost curtsies, almost a child again. Smiling she sits and takes the tiny porcelain cup from Regina's hands. "Of course, I will sit with you. I didn't intend to.... Well, let me just get my cigarettes, and tell that girl to bring me an ash tray." She picks up the mop and walks out the door. Halfway up the hallway she falls into the rhythm of the mop. In a few minutes, the dog comes slinking in, tail between his legs to hide under the dining room table.

"See what I told you? She forgot what she said. She's mopping in my room now; she chased the poor old dog out of there."

There is a loud steady rapping from the ground floor all the way up the stairs. A cane or an umbrella is being pulled across the wooden railings. Regina, puffing, runs to open. Teresa pauses in her mopping. Luisa and Debbie peek out the dining room door.

"*Buenos dias, queridas*! Here, Corna, take these bananas; they're perfect for lunch!"

"Cornelia is my mother. I'm Regina, *Madre.*"

"Huh," Teresa grunts between rhythmic swings of the mop.

Luisa waves her hand in the air, a blessing turned back on itself, "See! Those convents have ruined these girls. They took their money. They took their youth. They took their energy. Now they send them home to my house!"

# CHAPTER 8

# Luisa Is Called Back

### Medellín Colombia 1945

The world changed when Armando Gomez died--and not just for his children though they felt it more than anyone. All over the country, people asked in shock, staring into the eyes of the news bearer "*El Mago?*" Disbelief and sorrow hung in the air. The word traveled to pueblos all around the valley. In La Estrella, in the house of Faustino, there were bitter tears, for, as Faustino said and his son echoed, "He was a father to us. Now we are alone." Do not speak of what it did to Luisa, how she was knocked into a lonely and dark place. She shut the doors behind her and surrendered to grief. Adiela and Teresa bowed their heads under the weight of being true orphans, mother and father both gone. And the younger children, orphans they were now of father: Armando, a boy of fourteen, now the man of the house. Pablo, a willful twelve, Diana a toddler, who continued to refer to her father in the present, who continued to speak to him.

Luisa and Teresa stand outside her door to listen to the little girl after they hear her prayers and tuck her in. When Diana is alone in the dark, her childish voice loses its sob and grows animated. She tells him about the day, about her doll or her mother. She pauses as though listening and then answers. Hidden behind the door, Luisa and Teresa think it is a sign. They whisper to each other, "*Es posible?*" eyes wide and pained. "Believe it! It is possible," Luisa answers, praying to hear his voice too. When, day after day, these two hear no voice, they weep and cling to each other, musing. Who knows what an innocent might see and hear? Who can ever understand why a good man dies while others live and thrive! And to die when he was so needed! Look at the only daughter, a pretty little girl, orphaned so young. Luisa is lost in grief. Teresa raises the girl as she had been raised. She does what she can for the boys--

Armando at seven is most damaged by his father's death. He was special among the children because of his accident--the terrible accident. It happened with Armando the father away in the mountains busy working, and everyone, Luisa, Teresa, Adiela, Cornelia, busy ironing or sewing or reading, Armando and Pablo busy studying or playing, all busy and no one watching the baby. Two year old Diego found the doors to the balcony open, climbed up the railing and toppled head first to the sidewalk twenty-five feet below. His fall was broken by the telephone wires but his head was seriously damaged and there were no words to answer the question of why such a thing had happened. Such lamenting. So many tears. No one spoke words of blame then, but unvoiced accusations and remorse were heavy in the air. Diego grew to count his life from this day. Unwilling and unable to blame his mother or father or Cornelia, he would blame Adiela and Teresa forever after for his fall.

It was a concussion the doctor said. A terrible blow to the child's brain. And after that, he had terrible temper tantrums from which everyone ran. Everyone except his father. Only his father could calm him. The boy could not enter *El Colegio de San Jose* where his brothers went to school. No, it would not do. Too strict, too rigid for Diego. Such discipline would never suit him. A new school was opening. The Benedictine brothers were more modern, more understanding; they were seeking students. Don Armando made large donations to help their building fund and to ease his son's way. On his son's first day of school, the father was called from an important meeting at his office. He left everything, clients and ore samples and contracts and rushed to the principal's office for a meeting with the *profesores*. This became commonplace. Several times a week he was called to the school; he spent hours there pleading for his son. He even started leaving the office early to pick him up from school and thus spare the boy the bus ride that upset him so. At home, the father arranged a space on his own desk, the blotter just so and the pencils sharpened and set the boy in his big chair while he hovered over him to study the letters and write the words and add the oranges and apples on the work sheets. Diego, the son listened. He said his father could explain things as no one else in the world. After Armando the father died, the son said no one could explain anything. On that sad day, he put his head on the desk. He said he could not learn from anyone else.

About five years after his father's death, Diego had a second accident that would further mark his life. My father, he said a hundred times, wiggling his maimed fingers, my father loved mining. He loved me first and then the family and then his work of taking electricity to the *pueblos* and then he loved—he paused to make sure his mother was listening--mining. He liked to tease the family, seeking out weak points for each. His mother's weak point was mining in general and specifically his father's obsession with gold mines. Whenever the subject came up, Luisa would leave the room in a huff, to go to the kitchen to blow up to Cornelia. Luisa had two great *penas*: Armando her son and the mines and sometimes these two worries met. Her son's temper went so far beyond the normal family temper, explosive in itself, that for many days she wasted the precious water that Teresa had brought from Lourdes by putting large spoonfuls, accompanied by the miraculous novena, nine days of prayer, nine days of holy water in Diego's soup. For nothing. Perhaps her own temper improved. Her temper would flare when anyone talked about the mines. But with Diego, she did not dare disagree even about the mines. He would giggle to see Luisa's exasperation and prod her with questions. "Why does my mother hate the mines? Is it the time my father spent away from us? Was it the money spent on them? Was it some other reason? Speak, *Doña* Luisa!"

These conversations, or speeches since no one answers, clear the room. Pablo's normally calm face will cloud and he will walk out of the room. He disagrees with his younger brother about everything. Armando thought, and for once most agreed, that Luisa's hatred of the mines was because at the time of his father's death, the mines were worth nothing. Instead of leaving large sums of money that would cushion the family from life's hard rocks, as everyone expected, the famous mines left only a shoe box of useless memories which were stored in the family safe behind the largest mahogany armoire. A handful of nuggets were handled with glee by the children and with distaste by Luisa. A bundle of official deeds and mineral rights bright with stamps and seals faded and grew more and more brittle with age.

The family was just finishing the last of the funeral cakes when thick swatches of debts for salaries and severance pay and for equipment were delivered by boys with black hats on bicycles. "Perhaps she knew that would happen," Armando would wink. "My mother adored my father but--. But she didn't like any of the things he liked, not traveling or gambling or mining which was like gambling. He spent hours playing cards—for high stakes at the Country Club. And, did you hear that story about how my father gave that doctor at the Mayo Clinic a nugget from his mine?"

My father was special. He, Armando Gomez, was the one who lit up the valley of Abura. (Armando was wrong about this detail, but no one would correct him.) My father's name and address were known everywhere. Dozens of letters came to our house. No address, just his name and the city. Believe me, this is true. I loved to open the door when I heard that loud rapping in the stairway. Mail for my father, brought in *carriel* from the *flota*, beautiful stamps from all over the world, sometimes big wet burlap bags, samples of ore, I would drag across the floor leaving a damp path. Fancy stationary or notes printed with a pencil on wrapping paper. Later, after the city grew and the *flota* no longer delivered mail, a boy would come running up the stairs from the post office. He had a blue cap and shiny clips around his pants legs. I decided to grow up to do that work. I was a child and I would pick up pieces of paper and scribble on them and then run to my father's door, "A letter!" That's what I remember. "A letter for *Don* Armando!"

and the delivery boy would hand it to whoever answered the door, a letter typed on good paper with lots of stamps. My father gave me the stamps. No address was needed for my father, his name alone. When I was a little boy, he would take me everywhere with him, me alone of all the others. People would look at us and talk to us, to him, and they admired him. He would show me the lights in the little villages high up on the mountains and they were like stars. He would name each pueblito and tell how he had taken electricity there. Like stars in another sky. *Mi papá.* H e was called *el mago.* That he died so young is one of the ways my life was ruined.

When he went into the villages, in the early years on horses, he went in the lead on a beautiful grey gelding and the workers followed behind on mules and finally the machinery on *burros,* it was like a parade or procession how the people all came out to see and to call out, "Hola Mago!"

A few years later he drove the first car up the narrow mountain roads, a car bellowing and snorting and clanking, frightening the horses and oxen and the *peones* too! *Automoviles.* Cars. Cars bringing *el mago!* And bringing his magic too: big grey generators, each the size and color of a good- sized pig, and rolls of wire and pulleys as big as boys and tools whose name no one knew would all come together to make light bulbs bright and the radio play tangos by Gardel.

On the first visit to the villages, my father and my uncle Manuel would just talk to the people, the men to make the plans and draw the contract. They would meet on the sidewalk at a table of the most popular bar in the main square. All the old timers of the area would be there on this night, called together by some kind of magic. They stayed around because my father gave them the respect everyone deserved, rich and poor, from the mayor down to the *peon.* He knew how to give them all respect, even those who were ragged and barefoot. Each man had his *historia,* he observed as he listened to the stories far into the night with a bottle of aguardiente, magically renewed no matter how much they drank, in the lamplight. My father *Don* Armando would call them up, one by one to shake their hands, say their names and pour them a small glass of the anise flavored alcohol. He would ask them about the *tierras,* the minerals, the rocks, and in this way he accumulated many samples of rock and even Indian relics. He loved the adventure, the stories, the clues that would lead him to another mine. He was the *mago* who brought light, who found gold, who won the highest stakes. People remembered him forever.

When he died, his mining things stayed in the garage in a heap: all the tools, ropes, wheels of wire, pulleys, fifty pound drums of cyanide, gunny sacks of sample of ores and earth, explosives, wooden boxes with wicks, dynamite sticks wrapped in red oiled paper, and the blasting caps, shiny copper shells smaller than the fingers of a child.

Diego loved exploring in the garage with his friends from the Plaza. He poked here and there, naming the magical tools of mining, telling all the stories and bragging on his father. He did not say that his mother had never allowed him to go to the mines. It made him furious to recall how she had denied him that experience. Too young, she said. He would always regret the way his mother and sisters had confined him and changed his life forever. But he knew from his brothers how the workers would stick a length of wick into the copper blasting cap and then bite its thin shell until it held the wick. Yes, his brothers had described in infinite detail the enormous blasts, like bombs in the war. Kaboom! The whole earth exploded! His father could do that!

Diego had never seen it. Unfairly his mother had not allowed him to go. He was always singled out, always. The older boys had gone and they told how the *arriero* tied them onto the backs of mules to go up the side of the mountain, but once at the mine, they were free. It was the biggest adventure of their lives, far from the scolding and constraints of their mother and Teresa. They were boys, men, not sissies and they followed their father around, they thrilled to the shouts of warning, felt the ground shake when the blasting started. The boys had seen the workers prepare and plant dozens of these shiny shells in the crevices of the mines before the big explosion. They had described it to their little brother who tried that day in the garage with his friend to secure the wick in the blasting caps. Try as he would, his small teeth couldn't pinch the shell enough to get the wick to stay. Determined, they found a hammer and one held the wick in the cap while the other hammered.

That was a terrible day at the Plaza Zea: the explosion, the boys screaming, blood everywhere and the search for the fingers. When he was a middle- aged man and resigned to his life, he would say how he never wanted to be a surgeon anyway or a pianist. Laughing, he would wiggle the two stubs that remained on his left hand, "I tell children that this happened because I sucked my fingers. If they have that bad habit, they stop in a minute."

Diego blamed Teresa for that too. Adiela was in the convent, impervious to guilt though he sometimes forgot that and included her in the blame. He had to blame somebody and he loved his mother too much to blame her. Of course, his father was gone forever. It would never have happened if his father had been around.

When the boy was still in the hospital, Luisa called a man to bring his horse and cart, one of those many who supported his family by hauling what needed to be hauled, and with warnings against mining, she commanded him to clear out the garage and take everything related to mining. She warned the poor old man with the skinny horse against mines and cursed them a hundred times. She couldn't blame her husband in death as she had in life, so she blamed the mines and Armando's brother Enrique, and his whole family for encouraging the mining which not only took money when he was alive, years of his life, took money after his death and now the hand of her youngest son.

Luisa prayed day and night these days. She woke in the night in terror and every backfiring automobile sent her into shock. She wanted to hold onto Armando and her older boys too, to protect them against all the dangers in the world but they would not allow it. She retreated into her room in fear and astonishment at the dangers of the world. It was Teresa who ran the house and went out into the noisy streets to buy what was needed. It was Teresa who took the phone calls from teachers and went to visit schools. She harangued Luisa sometimes when the boys became too much for her. But it was no use. For several years Luisa withdrew from the world. The children, Teresa, and Cornelia (barefoot and for once unrebuked), stood silent, puzzled, defeated, in the doorway of Luisa's room.

Even in grief, Luisa's life went by in a flash. One day she awoke and Ines had come from Manizales and she and Teresa were cutting out a pattern from Burda magazine. When she asked what they were sewing, Teresa told her it was a dress for her, for Luisa, yes, the mother of the graduate, the oldest son Armando. That stretch of good wool, a serious grey with a slender pink pin stripe, on the dining room table, the crinkling hush of the tissue paper pattern, the bright pins, cracked open the shell that had held her for five years. She walked around for days repeating the good news that Armando was graduating from high school. She would stop Cornelia from her mopping to announce, studying her face to see if she showed disbelief, "Diego is graduating from high school." They all knew she was well when she bent over the sewing machine to examine a seam and insisted on pulling those threads and resewing it in a straighter and finer stitch. Over her bowed head, Ines and Teresa looked at each other in amazement and gratitude. Luisa was back. She entered into planning the celebration, and at Teresa's urging, she sold some tobacco stocks so they could buy a ticket for a three week tour of the United States. It was a good graduation present for Armando. He would fly from Medellín to New Orleans. New Orleans was still the United States, wasn't it? Luisa was afraid of the northern cities and was sure that gangsters still ruled Chicago with machine guns. Teresa assured her that Louisiana was very French and cultured and far from the movies with loose women and armed men. Yes, it was a grand gift for the graduate and Luisa never blamed Teresa for that idea even when the three weeks turned into three years and then more years. He sent letters from one city and another and finally he was in university.

Luisa and Teresa found their hands full with Pablo and Diana and Diego, whose problems consumed them as he was expelled from one school and another. The two women made novenas; they enlisted the whole convent where Adiela was and all the aunts in Manizales in a miraculous novena, a nine-times-nine with the holy mysteries of the sorrow of the mother doubled, once for the Holy Mother and once for Luisa. How they prayed! How they hated the phone calls from the school!

The phone rang many times a day and Luisa and Teresa would near sit by and listen to it. A fine family resemblance, the same shrug of the eyebrow, a brief twitch to the eye lids, the lips' hardening. Cornelia had gained the family ability to ignore ringing phones or raps on the door but Regina, Cornelia's daughter had not. One of the many times the phone rang, Regina was mopping in the room; she answered and it was the United States calling. She jumped up and down, shouting. She didn't want to put the receiver down, afraid to break the tenuous noisy connection. Finally, Teresa arrived, panting, to take the receiver in her hand. Armando. It was Armando calling from the United States. He had tried to call many times! Where were they? Unable to find words to answer that question, Teresa held out the phone to Luisa. Immediately, she took the phone and drank in her son's voice. News. Important news in Armando's own voice. He was getting married. To an American woman.

# CHAPTER 9

# Out of a Dark Place

### Medellín Colombia 1945

The voice of Armando with its good news called Luisa out of her dark place; it was a good thing too. Luisa had come close to following the example of her mother, called Mama Teresa. Mama Teresa had entered mourning not for forty days, the prescribed time for grief, but for forever as a nun's cell or a dead man's grave. It was in fact forty years after her first son committed suicide, though she did not ever say those terrible words out loud, forty years from his death until her death, forty years that she lived in deepest mourning. She said, over and over, so often that they stopped hearing, that it was hard to lose a child, and doubly hard to lose the first born. They only responded, they being the church, that suicide was the unforgivable sin. Pain upon pain and without solace! Hadn't she been raised in the church, devoted to the church, holy, Roman, Catholic and apostolic? And now--!

If she went to mass, the priest in his vestments was not a comfort but an accusation; the communion with its blood and broken body, well, wasn't that *his* blood and body too? She wanted to be like the *Santísima Virgen Maria* and offer her pain in serene surrender as was shown on all the images and paintings, but it was too hard. Her son, her first born son was dead and heaven was closed to him.

On a practical side, for she often thought of these matters, she could not take up ordinary life again, coming and going in an unthinking stride between her home and the market and the church because her son, her baby, her firstborn, was not buried in consecrated Christian earth. If she were to start going out on the streets like an ordinary mother, then on the day of his death, the date engraved in stone, on that date she would go into the cemetery as every mother must and then what? She imagined herself running up and down the rows of tall tiered mausoleums, reading the names followed by crosses, name after name after name--it was a city of the dead!--and never finding his name. Staggering, weeping dry eyed, an old woman searching and finding nothing. His name would not be followed by any cross. Suicide was the unforgivable sin and if she did not forgive the church, what use mass or communion?

Mama Teresa stayed in her own little room to pray and weep. Once a year for thirty years she put a black mantilla over her head, swept out of her room and marched out the big double doors and walked down the broad sidewalk to the Cathedral: Good Friday mass was one she did not miss, that mass when there was no communion, no body broken, no blood shed, when all the images were shrouded with purple and black, when not even the bell sounded, only a wooden clacker which was how the music of the world had sounded to her since that day.

Luisa also entered the cell of mourning after the death, unthinkable to her, of Armando. Only months after the death of father! Her father, Papa Jose left a huge hole in the world, not just for her but for many hundreds of friends and family. A whole city came to his funeral! How could the world go on without those two men, she would ask, the only men who were men, looking around her at the living, pale shadows of those two who had passed. The two deaths together sent Luisa into a miasma of death; she and her children too wandered as though lost for several years. Teresa, though still a student, was the adult in the house; she managed everything alone. In a terrible coincidence, Cornelia was deathly ill and stayed home with Regina who cared for her. It was Teresa who nursed Luisa and prayed with her and gave her tablespoons full of belladonna when her pain was too much. Teresa who cared for the children as much as they allowed, which in the case of the older boys was not much.

Armando and Pablo, both by grief and adolescence were determined to avoid all the comforts, influences, and rules of their mother and older sister. They would skip school to go to the *finca* to play in the creek. Pants rolled to the knee, they'd move stones and shape channels and trap minnows in the shallows. When the neighbors downstream sent to ask what had happened to the water, embarrassed, the boys would kick apart the dam and send the water tumbling on its way. Then they would scrub themselves and inspect each other. Mirrors to each other, "Look, there on your chin," Armando would say, rubbing his own chin as he directed his brother. They were careful to return home, trudging dejectedly through the sidewalk of the Plaza with their books, at the same time the other boys in their uniforms came home. Still, no matter how careful they were, the mud dried on their skin and clothes in pink chalky drops and streaks which Luisa and Teresa would ponder, suspicious but without proofs.

Other days they went to the Lido cinema where they thrilled with Tom Mix and Zorro. After the movies they took the bus to the finca to ride the horses and rope the cows the way the cowboys did in the movies. One of the best milk cows lost her milk. It dried up altogether, the mayordomo explained to Luisa, after being chased up and down by Armando and Diego who galloped after her, hooting and whirling ropes.

Feeling their power fading, the two women tried scolding and shame. It worked against them. Armando began to skip school more frequently and openly. When forced to the principal's office for a hearing of his case, he scowled and sulked while Luisa and Teresa tried to explain. The more the women pleaded for his special circumstances; see, he is an orphan, an orphan though of father only, the angrier the boy became. He was kicked out of San Jose and then the more lenient Benedictines let him go. Luisa feared he might not ever graduate from high school. What good school would accept him? Mediocre grades, bad attendance and the attitude of a rebel. He had taken to wearing tan shirts and pants with muddy boots and a slouch hat. He spent all his time on hunting trips, either alone or with another boy from his school. Luisa thanked God when she found out he was a decent boy from a good family, also orphaned of father. The two mothers commiserated. When Diego left the house with his belts of ammunition crossed over his narrow chest and a shot gun in his hand, a cigarette hanging from his mouth, he looked like a *bandido*. With his friend Juan Jose, or the neighbor Esteban, he found a whole group of hunters, men of all ages, who made long *paseo*s into the countryside, into the *monte*, wilderness, to hunt animals that hadn't been seen in Medellín for years.

Luisa prayed to her dead husband. It started as prayer in a tender pleading voice but ended in a shrill rebuke. *Armando, por Dios!* She berated him for being dead when the boys needed a father as much as they did. Only a man, a father, was capable of handling sons. She tried to understand her son, telling herself in her heart what she told everyone in the world about a boy, orphaned of father, trying to grow up. These hunting expeditions might have gone on for a long time, but Luisa would give credit to the Sacred Heart of Jesus who heard her -- though not as she twanted at the time. It came about because of the hounds.

One day Teresa was having a tea for all her friends. She had a good many old friends from high school at the *Enseñanza* who were now young married women. These elegant *Señoras* were invited, along with new university friends for the most elaborate social occasion Teresa had ever staged. She stayed up all night baking a rich black fruitcake which she doused with brandy carried in a cup by a boy from the bar down the street. Teresa brought in two new servants, highly recommended as having served in very upper-class houses, to polish the silver, mop the floors, dust the furniture. Then she stayed up that night to do it all again. Everything in the whole house sparkled. Despite her planning, on the day of the party, the new servants did not come and Regina was enlisted, much against her will but coerced by Cornelia and Luisa. Teresa dressed her in a new uniform and shoes, and rehearsed her manners, how she should answer the door (a modest smile, a short greeting, remember your place!) and carry trays of food ( Don't push people to eat. Don't praise the food. And don't drop anything!).

There were arrangements of lilies and orchids in the dining room and *petit fours* frosted in delicate yellow and lavender. Twenty young women, beautifully dressed and polished, carried on conversation that was intelligent, light, musical. In short, it was perfect until the hounds in the garage started to howl, bloodcurdling bawls which Teresa tried to explain as not only normal but a sign of their pedigree. "No," and she smiled slightly they were not howling because they were beaten. No, of course they did not have premonitions of tragedy." Although the hounds drowned out conversation, it was not the worst happening of that calamitous day.

Many and many years later tears would come to Teresa's eyes when she described little specks of pepper on her feet. Oh, she gasped, wondering how the specks could have escaped the shower she had taken. When she tried to brush them off, they jumped. That was really the end of the hounds. Not even Armando would argue it. Later that night when he was faced with the facts on his own khaki clad legs, he was speechless. Somehow in the middle of the tea, Teresa rushed Luisa into a room, closed the door and pointed at her legs. Gasping, the two hurried from the room to rush the guests out the door and down the stairs, praying and groaning and bobbing kisses and bows and smiling until their faces hurt from the strain of not looking at the many black dots that hopped on their legs. When the last of the ladies disappeared down the stairs, Luisa had to go to bed with a big spoon of belladonna while Teresa swore over and over, "*Maldito, maldito*! Damn, damn! The boys laughed at the scene and at their older sister who was finally saying the words they had been using for so long. Armando had to move his dogs and with the move, he lost some of his enthusiasm for hunting. Besides, he had discovered women. Dogs and hunting expeditions took a back seat.

At the same time Pablo began to visit his uncles on his father's side. Luisa shook her head at him. "You're just like Enrique, just like him." She stopped herself saying this for she hated to think that he might end up being the kind of man Enrique was, stuck in the back roads of life, but when the boy laughed at her, she realized he was just like him. Like Enrique, Pablo didn't care a *comino,* a cumin seed, what people said or thought. Luisa couldn't bear to think what might become of a man who didn't care what people thought. When he came in after a whole day away, she did not need to ask where he had been. He had been with his uncle. His shirt tail was always out, and he laughed at everything and at nothing.

The little ones were also affected. They too had ways of calling their mother's attention. "*No, por Dios*!" Luisa responded thus to every calamity, not daring to name what she feared. She would quickly move into a prayer in a voice loud enough to be heard all over the house. Little Diana would cling to Teresa, and little Pablo would pull away to kick at the door. The older boys closed their mouths, denying the response to the prayer that rose in their throats, that echoed from a place they could not stop. At this time Armando crossed his arms and said he would not pray either. Imagine, a small boy, jaw set, arms crossed, defying his mother and God Father, Son and Holy Spirit!

It seemed too much for Luisa but life just went on with all its problems and worries and the children growing up. The clock was eternally stuck at the hour of notes from the principals and a twelve year who refused to go to school. Somehow, probably with the help of a miracle novena, Armando graduated from high school. To celebrate, he was given a three-week vacation trip to the United States. Thrilled and nervous but he soon adapted. Then time began to fly as the three weeks became three months. He met people and got work. After a year, he began to study at a college run by priests. Then, although it was hard for Luisa to understand, he was enrolled in a university and working too.

Luisa and Teresa shook their heads and looked around. How could things have changed so? They got a letter from Armando asking them to buy a diamond ring, an engagement ring for his *novia*. Quickly, Teresa and Diana got passports and visas and airline tickets for the wedding. Luisa could not believe it. Armando was getting married. He had two degrees from an American university and was returning with his pregnant wife to find work and begin life as a married man. Pablo was at the university, and Armando was looking for suitable employment. The baby Diana was in high school. Luisa looked out onto the Plaza Zea and saw a bright new day.

# CHAPTER 10

## The Family Is Complete

### Medellín Colombia

Armando returned to Medellin after nine years, with a wife and several diplomas. Luisa had to change when Armando returned. His energetic presence and the force of his expectations forced Luisa back into the world. He who almost didn't graduate from high school was a *doctor* now. In relief she told everyone, and no one blamed her for bragging. Yes, he is a real *doctor,* not a medical doctor but a professional and married to a nice girl, yes, a *gringa* but very nice all the same, and she is expecting a baby. Luisa begins to sew again to help prepare for the new baby since the expectant mother does not sew at all. Luisa and Teresa, even Diana who was a teenager, laugh to see some needlework the *gringa* had done. *Pobrecita*! She shows them a tablecloth she made that was so botched, front and back, with huge knots and puckers that they have a hard time not laughing out loud. So Luisa starts to sew and to teach her daughter-in-law, difficult as it was, to sew and to speak the language. They talk, long rambling conversations because Debbie's Spanish is so poor that it takes a long time to tell the simplest story.

After so many years away from his homeland, Armando has a hard time adapting. It is harder for him than for Debbie who knows nothing and questions everything, because he has dreamed of Colombia, day and night for years. In the middle of the cold distrust he faced in Memphis, Tennessee, he longed for the open nature of his own people.

In the dark oil smelling noise of a factory in Davenport, Iowa, he dreamed of the cool quiet villages high in the green Andes. Every tree in the United States without a name or history brought to his mind the sixteen palm trees planted by his father. He would say, laughing grimly, if I die here, bury me with my head toward the South.

But once back in Colombia, he found a different reality. People were not so open and easy to understand as he remembered, and poverty and violence reigned. His hometown, the small town where everyone knew his father's name and house, now has more than a million citizens. Many live in splendor in marble mansions with high walls crowned with broken glass and closed by enormous wrought iron gates. Many many more live in misery in cardboard huts, beggars scratching scabs as they sit on greasy blankets in the middle of the sidewalk. "I can't believe how much it changed," he says, avoiding Debbie's eyes.

He immerses himself in his old life, but when he goes hunting with his old friends, the slums have crept further and further up the mountain and the forests are farther away. The hunters try to recall the last time they saw conejos *de monte* or peccaries. Even birds are gone, sacrificed to the DDT that killed mosquitos and saved so many from yellow fever. When the hunters walk through the little villages, conversations stop as the men and boys of the dusty plazas coldly scrutinize the hunters and their guns. Armando is a doctor now, a scientist, and he recognizes the poisonous nature of the yellow haze that settles around the smoke stacks of the factories, the turquoise blue jets of water flowing into the *Río* Medellín. The old friends are changed too. After a few hours of reminiscing over old days, they have little to talk about. "He's a doctor now, all right," they say and look down at the ground. A lot has changed, in Armando and in Colombia.

Luisa sees her son changed. He left a willful teenager, the worry of her life. Now he looks and even acts, in his energetic opinions and charged actions, like the man she fell in love with thirty years earlier. He is the image of his father. He is handsome and hardworking and well married and the world is before him. He lives there in the big house.

The return of Armando and Debbie brings *visitas* almost daily. The newlyweds and the visitors mean cleaning and cooking. The kitchen had not seen so much heat in years. Teresa does not know how to make any simple dishes like beans and rice but she makes coconut cakes and *macedonia de fruta* and roasted pork with Madeira sauce. Cornelia is sick again, another of a long string of liver attacks, so Luisa wades into the chaos of dirty dishes, the pans with burnt on crusts of rice and *platano*, the sticky puddled floor where someone spilled Coca-Cola. She does not resent it; she feels like Lazarus called back to life. She scrubs, polishes, cleans. Hours later, Debbie goes to look for her and finds her there in the kitchen, giving a last mop to the shining floor.

"Let me help you!" She would say sincerely but too late.

"No, Debbie. *Bendito sea Dios!*" Blessing God, Luisa would lead her daughter-in-law back into the *sala*. Everyone was home. Everyone was well. There would be a baby.

Of course, all the visitors who are family come into the family rooms, and onto the balcony. One day there is a new face leaning over the railing. Though the eyes are a pretty blue grey, they have a slant to them that is, as everyone says, *chino*. The rest of his face is ordinary boy: freckles, some soup dried on his chin, a nose that needs wiping. He is not *chino*, Chinese, and he is not an ordinary boy. He is Victor who is visiting with his mother Sola who was the sweetest and the most beautiful of all the Soto sisters. Victor is the same age as Diego, twenty six years old.

For no reason, Victor begins to call his mother. His low voice too announces his infirmity, the baritone of a man but the tone of a baby. "Sooo-la. Sooo-la." Sola is what he is saying. The name as a word means *alone* but no one ever thinks of Sola as being alone, and certainly not Victor, who is always at his mother's side. He calls her name because he feels uncomfortable with so many new faces. His mother's name is his prayer. He repeats it over and over until she comes. She comes, peeks around the corner to see if he is safe, and then goes back to her sisters. All the Soto sisters have arrived together from all over the country for a long visit.

They are all old grey-haired women--all except Maruja who dyes her hair that same black she remembers from her youth. Despite their years, they are giddy girls again. Laughing, telling stories on each other all day, they sleep two sisters to a bed, with the toes of one sticking out of the covers by the other's head. Luisa moves from the quiet murmurous haze of her grief to the bright sunlight of laughter and jokes and knocks on the door. All day she rushes to attend not just her sisters but all the *visitas* that arrive. Everyone comes to congratulate Armando and the family on the marriage. Visitors come every day, old friends, neighbors, even acquaintances of Don Armando so many years earlier, several different groups an afternoon. The silver tray for the little cups of coffee had to be polished. Potatoes must be peeled! Dishes washed! Luisa and Teresa can hardly keep up with all the demands of hospitality. Luisa sent a letter by *flota* to call Cornelia to come and work again but it was her daughter Regina who came clomping heavily up the stairs. At a glance, Luisa knew she had exactly the same faults as her mother. With a sigh, Luisa began to train her as she had Cornelia.

Teresa helps with visitors but her heart is in the new baby; she begins to knit little sweaters, the yellow of baby chicks, blue of a summer sky, white bonnets and booties laced with ribbon, and as she does, she ponders her life. Her soul-searching continues as she marches from store to store to find the perfect bassinet, white. She paints it again; it is not white enough. Then she shops for yards of white lace to create a bouffant skirt for the bassinet; she brings yards of broad satin ribbon for bows. Finally, she enters the storage room, called the *pieza de reblujo*, called Luisa's room to tease her about its clutter of cardboard boxes and mildewed leather bags, of old jackets on hangers and three armoires full of old musty smelling clothes. There, buried under years of discards, Teresa finds a box covered in yellowed tissue. Smiling, she unwraps, layer after layer, the little white baptismal dress used for Diana. She washes it, starches it, irons it. She watches Debbie's swelling belly and counts every day till the birth. These special preparations fill her life with joy. Everything she touches becomes perfect under her hands. But, when Ines arrives, and when Teresa sees her aunt Ines, one of the two

Soto sisters who has never married, the one who has loved other people's children all her life, she sees, with a jolt, herself.

Ines' life has been spent packing and unpacking. Whenever anyone has a baby, the family calls Ines, and she responds to every call. First, she gets a new permanent, and then she packs her little bag, the same bag always with the same dress and some underwear and her knitting needles and elastic stockings for her varicose veins. Immediately, depending on the urgings and the lifestyle of the family, she takes a taxi or an express bus or if need be the *flota* to the house. Not a plane though--even if they send the ticket. She needs the earth beneath her. It doesn't matter if she arrives quickly in luxury or days later after a bumpy ride, smiling, she takes her place. With a pot of *manzanilla* tea between her and the new mother, Ines knits little sweaters and booties while the mother nurses the baby. Then Ines carries the baby around, patting its back until it burps and not caring about spit-up on her shoulder. She loves everything about babies. So does Teresa, but unlike Ines, Teresa can not bear to think she will spend her life carrying someone else's child.

Teresa thinks Ines' life has been hard, going from house to house, from family to family. Soon after Mama Teresa and Papa Jose died, there was a fire. *Gracias a Dios* no one died, *gracias a Dios* the faceted mirrors from Spain were carried to safely. But the house, the special house built in Manizales by Papa José, a man unlike any other and a house unlike any other, the house was gone. The big house fourth from the cathedral burned down in a fire so fierce that nothing remained except ashes that stirred and rose to the sky when they walked through them, trying to find some material witness to their lives. They stumbled over heavy black jagged rocks which were identified as the silver tea service and silver goblets and silver trays, melted and fused with the mahogany table and nails from the floor. These chunks of metal are kept in the storage room, under an armoire so no one stubs a toe on them. Occasionally they are weighed in the sisters' hands and pondered: enormous nuggets of sterling and ash and lead that can never be separated. Only the mirrors, glittering memory of times past, survive to hang in the new house Maruja buys in a new neighborhood, far from the cathedral.

The sale of the property brings money for the new house for the two unmarried daughters: Ines and Maruja. But the new house was chosen by Maruja and kept as Maruja wanted, right down to the brand of soap and the precise measures of sugar per square of chocolate for their breakfast. So Ines took to traveling; she went wherever she was invited. Wherever she went, and she went to the houses of all her nieces and nephews, all the cousins and second cousins, the history of the family was in her head; she told all the old stories. She was welcomed and given a chair at the dining room table and in front of the television and in the *sala*, bent over her knitting needles, click, click, click, her glasses down over her nose. With her new permanent wave for every new *visita*, for every new baby, her grey curly head was part of the scene. Also, there was the smell of baby powder and sour milk, the sound of a new baby's cry and Ines' soothing voice, which was different from her everyday voice. "*A ver, a ver, mijito.*" Those simple welcoming words and then the patpatpat on the little back and sob sob, sigh, silence. Yes, Ines had a talent for babies.

Teresa saw herself becoming like Ines. Luisa's words about every woman needing to make a nest for herself were too true. What nest, what house, what family was hers? Now Teresa waits for Debbie's baby, she looks over her life. What to do? For all her travels and clothes and car, not much was hers. Not even her name. She had been named for her grandmother Mama Teresa and for her mother, Teresa-who-died-so-easily, who died giving birth to her, as everyone said sadly and in one breath.

She remembers all this when her aunts arrive. The whole family, aunts and uncles and cousins who hadn't been seen for years, come to see Armando grown with a *gringa* as wife. It was expected that the Soto sisters, every one of them, would arrive early and stay long, but for the first time since the father Armando's death, and to everyone's surprise, the Gomez brothers came.

Enrique and Manuel and Elisa came with Enrique's children, grown men and women but of course no one from Manuel's family. Manuel who stayed all his life with the same woman but never married her, could not bring her or his children to Luisa's house. Still he made brave to come. He took his nephew aside and whispered an invitation in his ear, he clapped him on the back and hoped he would come to the house, to the store, for a meal or just to visit. Unsure if the invitation to his house would insult the *gringa*, he hinted and blushed. Manuel looked at the young Armando and saw his brother Armando, vigorous, handsome, ambitious, yes, just as they had all been thirty years earlier. Diego looked at his uncle's proud smile and saw his father. Debbie thrilled at the emotional response to their homecoming. Armando was grinning, happy to have his uncles in the house. Diego stood in the background, an angry lanky adolescent, but he was there. Diana was much admired as a *señorita* though she followed Teresa's lead, and along with Luisa, spent most of her time in the kitchen. There in the kitchen, as they prepared coffee and arranged cookies on the silver platters, and even among themselves they did not say anything bad about the Gomez side of the family. No. They were together, they were family. It was a first. After the visits subside, Luisa and Teresa take Debbie to mass and to visit friends. She is introduced to all and she learns to extend her hand and say her own name. Since she is obviously pregnant, the new baby is the object of every conversation. Debbie learns that the first word, after the polite introductions, is *primogénito,* a word that makes everyone smile and coo with happiness. Debbie can pronounce the word but has a hard time understanding its importance. "First born?" she puzzles. "Oh, yes, as I am first born." The two older women giggle and exchange glances. "*Sí, sí, sí,* Debbie." It wasn't the same thing at all to be born first as a girl in a country far away. She suffers from more barbaric ideas and her ignorance is revealed. She had never heard of *dieta,* the days, forty days, of bed rest after child birth. She thought it meant *diet* and indeed it included diet with certain important foods to build strength and increase milk, but that was only part of it. Again the mother-to-be refused to understand the need to change her life after the birth. She intended to carry on her life as usual with a baby in her arms. In the middle of this lesson, she used the rude and common expression for nursing, *mamar*, and Luisa and Teresa laugh so hard they have to leave the room.

And though everyone takes a liking to Debbie, the new member of the family, Teresa sees that she must take on the planning for the many things a new baby needs. She phones the aunts in Manizales who sweep up the finest wools in the whole city. There's an ongoing clacking in the house like the conversation of small animals as all the sisters knit. They vie for the sweetest softest sweater sets with matching booties and cap. Debbie brought two little sweaters, machine made in the USA, and diapers and flannel blankets and pins shaped like little bunnies. She has a half dozen undershirts and night gowns. But these are nothing: no umbilical bands to hold in the belly button and nothing handmade for the newborn's soft skin.

Debbie is strong and healthy and refuses to allow herself to be pampered as she ought. When the baby is born, Luisa and Teresa bring a nurse maid, one highly recommended by one of Teresa's friends, to the house. Her job is to carry Debbie through the *dieta*. For forty days the nurse will bathe and care for mother and baby. She has special shopping list since she also cooks the special meals every mother needs. Luisa has to pay the taxi driver extra to drive the nurse to the plaza de mercado to get all the special foods for Debbie's *dieta*. Chicken soup with yellow bubbles and sprigs of green cilantro floating on top. Orange juice, freshly squeezed. Malt ale. The nurse and Luisa want the new mother to stay in bed day and night and call for the bed pan. They put a little bell at her bedside.

The nurse has a full day planned. She arrives the same day that Debbie and the baby come home from the hospital. She has a brilliantly white uniform and a schedule: the nurse brings baby to nurse, the nurse brings mother's breakfast, the nurse gives baby his bath, the nurse gives mother her bath, and then it starts all over again: baby nurses, mother's lunch, *siesta* for all. So goes the day. Before bedtime, the nurse brings the silver tray with a bottle of *malta*, room temperature since cold beverages might slow down milk production. The nurse pours the dark liquid into the pretty glass and puts it on the lace coaster on the platter.

Debbie picks up the glass and examines it. It looks like beer, smells a bit like beer. The look on her face when she tastes it makes everyone laugh. As soon as the nurse leaves the room, the young mother leaps out of bed and pours it out the window. The nurse returns and clucks approvingly at the empty glass. She has a serious responsibility and lots of knowledge. Only a few days advance before the nurse is openly thwarted. The lady mother will not stay in bed, she will not drink malt ale or flaxseed tea. *Gringas* are barbaric, the nurse declares and hopes she will not be held responsible. Luisa tries to explain but Debbie insists on bathing herself and washing her hair. She walks around like a peasant with the baby slung over her shoulder.

Every morning, after the first feeding, after the warm bath, the nurse wraps the baby first with the umbilical band and then the diaper and undershirt and then rolls him up into a tight cylinder in one of the receiving blankets. Over this she puts the sweater set and matching hat. "*Hermoso!*" is the call around the room. "Just like a little cigar!" Debbie unwraps him and delights at his kicks and wiggles. She carries him nude into the sun. The two old women stand by and whisper; the nurse nodding darkly as she tells stories of sickly infants and fallen female parts and death too from extreme exertion after child birth. Armando laughs at them all.

Despite Luisa's worries, she proclaims everything about the baby perfect. He has short fine golden hair and dark blue grey eyes and a wide forehead announcing great intelligence. When Tomás is a week old there begins another steady procession of visitors from all over the country to welcome the new baby and to congratulate the family. Luisa has not been so happy in her memory. She is busy and useful, telling Debbie about the family, teaching Regina, cradling the little golden-haired baby who is her grandson.

It is by accident that Luisa hears the discussion; Debbie and Teresa are bent over the baby. There's a pretty scene: Debbie nursing the new baby, a beautiful boy with such sweet features. Luisa is bringing a pot of tea for them. The cups tinkle on the silver tray as she comes up the hall toward the big bedroom where the *cama de matrimonio*, her marriage bed that has been empty so many years. Silent in the doorway, she enjoys the sight of the baby tugging noisily at the breast. She remembered that warm happiness. While enjoying that pleasant memory she happens to hear the question Teresa asks with a little laugh of embarrassment. She has said it as a joke, while drawing on her cigarette. Teresa concentrates on Debbie's face. If she sees some hesitation, she will deny her request and there will be no hard feelings. Wedding dress? The white lace wedding dress? Debbie, confused, repeats the question. Luisa however understands immediately why Teresa wants the white wedding dress and her heart stops.

# CHAPTER 11

## The Sisters

### Medellín Colombia

Now the family is together. As she cradles the baby, Teresa is elated that the *tías*, the women who raised her, are all united after so many years. All the Soto sisters are there in the little sala, the one with the falling apart leather sofa set that is for family. It is the first time they are all together, except for the funerals that came all in a row: Mama Teresa, Papa José, the big house, famous in the city of Manizales and their minds, the big house fourth from the Cathedral that burned to the ground. The third death was Armando's and it put an end to that cycle of misery. But here they were together for a happy occasion, a wedding, and a new baby.

Here are the sisters: Ines and Maruja who come from Manizales, the big house fourth from the Cathedral. They never married. Solita, her name, sad to think of, is given a musical twist to rob it of some of its misery, Solita is here with Victor of course, he is in the balcony window watching the busy sidewalks and streets. Even her daughter Rebecca is here. *Pobrecita* they all think, she married a drunk just like her father but no one speaks of that, at least on this day. Sofia came the longest distance, by *flota* all the way from Pereira, with her husband that good man Julio, but he disappeared quickly from the circle of the sisters. Of course one of the newlyweds, Debbie, is there in the middle of it, trying, poor thing, to follow the conversations, so full of laughter and family history. Armando accepted his congratulations, translated a few words and found an excuse to leave the house.

As Luisa's sisters renew their bonds, as the new baby brings them all together, other times, other babies come to mind and to heart. Luisa watches Teresa cradling the new baby and although Teresa is now close to forty years old, Luisa recalls her as a newborn. *O la niña, la niña*! She could see her, tiny and blue in the crude cage on the back of the man who had carried her across the mountains. Luisa remembers, and tears sting her eyes, how of all the sisters, it was she, Luisa, who finally warmed the little girl, who warmed the milk and held the bottle so she would suck. The little baby Teresa had chosen Luisa as her mother. Of course, she had become so engrossed in these other children, her children, of course but not orphans, not struggling for life as Teresa had.

Luisa brings in the tray and stands blinking in the light of the question about the wedding dress. She does not want to know the answer and when Debbie questions Teresa, foolishly thinking that Teresa might have a *novio* hidden somewhere, Luisa puts down the tray and stumbles back out the door. She hurries to the back patio where the tupiales shriek and clang their cages together in hopes of food. Unseeing, Luisa looks up at the sky, suddenly empty of clouds or sun.

She is reliving the day Adiela entered the convent. On that dark day as on many others, Teresa shared Luisa's sorrows. Teresa walked with her sister Adiela, and Luisa walked with Santiago Mejia, the best friend of Armando. In silence and two by two they walked to the convent and in through its wide doors. Armando had stayed at home, closed in his room. Luisa and Teresa and Santiago had walked in with Adiela and left her there. How they got home and what they said, she cannot remember.

Luisa leans against the wall, glad Armando is not here to relive the pain of that day.

Teresa of course is not remembering that day. She takes the baby from Debbie's arms and holds him on her shoulder, brushing his cheek with hers, inhaling the delicious smell of a new baby. She walks to the balcony and lets some sun shine on his little head, the hairs blonde in the light. She kisses him and called him *hermoso*. Carrying that little body, Teresa is reminded of a dream she once had of marriage and a husband and a life of her own, of children of her own and the warm nest of a family, her own family where no one is an orphan and everyone loves everyone. It wasn't to be. Instead she has given her youth to the family.

When Luisa heard the Teresa question Debbie about the wedding dress, she understood that it was about Teresa and the convent. Luisa was knocked backwards, oh so many days and years, into a fearful place of loss and grief and solitude. It didn't matter that she had her sons with her and that the two oldest at least were following their father's footsteps. Suddenly she didn't care that she had a daughter and a grandchild. Teresa was leaving.

Surely the name Teresa had a curse on it. Wasn't her mother's life, Mama Teresa's life full of pain? And look at her sister, mother of Adiela and Teresa, Teresa-who-died-so-easily.

Sisters were linked through blood and through names. The name Adiela for instance didn't mean a thing. And that's the way Adiela led her life, as though nothing mattered. Luisa too. A plain name, empty of meaning. Sofia. And Ines. But Sola. Sola, was short for *soledad* which sounded very pretty with a la-la like a song. But it was very hard; solitude was the hardest thing in life. Solitude was hard but having a child like Victor was harder. The name Teresa too carried a heavy weight. Teresa carries the baby and ponders her life. With the chatter of the *tias* in the kitchen, Teresa remembered all her aunts and how she lived with them in Manizales.

When she was very young, a *niña* living in the big house fourth from the Cathedral, her aunt Sola had had a *novio,* a serious boyfriend. Late at night, he brought serenades to Sola's window on the second floor. Teresa and Adiela insisted on peeking at the three musicians there in the lamplight and the handsome Uriel who sometimes sang the love words himself but mostly looked towards the window, where, inside, unseen, Sola swooned and her older sisters frowned in disapproval. Her mother and father slept in the quiet back bedrooms. Teresa could still remember those songs, songs she had memorized and sung to the applause of all but Papa Jose who did not understand where the *niña* could have learned such street songs, songs heard only on the radio and at bars. Sola's *novio*, Uriel, gave her little gifts, candy and books of poetry and letters, all by means of Teresa. She loved her job as messenger of the lovers. She could not use her position to lord it over Adiela--it was one of the greatest temptations of her early life. She had to keep the secret, something she learned early to do.

Teresa first learned the little song about a serenading sweetheart. Uriel always called around *siesta* time, when all the others were sleeping, with a whistle of the refrain, "I come unto your window." He stood against the wall near the window and when he heard the child running up to the window and saw her little hand reaching out the wrought iron grille, he would sing in a sweet tenor, just a whisper of itself, "Won't you come out to me?" That was because a *señorita* as strict as Sola could never go to the window by herself to receive anything from the hand of a man. Teresa understood this perfectly and so she became their messenger. She listened for the song of the man who called her little princess; she quietly delivered the small packages and envelopes to Sola. The child thought Uriel with his blue grey eyes and smooth brown hair was very handsome. *Novio*. *Novio* was a special word.

Yes, she had her hand in that tragedy. How many notes did she carry? Each one a nail in the coffin of Sola's happiness. Now Sola had been *sola*--- alone, almost abandoned for forty years, almost all her life. Of course Sola had to take blame for marrying Uriel who turned out to be the good for nothing Papa Jose said he was. Papa Jose never liked him. He had warned Sola and when she didn't listen, he made Mama Teresa come out of her room. Adiela and Teresa were dumbfounded to see their grandmother walking the halls of the big house. They followed her, clutching each other and shrieking, ducking behind doors and each other when she stopped or turned. She moved slowly from one cane to the other, her long black dress sweeping the floors to Sola's room, leaving behind her an odor of moth balls and candle wax and something else.

Even that momentous voice could not sway Sola. Too late. *Loca*, some said. *Boba* others said. She was under a spell. Sola was the second youngest of the *tias* and pretty and sweet. Ah Solita! For all his grey eyes and sweet voice, Teresa and the whole family soon came to despise Uriel. He was the very worst thing that a man could be. He was a drunkard. Always was, till the day he died. Drunk then too, God forgive him.

He started out an ordinary man though too handsome, too charming. Papa Jose saw the flaw in him right away. He worked for about six months at the job Papa Jose helped him get and lived in the house Papa Jose bought and furnished for them. Then one day there were loud discussions in Mama Teresa's room and weeping and Papa Jose *furioso* for days and Sola's name came into all the prayers of the house. After that, everything was quiet about Sola for a long time.

About three years after the marriage, Uriel walked out on Sola. Left her with Rene, just like him to give his first son a pretentious French name, just like him to leave his wife with Rene just starting to walk and a newborn daughter, Rebecca. If Maruja and Ines hadn't gone to visit Sola, if they hadn't broken with Papa Jose's wishes, then no one from the family would have ever known Solita was alone. If Maruja and Ines had not knocked on the door and discovered her coldly alone with babies and no money--God knows what would have happened, because Sola would never have told them. Uriel had cleared out the bank account and even sold some of the furniture. The *sinverguenza*. Never was a man a better example of *sinverguenza*, a man without shame, than Uriel.

The family just gave thanks that the brute was gone and Papa Jose went to the bank and set up a new account with more money and made Sola promise not to give any to Uriel. But what use was that promise? Sola was sad the whole time—several years he was gone--though she hid her sorrow and talked and visited with her sisters and brought her babies to play at the big house fourth from the cathedral. She knew she was needed there because it was quiet and sad with Luisa and the little girls Adiela and Teresa gone. Sola continued to do all the things she might have done if she were the happiest woman in the world. Then, unknown to the family, Uriel came back and what could she do? She did what a wife had to do and these lessons in matrimony confirmed Adiela's choice and made Teresa fearful. Just before dinner one fine evening, Uriel walked in the door. He stayed two months, sang all his songs, recited all his poems, took all the money and left Sola again, this time pregnant with Victor.

Of course everyone in the family blamed him for Victor. There was another name for his infirmity, a medical name, but no one could remember it. Victor from his earliest months showed evidence that for all his pretty blonde hair and grey eyes, he was *bobo,* retarded. The family didn't say it, and Sola just bowed her head a little lower. They called Sola the same word, *boba,* a fool, which shows how far a word can go. Sola was to go on all her life in love with gray eyes.

It was a cross for Sola! She had to raise those children, alone. Well, not exactly alone because she had to be with Victor every minute of every day. When he was still a baby, and already beginning to show signs of what he was, some of the servants said he would not live long. He would die young and innocent and that was the blessing of the illness he was born with. But it wasn't true. With his big head and eyes like a Chinaman's he lived to be an old man. Someone in the plaza taught him to smoke cigarettes as a joke. They would offer him lit cigarettes and show him how to inhale. How they laughed when he choked! But he learned and then he had another word he shouted at his mother: smoke! And even if there was no money for food she would search her pockets for a few *centavos* to carry to the candy and tobacco vender in the plaza. The man came to know her, and seeing her approach, he would pull two of the sweet strong Pielrojas out of the packet. She would hurry back to her house, head bowed, and little feet in soft slippers shuffling in the door. Seeing the satisfaction on her son's face when he drew a lungful of smoke made her happy. Poor Victor! Old and cranky and a tyrant over poor Sola; she loved him so much she could not even die for who would care for him if she did?

Sola's whole life would be like this. Hard. Couldn't have been harder. It made Teresa rejoice she had escaped motherhood. Teresa always wanted a child—she kisses the baby in her arms, but to have a son who wasn't complete! Sola's oldest son Rene turned out to be a drunk just like his father. The last the family had seen him he was tall thin boy with bad pimples. Now he was a man, married somewhere and abusing his wife no doubt. He never came around the family. They never saw Rebecca, Sola's daughter, either. The cousins didn't know each other as children. The curse of Uriel kept them away. The one and only time Teresa saw her cousin, she developed, instantly, a child's unreasonable hatred for her Rebecca's blond hair and gray eyes, like a real princess someone had said. Then Rebecca got married, too young, and Luisa sent a silver platter, but not one of the family went to the wedding. Uriel might have been there.

So Solita started a custom that lasted until just last year when she was finally too old, and the famous *flotas* gave way to ordinary buses. In the old days a *flota* bus driver had an assistant called the *fogonero*, the stoker, who had no engines to stoke but who helped with all the special cases. The *flota* would take, for instance a very old woman where she was going. The *fogonero* would treat her with respect, calling her *Doña*, helping her up the big step and into the uncomfortable bench seat. She would be carried safely to her destination and the same *fogonero* would take her hand and help her into the arms of her family who was waiting for her. Modern buses took none of these cares. Comfort yes, with a soft seat for each rump and always the same price, but no special cases. The modern bus drivers wouldn't let Sola get on the bus. "*Señora*, who's accompanying you?" And when they saw Victor behind her, Victor with his big head and shifty eyes, they snorted and threw the money back at her. But for all the years that the *flota* lasted, she came regularly, every fifteen days, with Victor of course, scrubbed and combed, to pay a formal visit. As though she were not a sister she would knock at the door at three in the afternoon and bring some little gift, not fancy candies or flowers but a nice avocado or a mango. And the family received her too as a proper *visita* and Victor too and took them into the *sala* and then into the dining room to have a nice *algo*, the best they had, cake or crackers with yellow cheese. They talked about a thousand things, but they never talked about *sinverguenza* Uriel or the fallen Rene.

Luisa helped her sister with Victor. Victor was a few months younger than Diego, a leader of the soccer game in the plaza, when Luisa helped

Sola teach Victor to talk, just a few words for politeness sake, *por favor* and *gracias*. He balked at *mucho gusto* and shaking hands because he already knew how people saw him. Together Sola and Luisa taught him to be polite and keep his tongue in his mouth the way all Christians do.

One day Sola brought a large shopping bag and in it a package wrapped in a pillow case. It was the photo album of Rebecca's wedding. She thanked them of course for the beautiful silver platter, but she didn't ask why they didn't come. In fact she hadn't sent them an invitation, conscious of her sisters' opinions of the marriage. The two sisters sat together on the sofa and opened the album. The photos showed that Rebecca, like her mother Sola, married a handsome man, a fair-haired man with blue eyes. She was a beautiful bride too-- though she soon looked like an old woman, as old as her mother. Because she too married a drunk, one who was even worse than her father. Her father at least treated them with some kind of respect; he only disappeared for months and years to drink all their money, but Rebecca married a brute. She paid for it too. She thought make up could cover the pain as it covered the bruises but it didn't.

So when Sola came to pay the *visita* with Victor, the sisters, after a few minutes of curious observation, paid no attention to Victor. Teresa who always prided herself on her manners was, for a few minutes anyway, very attentive to Victor. She talked to him, asking him how he was until he blushed and Sola interjected with an embarrassed laugh, "*Bien! Bien*, Victor, speak!" But he does not speak and Teresa turns away. She walks back into the room where the picture of the Sacred Heart of Jesus is smiling down on Debbie and the baby. Luisa rushes to pick up the tray and study Teresa's face. Did the question about the wedding dress mean that Teresa was following her sister's path? Was it possible that now Teresa was leaving?

It was possible and for once there was no discussion. She had lived helping Luisa, but now she would live for herself. A new life, and she prayed, a holy one. She would give her best years to the convent, to the church, to the Father, Son and Holy Ghost, amen.

# CHAPTER 12

# What's in a Name?

### Medellín Colombia 1960

Teresa, though her name was full of family pain, had traveled and gone to university. She owned her own little car. She was comparing her life to her aunts' lives. Teresa had friends, she traveled to Europe and brought back blessings from two popes and art books from the museums and a new hair cut and expensive make up from Miami, but what? Most of her life involved Luisa, the house and the children. And now they are grown. She was too busy to notice her life rushing by. Now with the house full of visitors and a new baby, she sees what she has become. Only one door is open to her. She will enter the convent, the *Sagrado Corazon*, a French religious order that runs the university where she studied. With their large white pleated bonnets and flowing black capes, they are holy women, devoted to the Sacred Heart of Jesus and teaching. Once Teresa has decided, she finds it hard to confine herself to life in an ordinary house. She drinks in the warmth and smells of the new baby while she can.

In those last days, when she is not carrying the baby, she sits in the dining room, alone at the table, smoking and drinking her black coffee. At Debbie's request, the large life-sized painting of Jesus now lives in the dining room. Teresa meditates on the painting of the Sacred Heart that is part of her earliest memories. Armando continues to progress, now with a good job with a respectable title. Diego has earned his university degree in architecture, a field that is both artistic and practical. Diana has had her *Quinceañera* party which, through Teresa's efforts is the most charming of parties with *petit fours* and marzipan made by Teresa's own hand.

With all the visitors, with the newlyweds in the biggest bedroom, and with Luisa in charge again, Teresa takes her black coffee and cigarettes and sleeps on the leather sofa. She is there, watching television and smoking when everyone goes to bed. The next morning, she is there, damp and smelling of Palmolive, dressed in a neatly ironed white blouse and dark skirt, running a comb through her curly hair as she sips hot black coffee and smokes Pielroja, the narrow oval cigarettes made of sweetened black tobacco. No one ever stays up late enough or gets up early enough to catch her sleeping. Sleep, she scoffs. She has never had time to sleep.

Now she has time and to spare. She takes on extra classes at the University and spends time there in her office. Of course, she has friends. But when she calls them, they have children's tennis classes and trips with their husbands. They have made, as Luisa always says, their lives into a nest around them, while she, Teresa, has not. Now she bides her time and talks to the Sacred Heart of Jesus. As she crumbles her bread at the table, she watches his pale fingers counting the hours. *Sí Señor*, she says in prayer. I'm coming.

Teresa's friends come later in the day to sit in the formal *sala* and drink *tinto* out of the little china cups with gold rims. The newlyweds, several times a day, had to enter there and bow and be introduced and accept the welcome and good wishes. Debbie hurries back to Luisa's sisters in the little family sala where they gossip and giggle and occasionally brush away a tear as they recall their sister Teresa-who-died-so-easily. With this eager new listener, they try to explain all the history of the family to Debbie. Luisa, delighted to find new ears, tells her sisters the story of the marriage. How Diego called to announce it on the telephone and she almost didn't pick up the phone. How he sent the picture and the letter. "Where? Where is it?" It is Solita who wants the whole story. Luisa runs to bring out the picture and everyone studies it and compares it to the real girl in front of them. They all read the letter. Even with the flesh and blood newlyweds in the house, the photo and the letter are studied. It is a beautiful story, *hermoso*! They repeat over and over. As for the girl, she does not look like a *gringa* and she isn't quite as pretty as the picture. She is not blond, not blue eyed, but she has a nice smile. "Pretty teeth," they say at last, nodding in approval. "*Gringa*," they say and exchange worried smiles. Luisa just laughs and pronounces, "*Bendito sea Dios*!"

Ines, the best knitter, has her needles and yarn on her lap. She remembers Adiela who was her girl in those early days and wishes she were among them. Adiela who could not leave her place in the convent for her father's death certainly can not leave for newlyweds. The *Madre Superiora* agrees, however, to a family visit. For the first time in twenty-five years, Adiela dials that old number and greets Luisa who is struck dumb and passes the phone to Ines who can only blubber and does not hear at all, and finally the gringa is tongue tied while Adiela speaks in her few words of English to the gringa. Only Teresa can speak and she helps set a day and time for all to come to visit the convent. There will be a wire grille and a grey gauze veil between them but Adiela will come close enough to touch fingers with them. After nine years, Armando is back in Colombia. Newlyweds in the house! God is good! And no one could disagree.

But close on the heels of happiness is sorrow. The perfect happiness of the newlyweds and the baby only lasted a short while. Standing in the door, observing, Luisa heard the Teresa question Debbie about the wedding dress. She understood that it was about Teresa and the convent. Luisa was knocked backwards, oh so many days and years, into a fearful place of loss and grief and solitude. It didn't matter that she had her sons with her and that the two oldest at least were following their father's footsteps. That she had a grandchild. Teresa was leaving the Plaza Zea.

She allowed no farewells or companions. She went alone, on the plane, carrying a small suit case. Once in Cali, a taxi carried her to the big convent with acres and acres of gardens and trees. She knocked on the big double doors and waited while the Mistress of Novitiates came to welcome her. She spent four years there, behind closed doors, four years in preparation, four years in discipline and submission. During the first year even phone calls were discouraged. There was one formal visit at the end of the second year when the whole family was allowed to visit. The four little boys, three of them born since Teresa left the Plaza Zea, were scrubbed and polished to be presented to the sisters in the convent. They went, all of the family, every adult with a child to carry or lead carefully by the hand. That helped. All the little boys, four of them, and Ines came from Manizales and it was quite a procession. Armando, like his father, did not go, though for vastly different reasons. The youngest son, was in the United States, a place where Luisa hoped he would find his life. Hadn't Armando gone to the United States a boy who hated school and studying and returned a doctor, a real doctor with a university degree and a wife? Sighing, Luisa weaves a prayer with a name as she has always done. *"Dios te salve María, O Dios,* Diego, Diego," Luisa prayed that he would be so transformed that after a few years he would return to get a good job and build a family as Armando was doing. Or he might come back and go to university like Pablo. Or get a good job in a good business. Or. Or. Those were Luisa's prayers that day at the convent. When Teresa, in the white lace wedding dress, emerged from the dark doors to walk alone down the center aisle to the altar, Luisa wept. Teresa, Teresa! There was her mother Teresa whose life had been a Calvary, and her sister Teresa-who-died-so-easily. Luisa wept for the little orphan babies and for this new pain in her heart. With solemnity and women's voices singing hymns to the Blessed Mother, Teresa professed her desire and her intention, and Luisa's prayers were a jumble of petitions and desperate pleas for solace.

In the assembly Luisa bowed her head. The four years that had brought Teresa to the altar had brought Luisa three new little boys. Only the little boys, her grandsons who were standing and hopping and crawling everywhere, who insisted on squirming into her lap to pat her face, brought her back out of the cave of grief. They would be woven into a picture of the loss of the baby Teresa and the woman Teresa and another loss. Diego, her son, seemed as lost to her as Armando her husband, twenty-five years gone.

Still, she prayed. She had hope that Diego, the youngest son, he who had suffered so much in life, would mend his life. He was away in the United States, a place full of temptations and gangsters. She did not say such because Debbie and Diego shushed her and laughed at her, but she knew. Her mother's heart knew the family was split up again. Everything they said about life being a vale of tears was true.

The whole family returned to the Plaza Zea, leaving Teresa to her vocation. But the world got crazy as every one began to grow up all at once. At times Luisa had a baby on her knee. She clapped those baby hands and sang the song of the baby chick, listening to the voice, laughing and imitating, "*Pio, pio pio.*" Then the same boy was in first grade and considered himself too old to sit on her knee and make baby chick sounds. There were other little boys born and growing and when they all came to her house, she had to run through the list of names, Tomás, Guillermo, Jeffrey, David! They laughed and squealed as they ran past her until she came to the right name and that little boy, one of so many in her life, wrapped his arms around her knees and called her *Abuelita*. God was good, God was very good. *Bendito sea Dios*! She bent over that little body, squeezing it and planting kisses on the squirming bundle of energy whose name she had already forgotten again.

One day Cornelia came in to help. She found a love letter to Diana from a boy. Folded into a lover's knot, it had been thrust in the pocket of Diana's uniform. Cornelia brought it to Luisa and there in the kitchen the two of them pored over the clumsy letters. They huddled over the cheap tablet paper and their fingers smudged the ink as they spelled out the words. *Imposible! Imposible! Dios mio*! Luisa put it in her pocket, there with all the keys to all the doors and all the armoires and her rosary from Jerusalem. The paper was proof. Proof! She pondered all that day what to do. She confided in Pablo, but she did not show him the note. Pablo was no help at all! His eyes grew big and his jaw fell down. "Are you sure? She's just a child. You're imagining things!" He looked serious but turned and walked away. Where was Armando!

The girl needed a father to make her respected in the world. That night there was a serenade.

There had been a serenade a week earlier but Luisa had foolishly thought it was for the silly Cordoba girl next door. The melodies, the protestations of love and promises of forever wormed their way into her sleep. Those songs! They were the same songs she had heard in Manizales as Sola's *sinverguenza* promised his adoration and love. Luisa threw her robe over her shoulders and without stopping for slippers she ran to the window. Yes, it was in front of her house. Three men, musicians and a thin dark figure under the very palm trees her husband had planted. She ran to Pablo. "Get up! Get up! See. It's just as I said! Go chase him away, the *sinverguenza*!"

He did get up. Grumbling, he went to the window of the sala and pulled the heavy lace curtains aside. "It's a serenade, all right." Luisa smoothed the curtains from Belgium, brought by her husband Armando on one of his trips and now the witnesses to this new danger. It was important to her that the *sinverguenza* in the street would not see any acknowledgment of his visit there. Luisa was growling in frustration.

Finally she hissed, "Can't I see it's a serenade?" Their faces were inches apart.

"I know those musicians. They hang around the bar--"

"The bar! Worse and worse!"

She hardly slept all night. The lyrics ran through her mind along with images of babies, little ones falling into dark holes where they cried and no one listened. The next morning she called Diego and Debbie. They laughed at her. They thought it was natural. Natural! How barbaric Americans were and her son was becoming an American. Who would help her with this? Teresa!

She called the operator and told her it was urgent. The phone at the convent rang for ten minutes but Luisa never thought of hanging up. Finally the door man answered. He couldn't understand who she was or why she needed to speak to the *Madre* Teresa who was not to be disturbed.

"*Señora*," the fool said. "The *Madre* Teresa is a nun. She's not allowed...."

Fortunately he was deaf.

"Death, you say, death? Is there a death in the family?"

"*Sí, sí, sí*!" Luisa's fears all poured out. She clenched the black receiver until she heard, after a long delay, Teresa's terrified voice. "Bisa, Bisa," the baby name she had invented for Luisa thirty years earlier, "who died? The baby? O *Jesus, Jose y María*!"

When she heard what had happened, she knew Luisa had done the right thing. Teresa agreed that that little lie about a death was justified. Diana with a *novio*? *Es posible*? Can it be, Can it be? The two voices were like tremulous in their exchange. Well, yes, it turned out. It was possible. The girl was sixteen. Hadn't they put together an elegant tea with friends from the school, the *Enseñanza* where Diana was now in her last year, to celebrate her fifteenth year? The *quinceañera* was traditionally a woman. But what to do now! Who was this boy?

"And last night there was a serenade--"

"A serenade!" In Teresa's mind she saw the handsome Uriel who called her *princesa* and taught her to sing, "Come to your window...."

"Luisa! *Por Dios*! You must do something."

Praying, weeping, lamenting, the two women determined to stop the romance.

The next morning Luisa roused Cornelia before dawn.

"There's no help for it. You have to walk her to school." Cornelia nodded and closed her door. She would find her street clothes and after a shower in the little *excusado*, the cement cubicle with a shower head and a toilet, not a proper bathroom the way rich people had with tiles and tubs and such but still better than what any *pobre* had, she readied herself. Luisa in the meantime started breakfast and waited for her daughter to appear.

"*Dios mio, Dios mio*!" She punctuated each orange, halved and squashed in the press. It took a dozen protestations to fill a glass. Diana came running out, cheerfully she reached for the glass and asked after Cornelia. Luisa turned to her, examined her frankly as she would another woman.

"Cornelia is getting ready to go out on the street."

"Oh." Suspiciously, "and what's the Corna going to do on the street so early?"

"Accompany you to school, *sinverguenza*!"

That word once out was like a fire. Cornelia came running out to calm the two who screamed at each other. The young woman was pale with anger but unable to deny the paper that Luisa pulled from her apron pocket and shook like a dirty rag in her face. Luisa, her motherly fears aroused, poured out years of anger. At this, Cornelia appeared, clad in her best outfit and carefully shod, patting her self into place.

"I won't walk with her. I won't walk down the street with a servant!" Cornelia's lip trembled.

"You can stay at home then. I talked to Teresa and we decided. And your brothers too. We won't let you see this *negro mala clase*! You're not a street girl! Remember that. You were raised to be somebody!"

Diana turned and ran sobbing back down the hallway and into her room. Luisa and Cornelia stood close but not looking into the other's face. They move a few steps one way and then the other. They moved their heads like cows in some vague search, swaying and silent. Cornelia started to go into her room to change out of her good street clothes, a special sweater and shoes from the United States and not at all like what servants wore, when Luisa stopped her with a hand.

"No, you must be ready to go if she goes. I'll do this."

For two weeks the house was turned upside down. Cornelia got up early and put on her best clothes. Luisa worked in the kitchen, burning not just the rice but potatoes and meat and her famous tomato pie. She scrubbed and complained and accused the kitchen and life itself of being ungrateful. "*Desagradecidos*!" to all of life and then "*Desagradecida*!" to her daughter. Somehow the serenades stopped. Somehow. It must have been prayer. Diana became again a school girl. Within a few months another young man began hanging around. Luisa immediately enlisted Pablo to find out his name, all his names, mother's mother and father, father's father and mother and their businesses and reputations. After she had the list, she called Teresa and they traced back his names, searching diligently for respectability. He came from a big family and lived in a big house. Not as big as the house, fourth from the Cathedral in Manizales, but still passable. The boy was just starting medical school.

With a sigh of relief, Luisa put away her worries about her daughter. The courtship was short but old fashioned with Debbie playing the chaperone to occasional movies. Once the wedding date was fixed Diana was allowed to walk to mass with her young man while Luisa watched them from the balcony. Luisa and Debbie bought magazines and cut out pictures of brides. Teresa, whose energy had made her important at the convent from the first week, took some liberties. She spent hours on the telephone conferring on the style of the gown, the menu for the brunch, the time and place.

Little Tomás, the first born, carried the rings and Diego, handsome in his white dinner jacket, escorted the beautiful bride to the altar. Then there was the reception with Regina and Cornelia enjoying the fiesta, observing the hired waiters, and appraising the gifts stacked high on tables. There were strangers everywhere, many of them now family since his family and hers were united. Teresa and Adiela both called from the convents, greeting Luisa first and enquiring about the party, the food, the nuptial mass. Both sisters called, only minutes apart, to give their warm blessing to both the bride and the groom. Teresa had helped to plan the honeymoon, nothing vulgar like Paris or Miami but a simple few days at one of the groom's family's fincas. The young couple, beautiful in their innocence drove away leaving Luisa and Debbie and Cornelia and Regina with many details of the wedding to recount and piles of dishes to wash.

It seemed to Luisa only minutes before there was another dark eyed little boy running up and down the hallway of the old house and calling her.

# CHAPTER 13

# Calling Their Names

### Medellín Colombia 1980

"Pablo. Tomás. Guillermo." These names mark the pendulum of her pace. "Diego. Armando. Jeffrey. Juan." The names of all the dark eyed strong- willed little boys of her life come to her like prayers. She repeats them, and then pauses before one of the several open doors off the hallway. She giggles, remembering how they hide from her, in the wardrobes behind the hanging dresses or standing, making themselves small, behind this very door. A smile creases her face as she recalls their hoots of delight, their arms around her knees when they leap out at her. "Juan. Armando. Tomás. Guillermo. Pablo. David," continuing. Mixing the generations. A rude girl comes laughing at her. She is not Cornelia or even Regina the daughter of Cornelia. She is, as she insists in a sassy tone of voice, the daughter of Regina and the granddaughter of Cornelia. *Impossible!* The old woman stops her pacing and naming the names to face a girl, a red faced country girl without any shoes. Surely she is Cornelia who never learned anything she didn't want to, like wearing shoes. Here she is, like Cornelia, taking liberties, grabbing the old woman by the arm and leading her to the dining room.

Ah, there they are. Old men. Old men who shake their heads and catch each other's eye. Stopping, flustered at first, then seeing their expressions, she giggles, then purses her lips and pulls down her chin, willing herself into dignity and back into the present time. "Ah hah.

Ah hah. Here are my sons." She can do this; she can will herself back to the present. She doesn't always know when she speaks out loud and when she speaks in her head. It suits her not to know. "They think they know everything but I'm here to tell them that they are ignorant. Completely ignorant of what happens in life!" She pokes her food with her fork, jabbing it into order as she murmurs to herself cautions. "*No, por Dios*, Luisa! Don't let them catch you--"

Abruptly she confronts them. She stands, picks up her plate, and pauses to observe in her old manner, the same voice with the same wry smile, that Cornelia-Regina-Ana, that girl in the kitchen who is of no use at all, burned the rice again and that there was no steak for the dog. Still enjoying their amazed expressions, she leaves the room. In the middle of life, surrounded by people, she can always bring herself back to this material world, but alone--.

Alone in the big house, and it seems like years she is alone, she walks from the balcony to the kitchen, from one end of the house, the public end that looked out onto the Plaza Zea with the palm trees Armando had planted, back to the other end, the kitchen and servants' rooms and the patio where the tupiales and the towels hanging on the line took the sun. If she passes through her bedroom, the Virgin winks at her and she must stop and fish the rosary out of her apron pocket, untangle it from the keys to the wardrobe where the money and the important papers are kept, separate its beads from the crumpled man's handkerchief and the wrinkled peso bills. She stands before the Virgin, the beautiful blue-eyed Virgin that has been her companion all her life and who has worked miracles in times past. Then she may hear a long litany of voices, all the voices of her life calling her to prayer and then her voice calling others to prayer–forever and ever since she could remember. With her head bowed and her eyes screwed shut tight tight, she calls in a loud voice, a voice loud enough to be heard all over the house, "*Dios te salve Maria llena eres de gracia*...." And then she slumps into silence as only the tupiales answer and what do they know of prayer. Alone, alone.

If she does not walk through her room but down the hallway, each shiny tile a step, then she calls the little boys as she did when they raced up and down this hall a hundred times a day. *No, por Dios*! a hundred times a day she called, Diego! Pablo, don't run, Tomás! Don't shout so! David, Juan, where are you, rascals! Hiding in the wardrobes just as that naughty Adiela and Teresa did, ruining the dresses and trampling the soft petticoats folded and stacked by color, everything pink here and the yellow there with matching blouses and silk stockings for when Armando came. "Adiela. Teresa. Diego." Then louder as if the time drew in synch, "Pablo! Pablo!" The old dog came and nudged her with his cold black nose. What? A dog in her house! It gives her a moment's start but now she remembers and pats his head. She walks back with him to the kitchen where she takes his pan and fills it with the dry dog food Diego insists on feeding him. Poking at it with her finger she decides that the dog, poor brute, deserves better since didn't he mourn just as she how the little boys are gone?

Why do they call them *brutes*? They're not. This dog is as smart as any Christian. He went crazy. The way any sane person might. With the faintest pricking of conscience, (didn't someone tell her not to give him meat or cheese?), she sets to work. How can it hurt him? Everyone knows that dogs like meat above all things. With the big shepherd walking at her knee she goes to the refrigerator, a fancy one brought by Diego from the United States. General of course. In this house there was only General Electric from the time when Armando was hired by Mister General.... Perhaps that wasn't quite right. What was that ugly man's name? *Pobrecito*. She always felt sorry for him. Opening the door, she stands for a few minutes there in the cold light. She takes out a chunk of *solomito*, the best cut for Armando who only eats the tenderest cuts of steak since he returned to live at her house. She holds it up; the beef hangs in a long ribbon with a border of fat where it had attached to the spine of the poor animal. She doesn't eat meat at all. Pablo too has done with meat. Like cows they eat grain and greens. So in spite of the price of the meat and the veterinarian's warning she sharpens the big butcher knife. With the dog sniffing and watching closely, she cuts half of it into tiny chunks and fries them in olive oil. She stands stirring them and remembering.

She remembers that first weekend after they had all left, all, all, Diego and Debbie and the little ones, all, little figures walking onto the tarmac and in through the door of the plane and then away far away. To distract herself, to forget, she thought to visit the *finca* and take the dog. It was Pablo's idea. She went along with it for the dog, Golo. But the dog could hardly stand it. He stood on the seat, his whole body in a tremble when they drew close to the finca where he had lived with his family, his little boys. And when they drove through the gate, all his good manners evaporated and who could blame him; he jumped over the seat and pushed Pablo out of the way so he could rush into the garage. He ran from one room to another as fast as he could, his nails slipping on the tile floors. He sniffed and made a noise in his throat, leaving trails of saliva. He made a terrible mess, poor thing. He ran into the bedrooms and sniffed the beds. He forgot his training in his *pena* and jumped on the beds, burying his nose under the sheets and tossing the blankets aside, snorting and crying in his throat. Then off he'd go, running fast in and out of the boys' rooms, in and out of Diego and Debbie's room, out the door and all around the house. *Loco* I said, *loco, loco,* look at him. He ran down to the stable. He did the same thing there and then ran back up to the house. I tried to help. I called him. He looked at me but just for a second, just to say--I hear you. Then he would go back to sniffing the beds, the closets, the hallways.

Searching. For the little boys. For Diego and Debbie. For that life there. *Bendito sea Dios. Bendito sea Dios.* Yes, God is good. The meat is browned and smells good. She mixes it with rice. It is hardly burned this time. She has made a special effort. It looks good enough for a Christian to eat she thinks as she blows on it, cooling it before she puts it on the floor. She pats his head, talks to him while she blows on the steaming meat. The bowl with the dried dog food she kicks into the corner. He might eat it later. Or maybe not. He isn't stupid like some dogs and some people too. She watches him eat, remembering.

After he searched the whole house and the fields and stable, his old nest in the garage, he sat down in the middle of the patio and put his head up to howl. Ooooh. What a sound! Who says they're *brutos*? It's crying, purely crying. Diego. Armando. David. Pablo. Yes, Pablo, get the car. Nobody can stand this. It's worse than all the rest. Let's go, let's get out of here and so we did.

Pablo goes to the finca, but we don't go back there. I don't and the dog. He has finished his steak and looks up at her in a kind of gratitude. *Sí, agradecido.* The two of them start walking back into the rooms. She slumps along, her fingers touching the coarse black hairs of his back. We stay here in the city now. We just don't care about the *finca* any more. "Isn't that right?" The dog raises his grizzled snout. He's getting old and I.... I don't know how we survived that time, but we did. When he got rheumatism--you see animals get all the same things people do--I got out the baby mattress. The very one all the babies used--I had it put away for something, but now I put it on the floor for him. He's grateful too. And old. Old. Old.

And I? I don't even know how old I am, as old as the Lazarus, and I think now I'm made of wood. I don't feel anything. Nothing gets me. I'm strong. I could go on for a long time. A loud thundering knock at the door stops her. The dog looks at her with his intelligent eyes. Oh! She starts. It must be Armando since the dog didn't bark. A smart dog, he learned quickly that Armando is one of the family despite his long absence. She moves quickly to open the door.

"*Buenos dias, Mamá.*" Then, sniffing the air. "Lunch smells good today."

The old woman has turned and is already down the hallway. Lunch, she forgot lunch. The piece of beef is still on the counter and a little bit of rice is crusted on the bottom of the pan. Not enough for both the boys though. She must hurry. *Dios mio*, where does time go? Armando and Pablo will be wanting their lunch. She turns all the burners on high. The dog goes to his mattress in the corner. Dishes clank; pans rattle and soon come the smells of burning oil and scorched rice.

# CHAPTER 14

## The Villa

### Medellín Colombia 1980

Esmeralda Ana, a heavy et girl with red cheeks and masses of curling black hair, giggles with pleasure as she stands at the door of the bus, the crowd surging toward her. She has succeeded. She has proved she didn't need all those warnings her mother and grandmother gave her. Old women! *Viejas!* They thought she was a fool, but here she is! *Bien, bien, bien*. Those warnings are for *bobas* and she is no fool! If anyone asks her name she will tell them Esmeralda and forget about the Ana part which is for old ladies. Giggling, almost dancing with self satisfaction, she thrills to the chorus of admiration she elicits going down the steps of the bus in her new skirt. This smile brings a new wave of calls and whistles from the factory workers who are lined up for the Fabricato Express. *Muy bien*! She chortles and stamps her feet in a little fandango. She's a modern girl who wants to be a worker in a factory and not a servant for some old lady, as her mother and grandmother have before her. But, coming to work for the very same old lady who has figured so large in her mother's life, this first morning alone, she is delighted. Here at this corner where so many buses meet, interesting things might happen. She smiles again. This job won't be so bad. It gets her out of the pueblo and away from the endless refrains of her mother and grandmother. She comes to take care of the old lady *Doña* Luisa. Remembering old ladies, her grandmother and *Doña* Luisa, she tugs her skirt down towards her knees.

Tossed about by the crowd waiting for busses, she looks up at the tall house that has filled her life. The villa in the Plaza Zea. This house, this park where her grandmother worked all her life and her mother was raised. Esmeralda sighs. She doesn't want to be a servant. Factory work is what she wants. Better money and more excitement. She sighs and cranes her neck again towards the balcony. It is the first time she's ever come to that corner alone, the first time she's looked up and not seen *Doña* Luisa on the balcony. The house is smaller and dirtier than she remembers and much smaller and dirtier than her mother and grandmother paint it in their stories. And the beautiful park they bragged that Don Armando built is not a park at all. Yes, the sixteen Royal Palms, she counts them, enjoying the smells and movement around her, planted by Don Armando, are still there, tossing their fancy heads above the dirty cracked sidewalk. Right now, the bells for eight o'clock mass sound. All those who hurry to mass crash into the thousands of people scrambling for a seat on the bus express to Fabricato. Others stand around waiting for the number 17 to Poblado. So many people. So many men. Everybody going someplace.

When she was very small she had come with Grandmother Cornelia who treated the Plaza Zea like it was a museum, pointing out the houses and naming all the old families with their important names, naming even the flowers in the park with respect. Hah. Nothing remains except this one old house. She looks up at the balcony. Still no one there. She can enjoy the morning a few minutes longer. All the fancy old houses are gone. The *Casa del Sacerdote* was there, a good reason for dressing as decent women, her mother said, since priests and even the bishop walked in and out of that door. Gone and in its place a mattress factory. The workers sit in the sun out on the sidewalk pulling huge needles and cord through coarse gaudy ticking. Two young men wink at her and murmur under their breath to each other as they stitch. She turns to look down the street for Doctor Cordoba's flower garden and pasture for the milk cow. It is a parking lot. *Doña* Luz's pretty little house with its dooryard rose garden where Regina and Esmeralda had nipped a rosebud now and then has a sign with flashing electric letters: *El Palacio del Osterizer*; that popular appliance is sold and repaired there. The Plaza is a low place, dirty and noisy and even this girl from the *pueblo* can see it.

Luisa doesn't realize this. Nor the sons who have problems of their own. It all happened so gradually.

When the loud rapping at the door finally catches Luisa's attention, she rushes, the dog at her side to open. There is a girl with a skirt that is too short and too tight, a girl with wild black hair, a girl with big earrings.

"*A la orden Señorita.*" Luisa is civil.

"*Doña* Luisa! It's me! Esmeralda. My grandmother sent me." She is moving in the door. Luisa steps into the door to block her and the big black nose of Golo follows.

"*Imposible*! Cornelia would never have a child like you! And she always named her children after the saints."

"*O Dios*!" the young woman lowers her head and pulls her eyebrows in a black line across her face, "You know me! It's only a few years ago. And then you called me" and her voice sinks into a respectful monotone, "Ana."

Luisa peers at her. Some recognition was happening. The black eyes and comeback voice. She also remembers the stacks of dirty dishes in the kitchen and the floors that have not been mopped. "But what about clothes? You have to cover yourself to work here!"

"Here's my mother's old uniform," she rattles a paper bag.

Minutes later she appears transformed. The uniform covers her from her neck to her ankles. She has tied her hair back under a white scarf which Luisa would later realize was a new dish towel. No matter. Ana looks very *decente*. Soon there is the sound of dishes clanking and cracking and a young voice singing love songs along with the radio.

Of the old families on the Plaza Zea, only the Gomez remain. Their house on the second floor with the street door at the bottom of a long L-shaped staircase has some protection from the traffic and the dust. That door at the bottom is a problem. It doesn't do much to keep people out; it is just one more door to be broken into. People lean against it while waiting for their bus until it almost sprang from its hinges. Out of boredom they twist the wrought iron arabesque covering the shuttered peephole. Someone with too much time on his hands stuck a piece of copper wire into the lock and jammed the works. Outside the door, the sidewalk is so covered with cigarette butts and candy wrappers and banana peels and ice cream bar sticks that an ordinary broom can not move the litter of a day.

Also, there are no public facilities for the thousands of people who move through here, no facilities at all. Leave the bottom door open for even a minute and someone will duck in gratefully! Even a minute offers shelter from the rain or privacy for the *necesidades* as even Pablo who is always the unlucky one cleaning the mess will admit.

Pablo does the work but he doesn't care. He mumbles if the mess is too bad. All that day he will screw up his face and hold down a gag, but he knows he's the one to do the work. He doesn't care much about the *villa* anymore though. Only Luisa cares about it. She knows its history which is her history. How Armando remodeled totally the old house where her sister, Teresa-who-died-so-easily, died giving birth to their second daughter that was Teresa, the nun who was also changing with the years. How then a few years later, *Don* Armando courted and married his first wife's sister, yes, Luisa. She will come to look out of the window on the balcony of the house he fixed up for her and his new family. How her children were all been born here, all grew up here. How the man who built the house died here and his wake was in the same parlor, its Louis XIV furniture now shrouded against the dust. How his remains are in the church around the corner. Luisa remembers all this. She has lived inside the fourteen foot-high walls for over fifty years, each wall eight inches thick of *tapia*, mud and wattle, smoothed the old way, by hand.

The villa has eleven rooms for family, more in the back for servants. All are connecting, all have several doors and spidery black keys which she carries on a ring on her belt. After her husband died, she did not care for a long time what went on in the outer world. She came back to live in the world for a while but when the little boys, her grandchildren moved away, she slumped again even more. There is an old dog that follows her from room to room and shares her unspoken hopes and fears: the children might return to stay; they may never return. There are other problems; she can hardly hear the bells tolling for mass for all the noise outside, and the doors of the church--which always stood open for prayer as they should--had to be closed and locked because someone stole the chalice right off the altar. This shook her faith; she became worried about the world and what it was coming to. She keeps her rosary at hand. When television news comes on and the announcer lists the names of the dead, she tries to remember their names so she can pray for them. Sometimes they show the faces too of the dead people and name their fathers and mothers and children and Luisa cries.

About this time, her children, Armando, away in the United States, and Diana with her new family and Pablo, the bachelor who stayed at home, have their own lives taken care of and they begin to take some notice. Not that they notice their mother, no, she is unchanging, but they notice the house. Of course, it is Diego home for a visit after many months away who first realizes how bad it is. He has to fight the crowd to enter his own door--wrestling with the Yale padlock while the ice cream bar vendors and the workers from the mattress factory watch and comment. Perhaps Armando happened to see his *mamá* leaving the house clutching a rosary in one hand, and droning *Ave Marías* while jabbing the crowds with her umbrella as she made her way to daily mass. No matter. They all suddenly notice that the Plaza and house have begun to fall too. The *villa* is an embarrassment.

All the sons get together and make plans to renovate another property that the family owns, a smaller house, near a church in a decent residential part of the city. The Plaza Zea, they say, is no longer safe. And of course, they are right by any standards. Their *mamá* should not continue to live in such a place! Nor with this rough girl who is caught talking to the mattress factory men from the balcony. She is warned.

The family struggles to teach Esmeralda Ana to comport herself like a *señorita* while they look for another girl to help in the new house. This is not easy and the days pass through their hands. Even the seemingly simple task of regaining custody of the newer smaller house in the nice neighborhood takes several years. The tenants did not want to leave. They did not believe there could be any good reason to force them out on the street to seek an apartment that would surely be more expensive and less pleasant. Pleas and lawsuits and threats follow with many unpleasant conversations and expenses but it had finally happens that the little house was ready for Luisa to inspect.

Understand that during all these years, there have been no attempts made to maintain the *villa*. After all, it would all be for nothing! The thick walls are cracking and bits of gravel and fine bone-colored dust filter out and down the long hallways. The macaws and the canaries and the yellow and black tupiales all have their way with the kitchen patio and while it rings with birdsong and chatter and the colors of rain forest, all these pecking creatures have sky showing through the roof in several places. Old walls are settling uneasily and noisily; the tiles of the floor uplift and crazy angles happen where there had once been parallel expanses.

So when the old lady goes to visit the new house, and it is thirty years newer, more modern, with shiny bathrooms where the tiles and the toilet and sinks all match, with low ceilings and quiet streets in front, in back, all around, it looks a much easier task to put into shape. She orders it completely painted, plastered, repaired. There will be a wonderful new patio just for the birds. The workmen move in and go to work. Some days Teresa comes and Luisa puts on her hat and they go in taxi to inspect the work and to give the workers hell! She wants the perfection she has not had for all those years. She asks for and gets new curtains, new carpets, matching towels. There is nothing it seems she cannot have.

The time comes when she will begin to move in. She walks around the sparkling little house, speaking to herself although Pablo is at her side. She points her cane to the wall where the mirrors brought from Spain by her grandfather, the same mirrors her sisters had all fought over, but she finally got, would be hung. Pablo makes little crosses on the wall. He whips out his measuring tape when she wonders out loud what distance there is from that corner to the other corner so the new blue drapes Diana has chosen will fit perfectly. Luisa inspects the windows, bends to look through her glasses at some smudges.

"Ah," she brightens, "these windows are on ground level so I can get to them and make sure they are clean." She sighs, remembering the problem of finding someone to get up on the rickety old ladder and clean her old windows, and old Desiderio, the only one who would do the job, though badly she would tell you, died last year.

"Who will clean my old windows?"

Pablo starts to fidget.

"What will happen to my old drapes? Your father brought those from Belgium. Not that you would know it, but they are very special."

At this she had begins to address her son, turning on her cane to look at him, to really speak to him-- "What will become of the old house?"-- and smiling at the old name, "the *villa*?"

When he does not answer, she looks sharply at him. She almost swoons at what she sees there.

"No, *por Dios*, I almost made a terrible mistake!" She walks out of the house as fast as she can without ever looking back. Her son slams shut the door and runs to the car. He starts the car, revving the little engine, going, it seems, on her steam.

"Where do you want to go?"

"Home, of course!" and she carries on the rest of the way home in a tone of voice too low to be understood but too intense to be interrupted or questioned. She walks in the door and without even taking off her hat, opens her purse and pays Esmeralda Ana in full and a little extra.

"Go back to the village, girl. The city will ruin you. And tell your grandmother I need her."

For once the girl does not argue. She shakes down her hair and takes off the tent-like uniform that covers her. In seconds she is transformed from Ana to Esmeralda. But her bravado fades as she packs her uniform in a paper bag and looks at the old woman.

"*Bien, Doña* Luisa. Pardon me if I didn't do like you wanted." For a few minutes she is little Ana who came there behind her grandmother's skirts.

"No, Ana. You did what you could. It's a mature person I need. Send your grandmother. Tomorrow early I'll look for her." And so she waves her out the door.

Luisa gets up early the next morning and stands in the window watching the busses unload their passengers. When the nine o'clock bells ring and Cornelia has not come, Luisa searches every drawer until she finds her glasses, the bifocals that still serve her best. She unlocks her armoire and digs out from under the new blouses and sweaters, still in red and green paper, her old address book, and carries it to the balcony, to the broad sun so she can decipher the number smudged from time.

"Put Cornelia on the phone." There is no time for manners. "No, Corna. Don't send those girls of yours. You're the only one who can help me with this."

When she hangs up with Cornelia, she makes another call to the corner store. "Votary candles. Two boxes of red ones. They're the best. I know that's twenty-four. That's enough for today." Then she goes to the balcony to wait and to pray.

When Cornelia, a heavy old woman with red cheeks, grumbling, but hurrying, comes an hour later, Luisa bends close to her and tells her something in a low tone of voice. No one is at home but still the two put their heads together. There is whispered agreement. Cornelia pokes around in the locked closet and unearths the old tea cart from the days when the *Señorita* Teresa was at home giving elegant tea parties. The dog that stood by Luisa during the greeting and conversation goes to his bed on the baby mattress and curls up there, tucking his nose under brush of his tail. The two old women scrub the cart which has not been used for tea for twenty years and then trundle it into Luisa's room where they carefully move the *Virgen del Rosario* onto its shiny table top. They add three votive candles plus the large candles. The bouquet of pink roses trembles. Cornelia pushes the cart while Luisa holds one out-stretched hand of the virgin. She steadies the three-foot tall statue with candles reflecting in its blue glass eyes. Roses drop their petals, soft crepe pinks like the skin of old women, and the candles leave a trail of red wax all over the house. The three make a pilgrimage around the old house, going from one room to another as though they were the Stations of the Cross, pausing in each while Luisa names their faults, the roof leaking, the floor heaving under them, the walls cracking and breaking. They pray, and their voices fill the rooms, for the faults of the house, for their own faults, for loneliness and old age and pain, leaving a trail of flower petals and red wax drippings.

The next day Diana comes and questions her mother, seriously and severely as befits such foolishness. Luisa is down on her knees scraping up the wax with a silver butter knife.

"What are you doing Mama down there on your knees like a servant?"

A grunt. The old woman bends nearer to the floor to examine the red shavings of wax.

"You know, *Mamá,* that this house is falling down."

Mumbling a prayer, she inches forward on her knees like a sinner in a Good Friday procession.

"Listen! *Mamá*! Look at me! The roof leaks!"

"Buckets!"

"The walls are crumbling!"

"More everyday!"

"The neighborhood isn't fit for a dog!"

"It's good enough for me!"

"What!"

The enormity of the statement makes the daughter go pale and the old lady chuckle and sit back on her heels.

"I said, find somebody else to live in that shoebox. This place is old and homely, just like me."

Outside the Royal Palms waved in the breezes as they always have.

# CHAPTER 15

## Turnabout

### Medellín Colombia 1985

"This has been a normal house but now everything is turned upside down." Adiela, dressed as nuns dress since Pope John VI took away their habits, in tunnel shaped dark skirts and heavy stockings and boys' black tennis shoes, sighs petulantly as she guides the thread through the intricate path of the old treadle machine. The Singer, pronounced *Seen-hair*, has served the house for fifty years, creating elegant women's dresses, mending little boys' pants and pajamas.

Sister Adiela is preparing to hem her sister's new house dress, her younger sister Teresa who had been the best seamstress in a house of fine handwork, who now sits studying the needle in her hand as if she doesn't know what it is. The nun is cynical; an attitude, she will defend, that comes only from her long years of experience. The truth is they are all at an age when they have a lot to explain and defend and forgive but no one in this house ever forgets. Remembering childish games of sixty years past, Adiela thinks Teresa might be only pretending, and she looks at her sharply, and then, taking the dress from her hands abruptly, peers at the long knotted stitches.

"You could do it if you'd only try! How can you have forgotten?"

The other, still holding the needle, jerks the thread tight so the material bunches up into a fist. Squinting at her older sister shrewdly, she declares, "You have to help me, Sister. I can't do this anymore. I just can't do it!"

Now the older sister is a nun; indeed, they are both nuns as well as sisters. But there's another thing turned around, for the younger sister who was the proudest of the sisters, yes, and the proudest of the nuns too, and the primmest and most proper, is day after day losing not just memory but tact, even shame, for she might say *mierda* or even *puta* if angry, and she gets angry enough too. The *Superiora* of the convent sent her home to rest when her mind first started to fail. That was ten years ago.

Yes, everything is turned upside down, Sister Adiela sighs and turns in time to see Luisa slumping and sliding almost out of her chair. As she rushes to straighten and settle her, the old woman opens her eyes and protests.

"Come, Bisa, let me help you," and as the old woman brushes her away, the nun cries, "Oh Lord, have mercy on our souls, how can Luisa have ended so?" As if she knows, and indeed she probably does know, the old woman propped in a large arm chair, her hands scrabbling in her lap, her glasses dangling from one ear, squirms as the nun perches her glasses on her nose and hooks them meticulously around her large protruding ears, squirms and as if in answer, she shakes her head so the glasses fall again. No more use to her who refuses to see.

She who had seen everything, she who could thread any needle, read any missal no matter how fine the print, now gazes emptily into space and repeats one word, only one word, over and over. "María, María, María, María, María, María." Her conversations had been a pleasure to her and all who knew her: what humor! with all the old wisdom, all the old sayings salted into long gossipy stories told with great gusto. Now, for as long as she is awake, she repeats only one word, regularly as the pendulum of the old clock, although amazingly, with all the inflections of her old voice: sometimes imperiously, many times with a chuckle. When this first happened the members of the family would raise their heads in unison, smiling, hoping, Luisa's back! but on listening, hear again only the *María*. Other times, the worst of times, she weeps for María, pleading pitifully.

Everyone in the house has theories about María. The youngest son thinks it is the maid she is calling or a nurse to ease her pain. There is some basis for this, since it had been Luisa's way, even when she was well, to call all the servants María, a name every Colombian woman has somewhere in her list of names, a short hand that kept Luisa from having to learn so many new names since there has been, for the past twenty years anyway, a steady procession of help into the house, and for one reason or another, all good reasons if it came down to it--the young women would pack up their things waving *adiós*, to which Luisa's voice would ring out: "*No sirven!*" a double duty message meaning they would not do, and they did not serve. Then Pablo, the quiet son with a college degree even though his projects were always small and poorly paid, but who takes care of the needs of the house, would go out to find another maid and pay her even more to see if she would stay.

Adiela thinks that Luisa had her stroke while praying or that when the stroke started, had the presence of mind to pray to the Holy Mother and so was stuck, rather like the needle on the old victrola they had enjoyed for so many years, on her call to María, full of grace, perhaps for deliverance from this crazy house.

Teresa, she who was a Sister of the Sacred Heart, but who has now lost that title and all its privileges, when she notices Luisa lost in her litany, shakes her head and intones with despairing and prophetic gestures, "Poor Bisa, she's lost, she's lost", and with the last lost, she wanders off into the house, perhaps to sweep.

No one can be blamed for his theory and so the youngest son who has felt so much pain and rejection and who will defend what has been his way all through life, of course sees his mother crying in pain. He knows. He has cried in pain he could tell you, or he could have cried but didn't because he was not allowed. He always tried to make up for his temper and yes, he did have a temper but he should not be blamed completely as his sisters let him fall on his head when he was a baby and also his life has been so hard.

Of course the sister Adiela's theory of prayer is easy to see, especially since she hopes, no prays, fervently, to be so elevated in prayer that her life in this vale of tears and *mierda*, a word she uses in her mind only, a word to describe her world full of rude students, crowded buses and her family now so turned around--that her world will transform suddenly and painlessly to highest heaven.

The youngest sister's theory is lost in the dark places of her mind in much the same way as her dearest belongings, her rosary and her best pantyhose and a tin of chocolate candies sent from the United States for her, and only for her, which she squirrels away and then, wild eyed, cannot find. She who has been terrified of men, loud noises, and the dark, now walks the hallways at night, her sallow face stern and searching; she visits, in the dark, the rooms of the others.

The younger brother carries long angers; the anger against his sisters for instance is fifty years old and growing. Growing up, he hid his anger in fun. Simple little jokes. He would yell to see them jump. They would freeze in their conversations and turn pale in midst of a laugh when he came around the corner. He would sometimes feel magnanimous and ignore them, though other times their fear infuriated him. Didn't they know he was a kind man? Then he would tower over them in a spitting frenzy.

Still other times he would say with calm concern to Teresa--"Poor thing, *pobrecita*. You must be going crazy. *Loca, pobrecita la loca*. It's not normal to be so nervous." After this, he would go his way chuckling, knowing that she was trembling behind him. That was exactly the way he had felt all his life and he liked someone else knowing what it was like. It was mostly a game to him but everyone knows that several old aunts and even great grandmother Josefa went a little off in their old age, so the accusation is full of dark promise.

He comes into the dining room late, after all the plates have been served and the older brother, Luisa, and the two sisters are picking at their food. Then he will shout, demanding an explanation for his misplaced Cross pen or an important telephone message badly noted. He always blames the younger sister, and indeed, in these matters, she is always guilty. It may or may not be important but on principle, he accuses her. He likes to see her tremble and stutter; he likes to see her freeze at her plate. Soon he recovers himself, and then he invites her, chuckling, to go on, go on, eat; he looks around the table so everyone except she, frozen and pale with the half-chewed meat a rock in her throat, rejoices that the temper tantrum is passing, joins in the good humor. He goes back to eating in an expansive mood, acting as the giver of food and of permission. "What's the matter?" he asks, smiling and waving his fork in blessing.

It's not that he's a bad man, but nothing happens the way he thinks. It's true, he hates to agree with Adiela, but everything IS turned upside down. He has lost two businesses and ends up living off his older brother whom he has always pitied. His brother never had a woman, never traveled, no life at all for a man. A university degree, and what's it worth? Pablo never had a decent job, never made near the money that he Armando, named for his father and more like him than any of the others, had made. Why he had made more money in a month than the brother made in a year! What good is a DR to put in front of his name?

Then, as close as Armando was to his mother and as much as he loved her, she deserted him in her old days; she had a stroke and now she is stuck in some other place, some world where she repeats over and over one word--is she calling her dead sister, is she praying to the Holy Mother, is it a maid she wants to bring her something? He is sure that he of all the children, more than his sisters or brothers, or the Doctor Builes or the Father Gomez, he can break through her fog. He imagines how it will be, how he will pull her back from the dark and they will be as close as he remembers in his childhood. He sits in front of her when no one is around and tries through mental exercise to communicate with her. She settles down, she smiles, she looks into his eyes and then she whispers--María.

He feels alone, finally, completely alone. He is bald and fat. He can't afford to buy the nice Italian shoes or the leather jackets from Spain. He can't afford any new girl friends; the ones he dumped know him too well. His old friend, his only friend is still being held in the States. Pablo hangs around the house, afraid to go out for fear of running into a creditor. He is so dejected by all these changes in his life that he forgets about his sister, the one he has bullied in small ways and large, all his life. She, at this very same time, loses the tenuous grasp she has had on her world. What he has always teased her about happens.

She opens his door quietly night after night and lays into him with a broom. The first time it happens, he lies there bellowing like a bull. She stops, holding the stick at her side and announces solemnly, "*Ahora sí,*" nodding in satisfaction. After that he can hardly sleep; he barricades the door but somehow, it seems like witchcraft to him, he finds her tiny pale form hovering over his bed in the dark. Silently and deliberately she flails him. He cannot bear that his mother or brother or the maids know, and so he hides her attacks, all the while quaking that he is finally in the hands of a mad woman.

During the day, all the days for the past ten years since she was sent home from the convent, she has swept the vast expanse of tile floor, moving chairs and even the sofa, sweeping as though her life depended on it. Now, she sweeps with concentration up and down the hall, looking neither right nor left, neither up nor down. If he walks by, she will suddenly--not always, but with the regularity of a failing mind, trip him or charge him with the broom.

Once, made bold by the family around him, by the broad sun everywhere, and his mother ensconced in her chair and smiling, he stood his ground and tried to yell his sister into shock, to turn her around, but she swung the broom, landing it in one great broad sweep on his bald pate. Everyone was transfixed. Luisa screamed: "María, María!" in alarm. Quickly Pablo, Esmeralda, Adiela shouted and charged her, trying to disarm her, to frighten her, but she began again to sweep, ignoring them and everything they attacked her with, and with no guilt, no shame, no anger, spoke: "Get out of the way. I am sweeping. Someone has to sweep."

# CHAPTER 16

## The Second Floor

### Medellín Colombia 1985

Of course they are right. The *villa*, the old house built by Don Armando in the Plaza Zea in 1930, is no longer a fitting residence for *Doña* Luisa. The family has arranged a new house for her. This new house has a balcony too and two floors. Both floors are sunny and modern. The second floor is in the same house as the first floor, with a kitchen and bathroom and three bedrooms and two patios: one next to the kitchen with clothes-lines and one by the *sala* for the birds and flowering plants. The second floor has all the comfortable old furniture from the *villa*.

In the *sala* of the second floor is the old green sofa set that has seen so many good times and bad. Sofia and her husband Julio re-upholstered it from its original scaly brown leather and sunken seats always leaking curls of wood filling. How pleased everyone was with its new dark green vinyl, a serious color Luisa said approvingly and one that wouldn't show the dirt. Important since at that time the little boys were climbing all over furniture and over all of their grandmother too as they practiced their walking from one end of the sofa to the other, up over a lap and back again. She remembers them so: one in each stage of walking, toddling, crawling, one right after the other.

There in the same *sala* on the coffee table in front of the green sofa is the larger than life-size *Niño Jesus*, the one who belongs in the

Christmas *pesebre*, with beautiful blue glass eyes and delicate hands and a hand made lace baby shirt, starched and ironed. This is since the boys are grown; they were always kissing him, their dirty little hands grasping his rosy head and trying to shake his outstretched hand. Now no one pays any attention except Teresa who dusts him very tenderly.

Another great thing about the second floor is the balcony. The balcony is the most entertaining spot in the house. From here all the neighbors' comings and goings are visible as well as the beggars and the men selling vegetables and newspapers and the cobbler who carries his shoe repair box on his shoulder, wandering the streets, calling up into the houses, "*Zapatos! Arreglo Zapatos!*" If shoes are thrown down to him, say some run-down-at-the-heel shoes, he will sit on the curb and pull an iron foot out of his box to hold the shoe and nail the new heel on, holding the nails in his mouth just as cobblers do in the fairy tale books. Then using a wickedly curved knife, and pulling it toward himself, he will cut around the heel so that it is pretty close to that original shape. He'll fix most problems right up, as best as can be done without a machine of course. He'll polish shoes too, going under the palm tree and spitting and polishing and then flirting with the neighbor's maid who finds so many excuses to get outside: shine, shine, smile, shine, with the brush. Esmeralda Ana will also find an excuse to go outside to chat. "*No, por Dios, no,*" Luisa will say. "María! Come back in the house like a decent girl. He can throw them up here!" And he will, with a smile, he'll throw them back up into the balcony with cautions --"Watch now, *Señora*, don't get hit!" and the *Señora* throws down the money, a few bills weighted with coins.

At night the balcony gives a beautiful view of the city lights. Since Medellín is such a large city and this house in the bottom of the valley, the lights from houses and highways going up the sides of the mountains seem to carry on right into the sky and there is no telling where the stars begin and the house lights leave off. Someone will be playing music. Teresa and Debbie hope it will be guitar and *romantico* but it might be loud and metallic. Still, that offers a chance for indignation, and whoever is on the balcony will look around for someone to talk to about it. It's like seeing the teenagers, called *Cocacolos,* with the extravagant new fashions. Then Teresa and Debbie criticize them, pointing out the colors of the hair, the bounce of the bosom, the amount of thigh exposed, oohing and being scandalized while Esmeralda giggles.

The second floor is fine except that it is alone.

In a country where children are taught to seek companionship at all times, where to be left alone is the greatest punishment, where solitude, even short term is full of boredom and pain, to sleep in a house alone, even if that house is directly above the house full of people, is to be in limbo, out of the light.

So when Teresa is chased upstairs either by her half brother or the clock, she weeps for a few minutes quietly. Only when her sister, Adiela, also a nun, also under fire for past sins, takes refuge in the second floor, then the two of them will shake from anger and from fright. Little by little, they calm each other by speaking of his fall, by remembering how it happened and how lucky he was to have lived.

So every night Teresa arms herself with pajamas and robe, and shuffles to the bathroom, sighing deeply and praying bits of prayers, asking help in this vale of tears, begging mercy, humming the latest Julio Iglesias tune. Shortly after she comes back with her little cotton house dress over her arm to check the locks on the doors--no matter, she will get up shortly to check them again. Her guarantee is to shake the balcony door to make sure it is out of its track and thus locked-- though it will take Esmeralda twenty minutes to put it back on track in the morning. If challenged, she will recite vivid details of cat burglars who scale house fronts like spiders and come in through the balconies that some innocent has left open to catch the breeze. *"Sí, sí, sí,"* she intones seriously all the way down the hall and into her room. She switches on the lamp, gets down on her knees to check under the bed and under her dresses hanging in the closet before closing the door and wedging a chair under the knob.

Once in bed, she will pray and read the psalms of the day and say the rosary and fall into a deep sleep from which she will wake with a start because the light is seeping in around the door and she has missed early prayers. True, it is past five a.m. prayers, and she was sent home from the convent years earlier, but old habits die hard. So, at six or shortly before, she'll get up and inevitably find her brothers in the bathrooms, taking their time over showers and shaving since they are men who must go out to the offices while she is a woman with no place to go. But her sense of urgency is great and she paces and sighs, and sighs and paces and peeks through the curtains into the street, but of course she will not go out on the balcony, nor down to the kitchen in her robe, something only children and *gringas* do. Soon enough the men leave the house and then she showers, and comes downstairs, neatly dressed, hair combed, to sit in a chair and wait for someone to bring her breakfast.

All day the second floor is alone. No one ever goes up there though it is quite comfortable and complete in its way. Luisa, Teresa and Esmeralda Ana pass their time below while the men are at work. Only when evening comes, or when Armando comes home unexpectedly during the day and catches the nuns taking their chocolate in the dining room for instance or watching the television is there a swift and silent pushing and scurrying to the upper floor. After commiserating with her sister and calming herself, the older nun, Adiela, will steal away, silently, silently down the stairs and out the street door--slam! Luisa who has never witnessed the confrontations and could not even imagine them, will query impatiently who leaves with out saying goodbye? Who slams the door? Why are the nuns so foolish? No one answers.

Most evenings after dinner the women are alone in the house. Teresa sits with Luisa and Esmeralda Ana watching television. They are like children, leaning forward in their chairs; sometimes in her excitement, Luisa almost slips out of her wheelchair. And the others, in their excitement do not even notice. They comment on everything and ask for explanations which no one has. They close the day by watching the news. At the endless lists of *muertos,* the daily roll call of the dead from natural tragedies like earthquakes or airplane crashes or murders from the vigilante right wing, from the guerilla left, from the drug lords, they pay attention to each name, repeating it and wondering aloud if the mother--or the wife, or the child--is listening. Together they mutter a prayer for the soul of that person and counting them, wonder, shaking their heads in unison, what is happening and if Colombia could be bad enough to deserve so much death. When, at eight o'clock or nine or ten, Luisa seizes her beads and begins praying, Esmeralda will--though often unwillingly--turn off the set. They will pray together and the last amen, the nun rises and shuffles upstairs, faintheartedly.

After just such an evening, Teresa was awakened by terrible noises in the street. She heard explosions and saw lights bursting. People screamed. Despite the terror she felt at going out into the dark hallway and down the dark stairway and standing even for a few minutes alone in the dark outside Luisa's bedroom, she got up shaking. Her head full of loud noises, voices raised in passion, lights flashing, with sirens and thunderous rumbles in the distance. Praying, rushed to Luisa's door and pounded and pounded and when no one answered, she pushed open the door and began shaking Luisa awake.

"Wake up, Luisa. Wake up! There's a war out there and they're killing even the devil."

"What? Can it be?" Then, convinced by the noises in the street, Luisa began calling and pounding on the wall with her cane so that her sons would come. Nothing.

Worn out with pounding on the wall, she begged in a tiny but urgent voice, "María Teresa, you have to go get the boys. Don't tell them about the war or they will run out on the street to see it and be killed."

"I'm not going back out there for anything, not for God or for the devil."

"You have to! There's no other way. If I could walk, I'd go in a minute. Are you going to let the boys be killed because you're a coward? Oh God help me!" And Luisa began to thrash around almost throwing herself out of the bed.

"I can't! How can I? What if they won't come?"

"You have to make them."

So Teresa bowed her head and ran down the hallway as though running through hail, from one door to the other, pounding, and calling their names. Over and over, at first softly, then *con gana* as

Colombians say, from one door to the other until both doors opened and there the two brothers stood, startled, nervous, too shaken to care that their hair was on end and they were barefoot on the cold tile.

"Luisa wants you in her room, right away."

Both men went immediately, and without question. When they came in the door, Luisa ordered Teresa to close the door.

"What is going on?" Pablo asked.

"Are you sick?" Armando peered at her.

"No, I'm fine but there is a war outside. What I always feared has finally happened. But if you stay here with me you'll be all right."

"War?" The two men exchanged horrified glances, but after a moment asked, for once in unison, "How do you know?"

"Listen, can't you hear it?"

The first sound from within the room was Pablo's squeaky little laugh as he turned and slipped out the door, then the other brother's baritone mumbling about the *manicomio* he lived in.

"Wait! Don't go!" Luisa commanded.

"Don't you know what day it is?"

"Day? Is there a day for this?"

"Go to sleep, Luisa. It's just the New Year."

The two women laughed and laughed and then tried to smother their laughter until tears showed in their eyes, and Esmeralda peeked crossly in the door at them.

"*Manicomio* is right." Luisa whispered, weak from laughing.

"*Sí*," Teresa nodded, "And I am the first *loca* here, but not the only one."

She was still laughing when she got back up to her room on the second floor. She imagined she could hear them all. It was a good laugh. *Bendito sea Dios.*

# CHAPTER 17

# The Years Do Not Come Alone

### Medellín Colombia 1985

Every morning a little brown dove perches on top of the high wall separating this house from the other houses in this row. Cocking its head first to one side and then to the other, it eyes the patio below, the three cages covered with old blankets, the plants wilting, the blue tiled pond, now empty, drained because of the canary who drowned there--.

"No." A voice comes from the bedroom directly in front of the patio. "The canary did not drown. It moved its little wings around, back and forth, back and forth, swimming--"

"Birds can't swim--"

"Of course they can swim. Look at ducks. Look at big heavy birds like swans. Lots of birds swim."

"But not canaries! --And ducks don't swim with their wings!"

"Aha. Aha. Of course not. I didn't say they did. I just said that the canary didn't die from drowning. None of my canaries ever died from anything except old age. And singing too. After it swam around for a little bit--SWAM I say, somebody--it must have been that girl in the kitchen--"

"Esmeralda Ana."

"*Sí*, María. She picked it up out of the water and put it on that ledge to dry off in the sun and it did and it was fine for a long time after that. A good singer."

The dove moves down into a long, gentle dive into the house. It is another day, one of so many. There in the patio are three quiet cages, bundled with ragged blankets. Around the small empty pond, runs a strip of grass with a rosebush, canna lilies, a hibiscus.

The voice continues from the bedroom.

"María...María... María..." The old lady goes on at regular and measured intervals. She is expressionless and motionless. She has some bulk to her in these later years and she forms a large twisted lump in the narrow bed.

At the fifth or sixth call, the bedroom door opens. Her son sticks his head in.

"Very good morning *Doña* Luisa. How are you? Better today? You must be, you're in good voice. You've been calling that poor girl for an hour."

"Where is she then?"

"*Mamá*! You can't even say Good--"

"Nooooo!" Exasperation fills her voice like a motor finally catching on all cylinders. "Good morning, Pablo. Good morning again. I think I said good morning this morning which was a long time ago now. Now. Now! Where is María! *Jesus, José y María!*"

True, they had already said good morning or something like that, several hours earlier when he, before dawn, rolled from his bed, the bed across from hers. Ever since her accident, since the days in the hospital, since the fracas with the live-in nurse who was turned out, yes, out! and who left in a huff, carrying her suitcase puffing down the stairs and out on the sidewalk while all the people in the house gave thanks, real thanks to all the virgins and saints to have escaped from her hands. Ever since that day, the old woman has lost her life-long old-fashioned modesty and now insists that her son keep her company, sleep there in the same room, in the bed across from hers.

She shelters herself inside a reserve as real as walls as she is dressed and undressed there in the bed, as she stands sturdily if unsteadily in the shower or sits placidly on the toilet.

Pablo laughs to himself. Everyday he assures himself of his mother's state by rousing her to a certain peak of exasperation and then, squeaking with contained laughter, he leaves her. Now, he turns in the doorway and almost runs into his half-sister, Teresa. A woman of sixty, she bobs in the doorway until he puts one hand gently on her shoulder to move her into the room. They do not speak.

"Good morning," Teresa says. "How are you today, Luisa?"

"Good morning, Teresa. Good morning! Is that girl out in the kitchen?"

"What girl, Luisa?"

"*Ay! Dios mío*! María!"

"Oh. That girl. I haven't seen her. Shall I go look for her? You look so uncomfortable, dear Luisa. I wish I could do something to help you. I'd do anything. Anything!"

Mumbling and shaking her head dramatically, she wanders into the hallway. She stands there watching the short dark girl, seventeen years old, who calls herself Esmeralda, tear the covers off the cages. The cages rattle and the birds inside them crash around squawking and flapping their wings at this brusque but usual morning call. The little brown dove retreats momentarily to the top of the wall.

"*Señora.*" Her voice is young too. Her expression is unchanged as she rushes from cage to cage answering in the same regular monotonous tone, the tock to the old woman's tick. A furious honking in the street stops her. Throwing the last blanket to the floor, the young woman begins a dash to the kitchen, stopped by Teresa who stands exactly in the center of the hallway keeping a worried eye on her. They step back and forth; at each step Esmeralda Ana takes to get around her, the older woman jumps with little gasps back into her path.

Both women are silent but an impatient keening comes from Esmeralda while Teresa begins to yelp and tug on the small wooden cross on a chain around her neck.

"What's going on out there? For God's sake will somebody come help me up from here? Will they leave me in bed until I stick to the sheets?"

I walk down the stairs and into the scene. I enter the bedroom and greet the old woman there.

"Good morning, Debbie." She is trying to take the impatience from her voice.

"Good morning, Luisa. You look terribly uncomfortable there."

"I am. Very. Very! But nobody will--"

"Why don't you move?"

"Move?"

"Here." I pull her feet, twisted into hand knit wool booties, down to the bottom of the bed.

"Here," I say, touching her hip, "move this over this way," and putting my weight behind it, I shove. Sometimes just reminding her she can move and saying it to her will do; other times she is made of lead and nothing works. I dash around the bed and try to pull her by one arm to straighten her from the lumpy S she forms in the bed. The bed is already wet so there is no hurry to get her up.

"Oh no! You still have your hair up in a bun, Luisa. You need to take your hair down at night. How can you sleep?"

"It's like sleeping on a stone. Hard. But I do it anyway because I have to. Isn't María here today?"

"Yes, but she's busy. And you have your bra on too! How can you sleep all tied up like that?"

"I like to be tied up. I always wear a bra day and night. You sent me some of these good ones."

"No, not I. I never buy those with wires. They're torture to me."

"And those are the very ones I like best. If I don't tie down these tubs, they move around, they bounce around. They fly around!"

She closes her mouth and eyes and laughs noiselessly at this and at Teresa's shocked response.

"María gets me out my clothes everyday: everything matches, everything is very nice, and I always wear a bra! María!"

"I'm coming in a minute, *Señora*. I have to buy the milk."

She rushes back through the hallway almost bowling over Teresa as the truck out front continues to honk.

"See how she runs? Just to go out on the street to gossip with the girls and talk to that man?"

Teresa begins to sing an old popular song, "Come out and talk to me." She rocks back and forth singing, "I'm waiting patiently...." She hobbles a little dance step as she goes to the balcony to watch.

The street is full of the girls, girls no matter their age, from the houses up and down this street. On occasion a lady or man from one of the houses will show his face, will walk directly to the truck, not bothering with the line, while the chattering girls wait, stilled. The milkman flirts with them; they are cool and practice responses to his advances. They take turns stepping up to the truck while the others laugh and call encouragement.

Esmeralda rushes--she has only one speed--back into the house, dodging Teresa who is coming down again to Luisa's bedroom. She throws the plastic liters of milk on the counter where I am fixing my coffee.

"I think *Doña* Luisa is calling you."

"Is she?" And throwing me an impish look over her shoulder she runs up the hallway, grasps Teresa firmly by the shoulders and moves around her and into the bedroom.

"Good morning *Doña* Luisa."

"Who's there?" A pitifully weak voice seeps from under the covers.

"Esmeralda." And she pulls the cover down from Luisa's eyes, "Ana." and sighing, "María."

"María? María? I thought you were gone. I thought you had left like that other time when you--"

"You always bring that up! I'm here. Come now. I'll get you up."

"Later. I'm going to sleep for a while longer. It's too cold to get up."

"It's not cold."

"No. Go away. I'll call you when I'm ready to get up."

"Teresa. Come and tell *Doña* Luisa it's not cold."

"Well, for me," and Teresa turns, rubbing her hands, into the room, "for me it's cold. I have been standing here shaking for an hour. I've been hoping someone would give me a cup of hot coffee--"

"No, it's not cold. The sun is up. Look into the patio. See the birds? See the sun? Blue sky. No clouds. *Doña* Debbie!"

I come into the room. Luisa is like a cigar store Indian, wrapped in her plaid wool blanket, straight faced, eyes closed. Teresa is standing by the bed patting Luisa's head and then rubbing her own arms with exaggerated shivering. Esmeralda can hardly bear to stand still; arrested in her run, she bobs there making a face to me, her full lips and dark eyes imploring me. I answer.

"Luisa. It's not cold. It's a beautiful day. Shall I help you?"

"No, Debbie. Thank you. Maria, get *Doña* Debbie some breakfast. The kind of coffee she likes."

"No, *Doña* Luisa. I'm not going to get her her breakfast."

At this Luisa opens her eyes, wide and wider, purses her lips and her eyes light on Teresa. The two of them take sharp breaths and exchange looks of shock.

"I can't, *Doña* Luisa, because you won't get up. You know I have to take care of you first."

"Anyway, Luisa," I add, "I get my own breakfast."

"Maria. I can't believe you talk to the lady like that. I better get up and take care of things."

She says this but doesn't stir. Esmeralda takes both the old woman's feet at the ankles and swivels them to the edge of the bed. Teresa and I move to the opposite sides of the bed. We each take a hand and begin to tug. It is a bad day. There are days when she forgets to bend and when she surrenders to gravity. This is such a day. Her legs extend over the edge of the bed but she is in a T with her arms stretched out to the side. Now Esmeralda runs to the other side of the bed and begins with enormously strong arms to lift Luisa's shoulders from the pillow.

"Up!" I shout, thinking to engage her mind in this act.

"Up! Up!" the other two shout while outside the beautiful yellow and black and white tupiales begin to squawk.

Throughout all the shouting and touching and tugging the old woman keeps a kind of stoic calm. Now she is a log on the edge of the bed, her long flannel nightgown up around her blue veined legs. I hold her up, getting my shoulder behind her shoulders, leaning into her.

Esmeralda Maria is trying to get the wheelchair close into the bed. Teresa stands in the way wringing her hands.

"Sit!" I back off suddenly. Now Luisa catches herself and drops into a sitting position on the edge of the bed. With the chair wedged up to the bed we all three begin to try to lift her into it. It isn't that she resists, it is that she is not there. From a high mountain she watches our efforts with mild amusement. We are all grunting with our exertion, and she still is in bed. Then, the girl and I each take an elbow, and as though someone had flipped a switch, she raises herself slowly but steadily to stand facing the wheelchair, one hand on each arm of the chair. Teresa kneels on the floor to direct her turn into the chair.

"Now move this foot!" She knocks on it like a door.

"No, Teresa, the other foot--" Esmeralda calls.

"The other way!" The two old feet collide and we all begin to laugh. Luisa rocks back and forth, her hands touching the chair.

"What good help I have!"

"Here, Teresa, you help me, please, please!" says Esmeralda as she thrusts a broom into Teresa's hands and pulls her out into the hallway. She takes it willingly and begins to sweep, getting into corners and under chairs, singing as she does, "Come out and talk to me. I'm waiting patiently, for just a little kiss."

The girl finally gets Luisa into the wheelchair and into the bathroom. The old woman grips the ceramic hand holds in the green tiled shower, and indifferent to the world going by, suffers the scrubbing with Esmeralda's none too tender hands. Her body is amazingly firm and white for her eighty plus years, breasts still large and round. Anyone walking by, her sons or the ironing lady or her other stepdaughter, will say hello and stand smiling for her response. She's fine we see. She's well. How beautiful she must have been sixty years ago when *Don* Armando took her home to his two little girls Teresa and Adiela.

I wander into the dining room while the girl bathes and dresses Luisa. This can take an hour. Teresa now has a broom in her hands and she will sweep until she is called to breakfast.

Finally, the old lady will be ensconced in her large stuffed chair in the hallway. There she will pass the day, commenting on the world, calling Maria, praying, snoring.

Eating too. Frequently and messily, another departure from her early days. Now for breakfast and all the in between snacks which are incorporated into the Colombian day with name and hour, *tragos* before breakfast; breakfast with eggs or meat for those who can afford it and *arepa* and coffee, the *mediamañana*, the mid-morning break, then lunch which should always have soup and rice and dessert. Lunch Luisa eats at the dining room table with a towel around her neck. Her sons cut her meat for her, push the soup bowl closer, cajole her.

"Please Luisa, another bite of chicken. It's so good!"

She picks at her food, irritated that she is the object of so much scrutiny.

"Oh God help me, they treat me like a barrel, shoving food into me. No. No. A person can only eat so much and then no more. And anyway, why are my sons fattening me up?" She addresses this question to the painting of the Sacred Heart of Jesus, the same one that has seen all the changes in this house. His smile, his calm hand signals an answer to Luisa's question.

In the afternoon, Luisa and Teresa have at least one *algo*, the something that breaks up the long afternoon, in their chairs, nodding. Sometimes they forget they have had it and ask for another and the girl brings it. She warms buns and milk, beats hot chocolate to a froth.

Dinner comes late and heavy, but there is more to come: *merienda*, the before bed snack. Luisa eats these at the table too, surrounded by her family. She picks at her food, mostly eschewing the fork and knife. Unconcerned for the chunks and crumbs that tumble down her bosom and into her lap, she examines piece after piece of food and pops it in her mouth.

Teresa sits on a bench nearby, also eating, also taking her pills. Every day she asks,

"What pills are these, Esmeralda?"

"I don't know, María Terre. The orange one's for your right eye and the red one's for your left eye."

"My eyes! That's the only thing I have that's any good! I better take them right away."

"Yes," Luisa intones, homing in on one of her favorite themes. "You don't know how lucky you are that you still have light left in your eyes. My sisters. Both my sisters, the only two alive are blind. Well, I know the doctor wouldn't call them blind, but that's a doctor for you. What does he know? They can't thread a needle. Eyeglasses. Have you seen the eyeglasses that Sola has to wear after such an expensive operation? And she still can't sew. Maruja is blind too. I think," and she lowers her voice to a stage whisper," that she ruined her eyes with paint."

"Oh, come now, Luisa, surely Maruja hasn't worn makeup for years. She must be seventy years old."

"Oooh!" a hoot at my naivete. "Seventy, on the fingers of one hand! and she wears more colors than a parrot. That she puts on in the dark because she can't see. When she goes to church--out in God's good daylight--well, the Virgin save us all from the foolishness of old age. And she won't listen! Not to anyone. The doctor. A good doctor, related to our cousin Luz in Manizales, who operated on her eyes and tried to save her said she should not wear makeup because that black stuff was poison to her eyes and she told him to mind his own business. That's my sister. There you have a picture of her. I have no eyes to speak of anymore. For example, there's something swimming in my coffee and I can't tell if it's alive."

"No, Luisa. It's a crumb of bread. You must have dropped it in there."

"I'm sure I did." Still she peers into the cup with a look of barely restrained disgust. "Are you sure? It looks like it's moving its wings."

"If it's like that, then just give it to me. But why does Maruja insist on wearing mascara?

"What's mascara? The black stuff? It's not just mascara. She also wears a pound of rouge a day. Probably gets that in her eyes too. She says it keeps her young and nobody wants her to stay young."

Teresa shakes her head and catches my eye. Five or six times a day, she becomes again, momentarily, the proper lady she was during the first sixty years of her life. Now she is embarrassed by Luisa's gossip.

Esmeralda comes for Luisa's plate and carries it away. Teresa goes into the bedroom and after rummaging around in a drawer comes out with several pair of elastic pantyhose. I go in and return with a pair of wool knee socks.

"Luisa," I say. "Let's put on these nice warm knee socks I brought you."

"Well, of course, Luisa," Teresa says, "if you want to just wear short socks like a schoolgirl, you can." Teresa folds her arms across her chest and looks out into the patio.

Luisa stretches out her hands and we dump both pair of socks into her lap. She picks them up, one after the other, pulls on them, and finally chooses the elastic support stockings.

"Here. These. I like the ones that hold in my veins. I can feel my veins today."

I groan. The girl has disappeared into the kitchen but she cackles there. She bathes and dresses Luisa but the shoes and stockings are our problem.

Teresa is smiling and concentrating. This is her responsibility for the day. She sits on the low bench and carefully dries Luisa's feet. She separates her toes, squeezed together for so many years that they crowd together even unshod, and dusts between them with powder. Then she smoothes out the stockings, checking the label.

"Made in the USA." She gathers up the foot of the sock and picks up Luisa's foot and begins to work the stockings on, one inch at a time, first one foot and then the other. Just getting them up to her knees can take ten minutes. Sometimes Teresa is distracted at this crucial point, for reinforcements are needed to finish the job. There are days when no one, not even Luisa, notices that her pantyhose are still around her knees. She will simply comment that some days she can hardly move her legs.

We have fallen into a routine. As Teresa gets the stockings on, I get out the hairbrush and let down Luisa's hair. It is very long, to the floor as she sits in her chair. It feels like my Great-aunt Celesta's hair. It makes a rope in my hands, strong strands of black, grey and white. I make small talk. Like her son, I'm always looking for the old Luisa beneath the surface of this woman, so heavy and smelling of old woman, so quiet.

"How shall we do it today? One braid rolled up? A bun? Two braids on top? Don't ask me to put the rat in because I can only remember when Don Eliberto stamped on the rat!"

"I remember that old fool. I ran out of the room so I could laugh at him. No, just make a braid and wrap it around. I used to wear it like that when I was a girl."

Something in her face makes me think that someone must have liked her hair like that. I brush it all back from her face and use heavy black bobby pins to fasten the thick braid in a flat round to the back of her head.

"Look Terre, what do you think?"

"I like it. For me, I like it. And now I'm ready for the next step in the stockings."

I bring the walker into position in front of the chair. Esmeralda runs by with a mop and a bucket; she lets me know she is not going to be involved. I consider distracting Teresa and leaving the stockings where they are, hidden by the skirt until the first trip to the bathroom. Then it will be Esmeralda's job. On this day however, Teresa is uncommonly centered.

"Debbie. We need your help here."

"Yes. Of course," I step to Luisa's right elbow and try to lift her. She pulls on the walker, on me, and on Teresa but does not lift her bottom. We brace for another try, the two of us straining while the old lady observes us. We both begin to call to her, to engage her attention and finally she stands, swaying, inside the curve of her walker. Now we must pull up the elastic stockings. With no ceremony, Teresa pulls up the old woman's skirt and plants herself on one side, prepared to pull on her side of the pantyhose. I do the same on my side. She smells like baby powder and as I grasp the stocking my hands touch her skin, soft and white like risen dough. We begin to pull.

"I'm going, I'm going, I'm--" With each word she wavers, and finally sits down.

"No, Luisa," we groan, "you must hold on to the walker!"

Again, we have her upright and rigid in the walker; we begin and as we begin, she quivers and calls, "I'm go--"

"Gone," we say with one voice, as she collapses. Now we see that we must support her as we pull the stockings up. The three of us are locked in this battle, Teresa and I giggling with each tug, and putting off Luisa's delicate balance with each tug, and we finally all topple over laughing into her chair.

"I give up," I say, still laughing but backing out of the welter of arms and legs.

"Esmeralda!"

"*Señora!*" She rushes by with a mop in her hands.

"Did she go by?" Luisa asks.

"She did," I say and intend to get lost in some other part of the house, just as the girl has.

Luisa and Teresa settle into their place in the hall to talk about the terrible changes in servants in this modern day. When that subject wanes, Teresa will search through drawers and pockets and bags for their rosaries, certain ones out of so many; one day the tiny brown beads, another day the crystal ones with the silver crucifix, choosing their company like old friends. Then sitting back, they finger their beads and gaze without seeing at the patio where the dove pecks in the dust under the cages.

"*Dios te salve María...*" Luisa's voice intones.

"*Bendito tu eres,..*" Teresa chimes in as the tupiales warble and the dove coos. The old women nod and pray while all their past prayers and intentions, sixty years worth, come sifting in, as light as sun or dust, on them and on us all.

# More Stories from Colombia

# STORY 1

# Ines Seeks her Mother

The phone began ringing just after dawn. Everyone in the old house was up but no one wanted to answer the phone. There was the man, his grey hair tousled, in suit pants and pajama shirt in one room and next door his old mother buttoning her blouse which sticks to her back, still wet from the shower. It would be hours yet before either of them would respond to calls, knocks or bells. The servant girl was busy in the kitchen; she wouldn't dare push open the doors that separated the family rooms from the halls and patios and kitchen, public rooms. She could not come inside where the people of the house lived, not until they were up and showered and dressed and moving about, ready to face the day. The two who lived inside liked to start slowly. They waked early, very early, hearing the milk bottles at the door and workers' busses in the street but both felt the same reluctance to start the day. Behind closed doors, in separate rooms, they mumbled and complained to see if the other would pick up the receiver.

The phone rings shrilly over and over again in the little room between bedrooms. Pablo hears it and tilts back in his chair at its insistent clangor; he is reading yesterday's paper and visualizing today's problems: a sick cow at the finca, a leaky faucet, bills. He will not stir until he has solved some of them, at least in his mind. The insistence of the telephone makes him stiffen in his chair. It's somebody with a bill or a worker who needs an advance on his salary.

The old mother of the house, now completely dressed, sits in the next room on her bed, brushing her long hair. Beside her on the bed are her tortoise shell hairpins, a net, and a brown rat of hair that once fell out on the floor in front of the singing teacher. That experience had taught her not to rush her hairstyling. With the hairpins in her mouth she mumbles, half laughing remembering. There he had been, Don Eliberto, standing at the door saying good-bye to all and giving some last minute special exercises to David for his voice, standing there as the old lady walked by and she had noticed again his smell of hair oil and the rum on his breath even at that hour of the day, when her hair net slipped and the singing teacher jumped with a shout of triumph to stomp on the little brown rat that had fallen from her hair. Everyone-- she, Don Eliberto, David, Pablo who happened to be passing through-- stood mouths open as he raised his foot and saw, not a dead mouse, but an old lady's hair piece. So she brushed and twisted and pinned the rope of black and grey hair over the rat that gave her hair some body, securing it from every point. She heard the phone too but did not even flinch.

Finally, in its tenth ring, a red-faced young woman came running in, her bare feet slapping the tile floor. She was the daughter of Cornelia who had worked in this house for so many years. Cornelia would never have come into the bedrooms at such an hour; she shared in fact her patrons' distaste for all ringing bells which likely announced strangers, but her daughter Regina who was giving her mother a few days off, helping while Cornelia recovered from an attack of bile, had the mind of a child. Regina was strong and good natured with only a few simple faults: she would not wear shoes, she loved to talk on the telephone and would drop her broom or dust cloth and run long distances to do so, and the third, which was the worst of all, was to listen to private conversations and then repeat them to her mother and the neighbors and God only knows who else. She rushes to the phone.

"Very good morning. This is the house of *Doña* Luisa....*Doña* Luisa! It's for you."

"Find out who it is and ask nicely."

"*Sí, Señora.* May I please ask who it is who is calling to the *Doña* Luisa? *Doña* Luisa! It's the convent calling about your sister."

Bad news. A very bad way to begin the day. Pablo began to grumble under his breath and rattle his newspaper. Luisa spit out the hairpins on the bed cover and went into the room to take the phone from Regina's grasp.

"Good morning, Sister. Please, Sister. Sister. We must be patient. You of all people...She did? She did what? Did she break anything? How is she now? Oh no. That's terrible."

Pablo is squirming, convinced that admitting anything is a big mistake. He is openly listening to the conversation as is Regina who stands on first one foot and then the other, looking back and forth between them anxiously, but Luisa pays no attention to either of them.

"Are you sure it won't hurt her? Did the doctor say so? Just give her half that much and wait for us. We'll be right there."

"Regina! Get back to the kitchen. Go put some shoes on. Don't talk to anybody while we're gone. Do something. Make yourself useful. And don't answer the telephone!"

Luisa rushed into the next room, her hands trembling in her hair; she pulled a jacket from the closet and called to her son.

"Pablo, *por Dios*, hurry! Get ready and get the car out!"

"*Mamá*! We are not going to bring her back--"

"Yes, we are. This instant."

"Luisa, Luisa. It's a long drive. It can wait till the weekend. I have to...."

"It can't wait. If you won't take me, I'll get a taxi."

"Pablo, are you purposely going slow?"

"Did she take her clothes off again?"

"No, Pablo, *por Dios*, don't talk so of your aunt."

"Well, she did once."

"Yes, yes, but she promised never to do that again and besides, there was more to that than you know."

"I suppose she is getting up at night and roaming around again."

"Well, yes, something like that."

"And doing crazy things!"

"Poor sister. Now I believe it's true. She's not just acting so we'll take her home again."

"I remember the last time we had to come because it was so urgent and it was just because she didn't like some new old lady who was at her table."

"I didn't blame her for that. You wouldn't like it either if someone took out her dentures and clacked them right in your face. No, this is different. This is serious. To tell the truth, Pablo, I didn't think it would go like this. She was so happy she even got a new permanent and started knitting again. She asked me to bring her some wool. Yellow. It was almost like the old days."

Both looked out the windows at the green mountains speeding past. For ten miles they were silent. The little houses crowded up to the roadside were full of flowers and here and there bare branches were wrapped with cotton and hung with tinsel.

"It's almost Christmas and the nuns had fixed up the manger scene and Ines had helped them and you know they have a big and very beautiful antique set of figures and the Virgin is pretty, pretty, pretty! Well, anyway they put them right in the chapel down the hall from Ines' room and it's true she was getting up at night but completely dressed and to go into the chapel to pray. It's just that she would get sad sometimes and begin to cry for our *mamá*...."

"Nothing there to make us drive this distance on a weekday...."

"Early this morning, at first prayers, the nuns found her in the manger. She had taken the Baby Jesus out--very carefully, even the nun had to admit that--and laid him on the bench and then she got into the manger. That's where they found her this morning. And when they tried to get her out and the Baby back--who knows what they might have said to her!-she went off, you know, off. They couldn't control her and she caused a terrible scandal crying that her mother would be looking to find her there. All the old people heard her and they got upset and started crying and everybody wants to go home now. So the nuns wanted to give her a tranquilizer and I said yes, but just half as much."

They pulled up at the large country house, its long shady corridor lined with rocking chairs but only one small figure slumped there. Nuns in white habits ran out to see who was in the car, then ran back to the porch, their veils floating in the early morning air.

"Inesita. Your sister is here for you. Now don't cry anymore."

Ines sat forward in the rocking chair, her head fallen so that all that could be seen were the tiny grey curls that covered her head. She did not look up but hugged her knitting bag to her breast; her sweater was buttoned up tight all the way to the top; her packed suitcase was at her feet. She paid no attention to the car or the woman who hurried up the steps to her side.

"Ines. Ines, *por Dios*! Wake up sister. I'm here."

"Bisa," she glanced up and no sooner did their eyes meet, than tears rushed down her cheeks. "Bisa," she cried, using the old childhood name, "take me home."

Mother and son struggled to put her in the back seat. Even the nuns were shocked at the effect of the drug on the old woman whose head lolled and feet would not move. Finally she was in, slumped in the corner of the back seat. Pablo got the little car started and turned out onto the road. They did not look back.

The two old sisters and the younger man made the long drive to the city, leaving the countryside with its flowers and sweet breezes, leaving the old country house with private rooms and windows that opened out on the garden and nuns to care for the old people, leaving the idea that Ines could be happy there.

The two in the front seat were quiet, sighing for all those good things that did not work out. It was a long ride with Pablo frowning and mumbling and Luisa breathing prayers while in the back seat Ines clutched her bag and wept quietly, *"Ay mamá, ay mamá."*

Days later, after the drugs passed, she would tell people she had to leave the nuns. Taking their elbow, she would bend close and whisper, "It's so my mother can find me. You would do the same."

# STORY 2

# On The Street

God knows how many kinds of deformity exist in the world, but Colombia has them and they are all out in plain sight. There is no protection for anyone from the bizarre, the deformed, the poor, the sick; they are all right there in the street. Since there are really no institutions to care for the cripples, the crazies, the merely strange, the families must care for them and they do. And only a few, the *locos*, have no one.

Every city has *cojo*s, crippled men who are conspicuous as they make their way down the crowded sidewalks with heavy leather "shoes" buckled to their knees. They hold in each hand a platform, padded where they hold it and rubber soled where it touches the ground. This gives the person an apelike gait as the arms reach far forward while the tiny legs swing around to catch up. Often these people sell lottery tickets, a good stationary profession; they are not pathetic enough to beg and survive at it.

A worse condition of the same malady finds those men--can it be only men? -whose legs are too weak or too deformed for them to walk at all. They have little carts, very low to the ground. They use the same kind of arm extenders to pull their carts along over concrete and dirt. But for all their tribulation, it is immediately clear that someone cares about them, that someone washes and irons their clothes; at noon a child, probably his own child, will bring a small aluminum pot with cooked white rice and a couple chunks of fried pork and another pot of coffee. These men are tremendously handicapped, but they belong to a family.

There was one who sold newspapers along Junín, the busy street that runs through the center of Medellín. He was alwayssmiling and calling in a big voice, "*Colombiano*!

*Espectador*!" He had a stack of newspapers on the back of his cart which was just a platform on roller skate wheels. Most of its red paint had chipped off, but up front was a little gilt altar with a figure of Saint Christopher, Patron Saint of Travelers. Every time this man went across the street, he was invisible to the drivers until, of course, they were on top of him. They would see him practically under their wheels and curse and swerve; he was cool. He would carry on at a good fast scurry across the street, smiling, his head at the same height as the wheels turning around him. Once at the other high curb, he would pull himself off his wagon and up onto the curb, settling his soft rubbery legs--so different from his strong muscular arms---down on the curb and then pull up the cart and get back on it. Every street. Every day. I ran across the street to drop all the money I had into his saint's box. What a smile he gave me, brilliant, not begging! And the customary thanks of a person who cannot reciprocate: *"Dios le pague."* God will repay you.

No, these men do not beg though there are many beggars in the streets. Beggars, the successful ones (and stories of their hidden wealth are common) are usually those with terrible sores, terrible deformities, or many children--something to awaken pity and make themselves stand out from all the others. It is said, and it may be true that none of the leprous looking beggars have anything wrong with them. They stake out a place on the crowded sidewalks where the pedestrian traffic is heavy and prosperous. Walk out of the bank patting your pocket and you will trip over a man whose extended leg oozes from a wound that seems to the bone. Who would look so closely at these sores to tell if the pus is real? Others say that beggars make a career of sores and practice picking scabs and rubbing dirt into their wounds so as to make more money.

There are people with great lumps on their heads, hands turned the wrong way, holes in their bodies exposing organs, freaks you could say, who might otherwise be in a circus but instead go to a public park, a street corner. The squeamish walk by without looking but the streets are full of others, perhaps with coins, who will poke at and scrutinize.

The other group of successful beggars are mothers with children. These mothers will set up camp with a dirty blanket or sometimes just newspapers to cover the children, two or three or even four. Cynics say the children are not the natural children of the woman but perhaps are rented for the purpose, or worse yet, stolen from a good family. However it may be, children there are, all up and down the streets of Colombia.

Of course, most are dark skinned but from the life they lead, where water is an impossibility and soap, even if they wanted it, a luxury of the highest order, the children take on a dusky grey color with streaks of actual dirt, feces, food, and snot. Their hair is straw-colored, cottony, matted. The children, and it does not seem rehearsed, are always crying. They run to the passerby and accost her with outstretched dirty hands and a piteous voice, "*Doña, Doña, centavos por el amor de Dios.*" A few pennies for the love of God.

One wonders where the love of God comes in--it is as hidden as the secret lives of these people. Some may have a life off the streets, a place where they go and relax and eat and talk and laugh and hug their babies. Most live, day and night, on their corner of the sidewalk; by night blanketed by newspapers, by day begging, eating, fighting, there in the open. The children squat on the sidewalk. One more obstacle for the pedestrian. Several times a day they parade down the sidewalk. Mothers, clutching a baby, crying of course, lead the way. The others follow, dragging blankets or smaller children. They have a destination. A good mother makes a contact with one of the large houses, a maid, or the *señora de casa*. If the there is a welcome, the mother will lead her family up the sidewalk and right up to the door. She'll knock, and hand over a large cracker tin, smiling of course, and bowing and trying to keep her children from crying and disturbing the family. The maid will scrape the lunch plates into the can in some houses; others give them fruit or bread. The mother then hunkers down with her little ones to eat there on the sidewalk, they eat with their hands, the rice and the green peas and chunks of fat that the old man carefully carved off his steak, all congealing at the bottom of their can.

Sadder and more frightening are the *locos*. Every city has a number of these and there are as many women as men. These are without any doubt outside the limits of family, of any caring human being. They do not, as the begging mothers sometimes do, band together. The most terrible thing about the *loco* is his absolute solitude. His first and last trademark though is dirt. Colombians are scrupulously clean and the crazy man on the street has skin and hair all the same grimy color as his torn clothes, torn always it seems to expose his dirty buttocks. He or she is fair game for the gamins, the street urchins who pick pockets or steal to survive. They bait the *locos* who are not smart enough or fast enough to steal or even to defend themselves from the gamins. A *loco* might sometimes beg, but all the other beggars will chase him away; he is bad for business. This is probably one reason the *loco* is far ranging. The same man is seen all over the city, shouting obscenities, pissing in public, terrorizing decent people by his presence.

Most *locos* are in the cities but they also exist in the countryside. *La Mona* was a *loca,* one who actually had a little house, a very tiny one with one door and one window and a dirt floor. She also had a grandson that she cared for but no income that anyone could see. Her son--father of the boy she cared for--came every two weeks walking from the bus stop with a burlap bag of necessities: rice, potatoes, beans. But no coal to cook with, no cigarettes, so *La Mona* and her little grandson would spend most of every day walking up and down the roads and paths, all the places where others walked and threw away cigarette butts and soda bottles. She would pick up all these and many other good things, as well as horse and cow manure to sell.

She was a little old woman whose mouth, since she had no teeth, had collapsed into her face. Her chin and nose almost touched, just like the witches in the old picture books. Though old, her hair was very black, completely black and matted, uncombed it seemed forever. She wore layer upon layer of black dresses, each showing through the holes of the other. The one on top had a greenish sheen as if it were mossy. She was always barefoot, her toes like tiny clayey potatoes. She carried a large stick and when the mean town boys teased her with calls of *loca* and witch, she would go into a frenzy and throw all the manure her grandson had so carefully picked up. Bent double with rage, her face purple, she would call down curses on her tormentors, at which their bravado would melt. The grandson who ran to hide in her skirts when the town boys approached, would get far out of her reach when the fit was on her. He would stand at a distance, stork like, on one thin brown leg, sucking his thumb until she calmed down.

Still, she had her peaceful moments when she would sit like a large black hen, all the ragged hems of her skirts like feathers fluffed out in the dust in front of her house. There she would smoke the large cigarettes she rolled of the tobacco from the butts she collected and smile toothlessly while the little one cuddled up beside. On Christmas day, a passer-by might give the old woman a whole pack of cigarettes and the boy a chocolate candy bar. They would chatter back and forth with their treasures, the two who were always silent.

There are persons who are judged *locas* in Colombia who would not be in many other places. There was a woman, a peasant woman, but one who could read and write and keep track of money who was judged a *loca* by her peers. Ismenia, God rest her soul, was what they called a *marimacho*. The word says something about her and something about Colombia too: *Mary*--feminine, *macho, male*. She was a big woman, a head taller than any man around with a big belly that preceded when she walked. She had a loud voice and laugh and manner. She even had a job as a *mayordoma*--her success at it was thought proof she was not normal. This work of keeping a *finca* going, taking care of the cows and chickens, guarding against thieves, maintaining the grounds is clearly man's work, but she did it well for many years. She wore a machete on a belt around her as her badge. Not many crossed her path; she didn't mince words and wasn't afraid, as she herself would say, of *Dios ni el diablo*. What chance did a man have with a woman who wasn't afraid of God or the devil?

Still she was married, married to a tiny man perhaps thirty or forty years her senior and she was doggish in her devotion to him. She spent hours fixing meals to tempt his failing appetite; she fed him with a spoon. The truth was that she was a kind and conscientious nurse, and this was why people from all around would bring their sick animals for her to care for even as they made fun of her being so masculine and loud.

Once, in the seventies when there were so many *gringos* in Colombia getting into cheap drugs, foolishly venturing into areas that no *Colombiano* would approach, a young man named Charlie brought Ismenia a charge. He had experimented with a jungle herb, a hallucinogen from a tribe of Amazon natives and had taken this Colombian girl along. This young woman was now completely *loca;* her craziness was unpredictable, and her running away from home with a crazy hippie had left her bereft of home and mother.

Ismenia took her in. The first thing she had to do was to rearrange her house for there could be no knives or matches left in the way of the *loca* who would occasionally be called out of her haze to do damage to herself and whoever tried to stop her. During the day when Ismenia had to go to the town to buy food or down to the stable to milk the cows, she would tie a rope around the *loca's* waist and tie her to an orange tree in the courtyard. There she would sit dreamily staring into space until someone came to get her and lead her to another place. This is a homely remedy for such situations.

Ismenia had no children of her own but she loved, in her own gruff way, a number of children, nephews, neighbor children, *la loca*. She would make enormous meat pies for her *niños*, give them bear hugs, and laugh hugely at any mischief they got into.

She goes to show how some of the ones who are on the street, abandoned even by God, will be cared for by another outsider.

God will repay her.

# STORY 3

# Don Samuel and His Science

He kept us waiting. It was always his way to come in at least twenty minutes late, bowing and smiling and kissing the women's hands all around. Then he would sit, very upright as was his manner, and clapping his hands, call the waiters although we already had drinks.

"Here and here," jabbing his fingers at us, "drinks all around. Not for me, I can't tonight," and this night he rolled his eyes and held his arms around his tightly muscled waist and winked. We all laughed. His good health, his strength was famous, just as his story telling. He had called us together. He had a story, so we waited until he had his glass, tonight with seltzer rather than his usual aged rum. He started his story by asking after all our children by their pet names, and our parents, and our businesses. We responded by asking after his.

"You are having some troubles at your *finca*, we heard."

"Was having," Jaime punctuated the past tense, "but Samuel took care of his problem without the help of any *expertos cientificios*."

"There is science and science. It's not that I believe in this--" Samuel bent over the table and scooted his chair in, "I say to you, I don't believe in all these old stories. I'm not superstitious. I'm not a *Doctor* as you are," and his black eyes stopped briefly on each of the men," but on the other hand I'm not a complete innocent." With this he paused while the table made noises of appreciation of his wit. Innocent indeed!

With a smile he held up a strong forefinger that bristled with black hair and when he had everyone's attention, he began again in a soft voice. "One thing I know well. I must defend my-self against all the others who do believe in superstitions. So sometimes I have to make deals with people I would otherwise avoid."

He grimaced as though the thought of it were distasteful. "I first got the idea when I was getting a divorce--and anyone who knows my ex-wife would comprehend perfectly--if I had to make a deal with the devil, it was because she would make ten deals--she would do anything to get at me and she did. It didn't turn out the way she wanted though, because God is good, and I keep my eyes open," at this he used his thumb and forefinger to widen his already large black eyes, to push back the curly grey eyebrows behind his thick square fingers, and peer all around the table, not stopping until we were all laughing.

Laughing then himself, taking a drink and then with a flourish of his hand, brushing it all away--he continued, "but I found a man, I always go with the men, the *brujos*, there's no doubt they have more power, if you believe in that kind of thing. Well, you can decide after I tell you the story. My ex-wife was after every cent I had worked for over the years. She didn't stop there; she wanted to take everything! Even my sons and my only daughter. She tried to poison their minds against me! She threatened me with some other bad business, but the bitch was wrong there too--forgive me for saying such."

After a brief silence, he raised his head, "It's not like me, I wasn't raised to speak of women thus but she pushed me to it. Not only my children, she wanted my money. Well, as I say, I'm no fool." He closed his eyes modestly at the flurry of affirmations that went around the table. "I know how to look around and defend what's mine. So first I hired the best lawyer in the city. I don't stick at the cost, and I don't examine his reputation at the bar or his fancy office. I want someone who gets action, someone like me!"

"After I got him working-- 'Here,' I said--'anything you need.'" As if to punctuate this, he clapped his hands again and four waiters materialized. He drew a very thick wallet from the small leather shoulder bag he carried and laid it in the middle of the table while they filled everyone's glasses.

"So the lawyer with all the papers on his wall, says: 'Sorry, *Don* Samuel, but you have to pay. The law is clear that the spouse gets half of the estate,'" he said, glaring all around.

"That's what the son of a bitch said--which led me to see that she probably had her powers working--and don't underestimate the powers of a woman like that; she was just a poor soul, ignorant but for hate, for hate she excelled and here was the proof. That's when I knew I had to get some other help so I went to the *brujo*. I told him the whole story from beginning to end. He's more intelligent than the lawyer; he wanted to know a lot of details about her and about us, and as I say I was a desperate man! That woman is terrifying to me!"

He pantomimed wiping sweat from his brow and flinging it on the floor. When we were all laughing, he continued reflectively. "It's funny, nobody would believe that such an ordinary looking man as *Don* Elias could even understand what I was saying, but he listened very carefully, never writing anything down. Later, his *secretario*, a man just as simple looking as his boss, came knocking on my door and handed me this folded over piece of kids' tablet paper with some numbers scratched in pencil. That was the bill; he charged me almost as much as the lawyer with his fancy office. I didn't regret it, I said I was glad to pay as long as he guaranteed results. He just closed his eyes as if to say I had said too much. You know the lawyer wouldn't be that *correcto*."

Samuel pushed back in the chair and began to windmill with his arms. "I remember the day he came to my house; he had to enter to my house where I lived with my ex-wife together for thirteen years-- Now, it wasn't easy to get her out so she wouldn't know, but I did it. *Don* Elias closed the door and went from one corner of the room to the other--'here,' he said, pointing--'*del Oriente al alto de Santa Elena- -hasta el Boquerón--al alto de Minas-- al alto Matasano*'! He named all the mountains that circle the valley of Aburra where we live, we and three million other Christians."

He was almost whispering now; we all bent closer.

"I was in a sweat. I couldn't move just watching him do these simple things," Samuel again swept his arms in a large circle all around the table, "and he said some things I couldn't understand and finally he smiled and said, 'You're safe.'"

Samuel sagged momentarily in his chair.

"-- the lawyer?" I asked.

"The lawyer says I have to pay--but Don Elias just opened his eyes and said very seriously, 'Don Samuel, believe me. You're safe and she can never touch a penny that is yours.'"

After a brief silence, Samuel continued in his ordinary voice.

"And then we got out of that house--in plain daylight--without anyone seeing us. And everything," he spread his hands out, pressing them down on the table, "everything, he said has been true. It's been five years and she has a whole team of lawyers who run around with their hands full of papers and books and laws, and I just laugh. My lawyer, he can't believe it either. I don't tell him about my other protection, I just tell him to relax. Even, the best thing, even my children are coming back to know me and love me. That's inevitable when a man is good."

All of us congratulate him on his reconciliation with his children, especially his only daughter. He bows his head and crosses himself, ending by kissing his thumbnail, a monkish touch from his days with the Jesuits.

"*Sì, Bendito sea Dios!* So when I started having problems up at the finca, I knew what to do. I take good care of my things. I have a good herd of cows up there and a good *mayordomo* who knows how to take care of them, and I buy them best feed, and well, you name it, I do it.

No one could find any reason why all of a sudden the calves started dying. Beautiful calves. Healthy calves. Healthy when they're born and they just go down, down. After the third one died, I got the idea that maybe they were starving to death; that's how they looked, so 'Stop,' I said, 'selling the milk. Leave all the milk to the calves!' but it didn't matter and we just stood there and watched them die, watched the life just go out of them little by little. I called in the best vet in the valley and he couldn't figure it and wanted to do an autopsy, but even though I believe in science, I can't see cutting up the poor beasts so I said no and I went back to my man."

He paused and women's voices chimed in, "Oh, Samuel, what a shame!"

"It's terrible to watch the creatures die."

"Who could do such a thing?"

Bowing and smiling, he nodded, "But it wasn't just the cows. At the same time I bought a nice four wheel drive vehicle. The best, because you see, money isn't important if I need something. So I bought this brand new Landrover so I could get all around the farm, up the mountains even where there was no road, and the son of a bitch car," here he slowed, hissing each syllable, "brand new out of the dealers, would take me up the mountain or down to the creek or up to the stoplight, with three hundred cars behind me honking, and stop. Just stop and nothing would work. I towed it to the dealers. They couldn't find anything. I called this mechanic I know--he owes me some favors, and I said, 'Just ride around with me for a couple days,' and he did and nothing happened. But the first time I went out alone, the damned car stopped. I had it towed back to the dealers and I told them to keep it."

"So I called back my man, *Don* Elias, and he came out to the finca, brought by his brother-in-law or his political uncle, you know how those people have all their relatives around to serve as *secretarios*, and they came up the road to the driveway but there they sat, wouldn't come through the gate. I sent the *mayordomo* out to find out why in the devil they were sitting out there honking and they sent back word--*Don* Elias sent back word--for me to go out there so I did, but I didn't like it.

"I mean I don't come at just anyone's bidding, but there was something to this--I don't know how to say what it was--so I walked out. I wasn't happy that everybody would see me so I sent the *mayordomo* and his wife inside the house to do something--I don't want people to get the idea that I believe in this stuff, and I went out to the cattle grid at the gate and as I started across, *Don* Elias called out--'*Alto! Don* Samuel!' I was startled and stopped right there and he held up his hand--what he does with his money is a mystery because he doesn't spend it on cars. This was just a little old grey Renault, and he was sitting there in the passenger's seat while his *secretario* sat perfectly quiet and watched him. Well, *Don* Elias has his eyes closed and he's sitting there dressed as always like some little clerk or something. The only thing different from a clerk is a big gold cross on a chain around his neck, first thing you see about him, but the spooky thing is how he just sits there and starts to shake or something so he called again, '*Alto! Don Samuel!*' and I did and I started sweating. So I was balancing there on the metal cattle grid when he said something I couldn't hear and his man ran around the car and opened the door and *Don* Elias got out and stood looking around and around, and then there at the power box--you know where the electricity comes into the land there at the gate and the meter is closed up in a metal box--with a stick, a bamboo rod he always carries, he touched the metal box and it opened--"Here Samuel starts to shudder, his eyebrows are raised into his head, he gasps, catches his breath and continues--"there was the *maleficio*. The curse. The voodoo. It looked at first like a bird nest or something natural there in the bottom but as the *brujo* began to poke at it with his stick--all the while he's praying in some kind of language, fast, fast, it started a terrible stink, terrible! It's not like a natural stink like something rotten or dead, but one that made my hair stand up, and bones, human bones--there no mistaking them and pieces of shriveled skin, bits of intestines and something metal and I almost fell over but *Don* Elias was praying, faster and faster and rolling his eyes around and poking it with his rod and in a while, I don't even know how long, it was all gone, all crumbled into the dirt and rocks and grass of the road."

Samuel stopped to drain his glass of water; then he clapped and ordered a double of dark rum which he swallowed while we waited in silence. When the color had come back to his face, he continued, "So after this, the *brujo*, as calm as you please, walked across the grid, smiling just a little bit. He never really smiles, but he invited ME to go all around the property, MY property. We did. We went up to the highest point, up in the pines and he just stood there and looked, but he doesn't LOOK like most people, and he doesn't say much either. He just stands, almost like a dog does sniffing the air, and gazes into the distance, across the mountains, and then he goes on, with me behind him like a puppy-dog or his *secretario*--who's with him all the time, a shadow--but I wasn't about to argue after what he found down at the gate. And we went down to the creek and followed that for a ways and then into the stable where the cows were all gathered and now only one calf of the seven that were born lives and still lives and we gave it a name to keep it alive and *Don* Elias just sort of soaked up atmosphere there and finally to the house and he walked slowly around the house--he wouldn't go in even though the *mayordoma* came out an offered us coffee she had made, but he just shook his head nodding and all. It isn't that he's bad mannered, but he's still concentrating and there at the back wall, he brushes back some branches, tapping the wall with his stick, and his *secretario* says, 'Bring a pick-axe and knock this down,' and the wall almost exploded when we touched it and there was another *maleficio*. Same as the other or worse with a stench that made the *mayordomos* and me cough for air. I don't know how we even lived with all that so close."

"So you can see that this man earns his money! And I'll ask you too if you believe even a little bit in this science? Well, his work wasn't done yet. Remember that car that was giving me so much trouble? Well, he had never even seen it. It was at the dealers. *Sí, Señores*, that's the way I do things. 'Take that son of a bitch back and put it on the line and go through it! I told them. Well, they did and then they sent it back to me and charged me a lot of money and said they had made some adjustments, but would you believe? First thing that happened, I took it up to the mountain and it got up there and stopped. So I had to have it towed down with the neighbor's oxen. Yes, oxen, what else with no road?"

"So the oxen towed it to the village where I got a tow truck and took it right over to *Don* Elias' house. He came out and walked around and around and then tapped with his stick--see, he never touches things with his hand, he never even shakes hands--on the driver's door. I opened it. I'm getting so I understand him too! Anyway, he stood there going into that kind of trance when his secretary tells me to take the driver's seat out. 'Out?' I couldn't believe it. But he just nods with his eyes closed.

So I do, with a wrench and plenty of sweat because it was so tight and then with his rod he flips up the carpet and there it was! Right under the seat where I sit! Another *maleficio*! *Dios mio Bendito*! I live in great danger! It's a miracle the only thing that happened was with the car. It might have had serious effects on my being!"

He stood up, smoothed his forehead and forced a laugh. "Here," he began to help the ladies out of their chairs and signaled to the waiters. "We're ready to go into the dining room."

Then taking me by the arm, he leaned over to whisper in my ear. "Pardon me if I don't have anything to eat--What? No, nothing wrong. A little discomfort in my gut. It's nothing. I know how to take care of myself."

# STORY 4

# La Pecoralia

There are places so remote, so far from the big cities, far even from villages and little huts perched on the upper ridges of the mountains, so far that it takes hours in car over good roads, more hours in jeep over poor roads, to a river bank where a man in a boat fishes as he waits. When the people come, he will pole them down the mud colored river called Rio Man to where there are horses, saddled and standing as horses everywhere do, on three legs, ears back, tails flicking at the many flies and gnats, waiting to carry the visitors to the ranch called La Pecoralia, named for the creek that cuts through it.

It is an all-day trip, not much time actually to go back several centuries and see, feel, live the sweat of each of them. Here was a trip, taken by a Colombian man, *el doctor*, as they called him in Colombia, and his wife. He has been before to La Pecoralia; he goes now to offer some help to the people who struggle to live there; she goes to see what she will see.

There is a man on horseback waiting with the horses. He is dark, small and wiry, barefoot; he has a machete in his belt, a hat shades his black eyes that study but never meet the eyes of the visitors. He has been sent to meet them by Clemente who is his boss, the boss of many in the area. He came leading a bay and the good *mula rucia*. The gray mule is for the woman; the mule is the best mount on the ranch; she will take care of the woman, keep her from danger no matter how stupid she is. For although visitors are not new, a woman is, and an American woman unthought-of. They continue, three specks on horseback while the boat man turns back. There are a few trees on the bank of the river, small ones that have grown up since the jungle was cleared. Turning from the river is like turning to the sky. The land, the horizons are far, far away. The hills roll and peak and break; in the east, north and west, the horizon is bare. Here and there incredibly tall trees dot, spike the scene. The few large trees that remain are giants that survived the fires that cleared the land. They had grown without branches up to the top canopy of the jungle, a tiny umbrella of leaves at the very top to catch the sun; now they offer the tiny spots of shade in the otherwise relentless sun. To the south, still rain forest, trees cloud the horizon.

They ride for several hours; the visitors in front, looking, looking, and soon *vaqueros* come in from all directions. They touch their hats, mumble a greeting, steal respectful glances, and fall in the rear of the caravan. They hesitate, uncertain, eyes flashing back and forth to each other, at the woman's many questions. They confer--what is the name of that tree? and present diffident answers, half pleased, half embarrassed. Within another hour, they approach the compound, a fenced in rectangle measuring perhaps some 50 meters by 100 meters, tightly strung with six rows of barbed wire. There is only one gate and a dirt road leading up to it. Coconut palms stand swaying sentinels at each corner of the compound. These are the only trees for a half an hour's ride. Clemente, the *colono*, waits at the gate to greet the visitors. He is the colonizer, the one is charge, and the one who--although his background is much the same as the others here--took on the responsibility, got in with the government, signed the papers; the land, three thousand acres that he burnt off and defends, is his, or will be once he completes his fifteen years of making improvements, of holding back the jungle. He shakes hands with *el doctor*, this title that is more a sign of respect than recognition of a degree; he helps the woman down off the mule. They stand at the gate of the compound. The compound is bare dirt, red dirt, scarred by the stiff brooms that Josefa and her helpers wield everyday. There is not a blade of grass or a plant anywhere. The jungle that resisted them so fiercely is kept back! Small wiry pigs by threes and fours wander around, eyes and snouts on the ground.

They scavenge, following the flocks of chickens that also wander freely. The ground, large as it is, is spotless; the pigs eat the chicken droppings, the dogs, last in the eating order because they alone are not food for humans, follow the pigs and clean up after them.

There are four large thatched huts, a number of smaller ones; the largest belongs to Clemente and his wife. Sadly, they have no children of their own, but they have adopted, informally, their nephew to help them and to inherit the ranch. Josefa waits at the door of her home; she steps out into the sun as the guests draw near.

Josefa is dark and large for a Colombian peasant woman; she is the size of an average American, her visitor. She glances at her guests and then looks away. She does not extend her hand but ducks an awkward curtsey while she sizes up the situation. This is something out of the ordinary: a lady out in the wilds!

She invites them into her home. The place they enter is only a larger version of all the other huts. The walls are of bamboo that has been split into thin slats and nailed vertically to form a privacy wall that allows the breeze to flow through. The roof is of thatched soft silvery straw; from the outside it looks like a slide, a mountain of straw; from the inside the plaited pattern of stalks twisted and tucked is revealed. There are no closets; everything is hung from the ceiling struts, or hooks on the walls. The fancy saddles, the Sunday clothes, the blankets, the hammocks, and bags of charcoal hang around the room.

Josefa's hut is divided, a sign of her position, into two rooms. In her bedroom, another sign of prestige is a bed rather than the more portable and cooler hammock. She offers the *gringa* the bed, the only bed for a hundred miles. This is not only an act of hospitality but a way of showing her knowledge of the bigger world outside her hut. The bed has a high, ornately carved headboard where a crucifix hangs; it has a mattress stuffed with horsehair, hard, hot, and prickly even through the coarse sheets and pink chenille bedspread. No, thank you, the lady insists gently on a hammock. Josefina finally laughs that someone might never have slept on a hammock and would want to.

"Very well, then, very well!" she smiles broadly, "Clemente will string up a hammock. There, that striped one will be just right for your sleeping."

Now she is relaxed and enjoying this rarest of visits. She inquires after the family, calling the woman Blanca.

"Four sons! God blessed the Blanca with four sons!"

*El doctor*, whom she has met before, corrects her, "Her name is Debbie."

"*Sí, Sí*. Blanca." She has decided and she has her way here. She leads the visitors outside where four straight back chairs stand. There in the shade of the overhang, the two guests and Clemente sit down.

Some of the twenty-five or thirty other people who live on the grounds, workers or related to the workers, come near to look and listen. They have never seen an American. They exchange amazed and pleased glances.

She speaks! They can almost understand her! The three lean back into the shade of the overhang, tipping the chairs back against the bamboo wall, getting comfortable while the people and chickens and pigs and dogs move in front of them.

Josefa returns with a bottle of aguardiente on a tray, four shot glasses, and a small bowl with chunks of raw coconut. She will not drink or sit--it would not be proper--but the woman who is a guest and a *gringa* is expected to. Aguardiente is a 100 proof anise-flavored clear liquor that is always drunk straight, not sipped but gulped. It is used in the countryside, as an antiseptic poured on wounds, a preventative for malaria, an intoxicant, and common cup to toast friendship. This means there is always a good reason to drink it down fast without too much grimacing and follow it fast with a chunk of fruit, orange or coconut, chewing meditatively while the alcohol spreads from the throat to the fingertips.

The extra glass is to be shared by those whom Clemente calls from the crowd. Some will be favored so, singled out, called by name, offered the glass full of aguardiente and introduced to *el doctor*. The lucky one will throw the liquor back in one gulp, give thanks as he tips his hat, and step back into the many.

This drinking and conversing are serious business and will go on for hours. The *gringa* soon begs for her bed. Clemente measures her with a shrewd eye, gauging her weight so the hammock is suspended at the right angle, neither too taut nor too slack. She collapses into it while the broody hen clucks and scratches in the pink dirt underneath her and the men's voices outside drone on. She wakes in the morning to the rooster's crow and a pig squealing his last bloodcurdling squeal: he will be dinner. The two visitors step outside; shy children come to watch the strangers. There are no bathrooms, not even outhouses; the people who live here have a system, places where women go, other places for men. The strangers improvise out in the sugar cane fields playing sentinel for each other.

Josefa waits with a tray with bowls of coffee. She has decided that Blanca must have fresh fish for breakfast and she sent a *vaquero* on horseback to the river. In the meantime, to hold back hunger, she serves them thick strong coffee sweetened with *panela*. *Panela* is the crudest form of sugar; it comes in hard brown cakes and is broken and boiled in huge pots to dissolve its sweetness and purify the water. It is served with coffee or chocolate in the morning and when cool with lemons squeezed and floating in it.

Soon a man comes at full gallop, a *pez dorada* as long as his arm still gasping air dangles from his line. The cooking hut, for no one cooks in his sleeping hut, becomes the center of activity; a fish goes in, the pig is being butchered close by; boys are laughing, splotched with blood, they carry arms full of pig meat into the hut. The bounty is already shared out as chickens scratch at the guts, the dogs tag the boy's heels begging for bites, even the other pigs watch at close hand, shaking their heads at all the activity. Since there is no refrigeration, all the meat must be eaten within twenty-four hours; everyone will eat meat this day. Overhead, vultures circle, the ones called the King of the Buzzards, white and black with red heads, but they will have none.

There are children everywhere running, as the chickens and pigs do in little groups, here and there, in fits and starts; they stop and giggle, then scatter when the strangers speak to them. As the visitors sit down to breakfast, the fish, scored then deep fried, split between them and Clemente, served with a mound of rice garnished with sliced onion and tomato, fried plantains, more coffee with *agua panela*, now clouded with milk, in the shade of the straw overhang. There is always an audience to watch the strangers eat. "Ah," they say out loud, "She likes that fish!" and they exchange pleased glances. The dogs too gather around; one a pitifully pregnant bitch, a hound, long eared, her black and white spots run together in a muddy grey; she has mange and scabs and not only do her ribs show but each knobby vertebra of her spine. The *gringa* gives her leftovers and the observers learn another caprice of *Norteamericanas*: they talk to dogs; they feed them!

The horses are waiting at nine when the meal is finished. Now they will go out with the work crew to ride the fences, to see all the herds, to visit the planted fields. The grey mule is third in the file that stretches out on the pale orange road away from the compounds. As the day goes on, hour after hour, the mule gets nearer and nearer the end of the line; at a nod from Clemente, cowboys dash back to see where the woman has got to. During this nine-hour day, a holiday schedule for the *vaqueros* and Clemente, they will cross small parcels of land belonging to other *colonos*, smaller landowners. These come out to see who comes; people are always welcome. They offer something, whatever they have and there is a serious obligation to accept it. So the group receives *aguardiente*, no matter the hour, from those who have it, and *agua panela* with lemon from the poorer households.

After three or four hours in the saddle, even on a very good mule, and three or four shots of 100 proof liquor, the tropical sun and the day becomes a trial. The woman concentrates on lasting the day. She does, by riding last, riding slowly, spending her energy on seeing the towering ceiba trees, the pairs of parrots that fly squawking overhead.

In some places they ride close to the jungle where the monkeys scream and crash through the branches. There are always the graceful Zebu cattle to watch, always the *vaquero*s as they ride, talk, sometimes sing a comealong to the cattle. It is a long day; it is a day out of another century. She cannot even get down out of the saddle by herself when they finally ride back into the compound.

Josefa waits with food. Here is the pig; the guests are given the best parts and in great abundance. Also there is *yucca* and rice and a sweet made with *panela* and milk: a feast. Again the audience gathers to watch them eat; the children have now been fed; their faces are greasy and smiling and the strangers not so strange. Still they know their place and become shy and ashamed if their voices become too loud. The animals draw near too, less urgently than the day before. Only the black and white bitch is not there.

"Please, Josefa, where is the spotted bitch?"

"Ah, don't worry, Blanca, that bitch got what she was waiting for. She is over there somewhere."

"You mean she had her puppies? May I see?"

Children swarm around her as she steps into the yard, calling her now that they are out of Josefa's range, to look here, to see that. They duck close to her and then dash away as they lead her through the compound. Men are hunkered in the shade of their huts, eating; the women serve them their meals and then stand by. The *vaqueros* eat first and they get the largest portions. The other workers, those who plant or dig must wait. They sit around playing cards or dominoes. Their conversations stop as the *gringa* and the children approach.

They lead her behind a hut, and there in the pink dust is the dog. She is breathing shallowly but she lies belly outstretched for her four puppies to find what they can. They are the brightest things in this dusty place, their mouths brilliant pink, coats shiny black and white. The dog has to be coaxed to take the scraps of meat.

"Oh," the children say with something like pride, "the lady is a friend to dogs!"

Josefa laughs too when they return. "Don't worry Blanca, I will send food for that poor old bitch."

And perhaps she would.

The holiday atmosphere continues after the meal as men gather in front of the hut to listen to the talk and perhaps to be called to drink.

Clemente brings out his battery operated radio; they will listen to broadcasts from the *guerrilleros* and sometimes they also intercept the Army trying to track the *guerrillero*s; thus they follow and avoid the battles. This leads to politics; then, drunker and closer to their hearts, they talk beef and fences and more land to buy and clear but the *gringa* does not hear it. She falls asleep immediately swaying in her hammock. She will leave the next morning early, retracing her footsteps into the twentieth century.

In the morning there are thanks to be given, names remembered.

"*Adiós* Clemente. *Adiós* Josefina. *Adiós*, Eladio, Miguel Angel, *niños*," each name with a handshake and thanks.

Josefa always remembers the *gringa* and asks after her. The people there at the Pecoralia laugh and remember the funny things she did and said; La Blanca was their *gringa*; she had visited them.

Josefa would continue to tell this story even after she returned to her little village, to her mother's hut, returned from being *Doña* Josefa to the whole countryside, returned carrying her pink chenille bedspread, the crucifix, and Clemente's radio, to being just Josefina, Magdalena's daughter. This was after Clemente and his step-son were ambushed, shot dead with shotguns on their way home from the village.

They were not robbed; they were being paid back by some who were envious, or some who had been fired from the ranch, or perhaps just because that is the way life is.

# STORY 5

# Services

In the plaza of the *Palacio Municipal*, on the wide broken sidewalks under the dusty leaved trees, business begins early. Some old women with aprons and kerchiefed heads sell the typical Colombian breakfast of milky coffee, sweet rolls and corn bread with cheese. They walk up and down, clicking their tongs and calling out,"*Café con leche, arepas con queso*," click, click, click. At first, they amble along, hips swinging, exchanging casual conversation, but soon the pace picks up. The church bells for masses all around the city begin to clatter, old women rush by, mantillas and rosaries waving, and the first crowded busses arrive.

About this time come the amanuenses. They are what make this plaza different from any other here in this large city. There are many amanuenses (or *escribano*s as they are called in Colombia) for the letters and forms and accusations and denunciations that will be needed this day are many too. These important men, for they are all men, are a bridge between the world of the *Palacio Municipal* and all those who cannot read or write.

Like the sellers of sweet rolls who advertise their hygiene with a clatter of aluminum tongs, the *escribanos* show their vocation by their typewriters and suits, imitating the trappings of the later arrivals to the *Palacio Municipal*, the lawyers and the judges. These, dressed in business suits and white shirts, carry brief cases to offices hidden behind heavy doors and ranks of bored secretaries; the amanuenses carry their offices with them, large wooden boxes with handles that open into tables with drawers for paper and envelopes, portable typewriters, folding chairs. They cart these to and from their homes everyday by bus.

All the *escribanos* wear suits. Stained perhaps, and rumpled, and more often than not the pants and the jacket do not match or fit, but suits nonetheless come together, all appearing finally to be the same color of the building or the sidewalk or the tree bark. They all wear white shirts, too, shirts which once were starched and folded to a military crease; yellow lingers along the fold lines, blends with the grey of the worn cuffs and collars. The ties, an essential badge, are a museum's display of neckwear for the past thirty years.

As these writers set up shop, fussing with the rickety tables, settling the chairs, counting papers and stamps and envelopes, they may sip thick sweet coffee, they may have their heavy cracked shoes polished by the boys who haunt all the streets, squatting with their boxes of brushes and polish wherever someone gestures. Finally, the scribes are ready; they need only wait for a client to arrive to dictate a letter home, or make a request for a formal hearing, a delay in prosecution, mercy.

By eight in the morning the sidewalks are crammed, the buses, screeching to a halt at this crucial intersection, have deposited hundreds and hundreds of people in only a few minutes. The wide sidewalk is jammed with people who enter the huge building, two hundred years old, built as a fort and a symbol of Spain's power, built to last and to intimidate all who enter there, staffed then and now by public servants immune to pity and justice and civility.

And all must go there, although the rich may pay someone else to go and stand in line for them. This is where the workers get their working papers, the drivers get their drivers' licenses, the travelers get their passports; I say get, but these essential papers, duly stamped and notarized may just as easily be refused as given. Here too the unfortunate make formal claims for lost or stolen goods; they declare bankruptcy, certify deaths and appear for trials.

Nobody sees more of the misery that comes and goes here than the *escribano*. He steels himself with a look of bland cynicism. He rolls a piece of blank paper into his high black typewriter. The letters reach out like old black crooked fingers to stamp the page. The Indian woman stands slightly behind him; their eyes will never meet. She relaxes finally into this magic, her voice falling into a rhythmical recital which is translated into black marks. Somehow she trusts this will all go home to her family. So she gazes into the sky, her eyes flickering to the page and the black machine.

*---My very much remembered little mother and father and all my sisters and brothers. Has my sister's new little one come yet to grow and be well and the chickens and the garden? There is no green here and the sky looks false. It comes down in yellow clouds that sting the eyes. This is no place for humans, but I almost have my papers for work and I will earn money and come home home home---*

The man typing has repeated the word. Now he stops and waits; he too looks up at the sky as though some answer might come from there.

Church bells ring. Another bus load of busy people arrives.

# STORY 6

# A New Order

Mornings before the sun is up high enough to burn off the cold, people who can, turn over and cuddle up with their spouse or brothers and sisters, warm in the nest of bodies. Everyone sleeps with someone. In this little *finca* sleep now close to a dozen people. There is the *mayordomo* and his wife and seven children, one right after the other as regularly as babies to good active Catholics, in three beds. Their *mamá* will be the first to stir, to open her blouse to the latest red cheeked little one beside her.

These are simple people who farm the farm, caring for, with the help of their children, the fifty or so milk goats, white, graceful animals who get through fences and into everything but who are ultimately as fertile and good natured as the mayordomo and his wife. Magdalena is an endlessly smiling woman, small, close to the ground in her long skirts, always with one child in arms and another by the hand and two more just behind. The oldest son is in the village on most weekdays. He is José, the malcontent who has been ruined some by his schooling, schooling insisted upon by the *patrones* and who now are blamed so by the same proud bitter young man. The mother sighs as she thinks of him.

The father, Libardo, chases the goats from one pasture to the other so they don't eat the grass to the roots or cut it to bits with their tiny sharp hooves. He must watch for sick ones and overdue ones and keep the kids from the dams so there will be milk, and herd them in to the stable and then milk them up on the high table designed by the patron so that he did not have to bend so, keeping the milk clean and carrying it to the house. Later in the day, he will be shoveling the manure and feeding the animals and making sure their water is clean and plenty. Then there are fences to keep and the garden.

Magdalena is in charge of making the cheeses: straining the milk with the cheesecloths she sterilizes by boiling them and boiling the pots too so the milk won't sour, measuring the salt and the *cuajo*, that magical white powder that makes it all happen, and finally turning the curds into the molds and packing them away until the *señora* comes to check them, to wrap them and to carry them away to the city to sell.

A hard life you might say, thinking of the milking and feeding and chasing of the goats along with all unnamed tasks work of raising a large family. But they have a little house, land, some money. The whey they use to feed pigs, theirs to eat or sell, and there is always milk for the *niños* and potatoes and onions that grow outside the kitchen--as long as the goats don't get into them--and so they are all as healthy, well fed and contented as *campesinos* can be in the poor region of a poor country like Colombia.

Two more sleep here this night, Jorge and Marilyn Gomez. These stayed in bed, *haciendo pereza* as they say in Spanish, the delicious laziness of those not used to it, enjoying this holiday, a third day of weekend far from telephones and mail and perpetual knocking on the door. These did not exactly own the *finca*--except in the minds of the simple people who shared their roof.

The fine points of ownership were lost in the reality of the relationship: *patron*--and not *peon*--but *campesino*. Jorge and Marilyn were trying to break old patterns of *paternalismo*, to create new human alliances. They had signed over all their earthly goods to the campesino communities they founded. Still they administered and led this little ship of goats and cheese in this idyllic setting. Jorge had a degree in electrical engineering from MIT but he had not stepped inside an office or worn a tie for thirty years. The coarse wool blankets on the bed were woven by Marilyn from wool she spun, carded and wove into slightly knobby irregular squares. The house was simple adobe with a fireplace with copper tubes running through it that Jorge designed so they could bathe with hot water. The only concession to the twentieth century was a stereo, the boom box that only booms Bach he would say, his kind of joke--oh, and a cordless telephone for emergencies to their house down in the village.

The mothers of these two families greeted the first signs of dawn with reveries on their children. Marilyn mused on her four children, studying abroad, distant from the life she had chosen. Only one remained near them, the cellist who for ten years woke up the family with his early morning practice. So the two mothers, the first awake, ran through their children, pausing over the cares and burdens of each. Marilyn prayed for her son's marriage; Magdalena awoke heavy with the memory of how her first born had returned unexpectedly in new tennis shoes, the kind the sons of rich people wore, with the explanation that he had earned them, and defiantly refused to say how or concede that she might have had a better use for the money.

There was a sound in the yard. The dog barked furiously for a few moments. Inside the house, the sleepers stirred, then returned to their sleep, the baby tugging at the breast creating a calm place in the mother's mind of work. Soon there were shuffling sounds on the front veranda of the finca. Medellín, seen from the veranda, seemed free from all the dirt and pain of the city.

The two patrones, for no matter how they tried, they could never erase that title, were wakened by a heavy knocking on the shutter of their bedroom window. This echoed throughout the house but the dog's bark was cut off.

"*Buenos días*" the gruff voice began with a greeting. The two opened their eyes to the whitewashed ceiling and saw their breaths in the cool mountain air. They exchanged patient glances, hiding their reluctance to go out to yet another problem of the hundred that they took on as part of their daily work.

"*Muy buenos!*" Jorge answered, always jovial.

"*Por favor, los señores,*" and the voice held a note that scraped them even as the front doors of the house, unlocked in the age old tradition of the high mountains, scraped across the uneven floorboards. Now the *mayordomo* and his wife exchanged perplexed looks. Their house was the center of visitors at all hours, all were made welcome, but no one had yet pushed open the door--

"*A la orden,*" Jorge was out of bed, struggling to put on his pants and keep his calm, to meet whoever was entering the front of the house, where now there was the tramping and grunting of several men, moving and pushing each other into a desperate quiet. The door to their bedroom was flung open; there in the doorway stood two armed men. Marilyn shrank into the sheets as her husband stepped between her and the men.

"You need to get up. Everyone needs to come here into the *sala.* Get your workers and all the children. *Rápido.*" They backed out of the room and voices were heard around the house. Now men's voices came from all directions. The dog yelped, then went silent.

"What can it be?"

"God knows." They held hands, their foreheads touched in a momentary prayer before they walked out into their *sala* where the *mayordomos* stood, afraid and looking to Jorge for an explanation. The children whimpered at their mother's skirts. Only the oldest son stood apart somewhat, pale, his eyes darting around the room at the armed men in front of the now open shutters and flung open double doors.

Jorge's voice was low and musical even as he asked them their business. The two who seemed to be in charge waved their pistol about and stuttered, uncertain of how to proceed. They motioned the men on the outside to close the circle. Now every window and door was filled with strange men, armed men nervous and standing on edge around the small house.

"Well, we are members of the Narcotics police--on an investigation."

This astonished the four adults. Yes, there had been raids on *fincas* in other areas. So these were police! There was a sigh of relief all around.

"Please investigate, *Señores.* In fact, allow us to help you, this is a simple farm, goats and cheese and..." The man with the gun poked Jorge with the pistol and sent him back into his chair. "But it's true, *Sí, Señor,* you can look anyplace--" The *mayordomo* was silenced by a shove that sent him into his place between his oldest son and his wife and little ones.

"Yes, we know, we know!" With each word the voice escalated. "You have everything well hidden, well disguised. You are just pretending with all of this!" As he spoke, his eyes ranged and his voice got louder and more desperate. The children began to cry and Magdalena crumpled slightly, pale with fear that her children's tears would antagonize the men. She pulled her children away from the man who, voice quavering, continued, "You will not fool us! We are not fools. Don't even think about it!"

Now a third man stepped into the room. The other two shied away from him, leaving him the center of the floor. His hands held only a walkie talkie that occasionally crackled with an almost human voice.

"*Señores*. The truth is that we are members of a group working for social justice in the country. We, like you, are trying to establish a new order in this country. We know about you. We have seen you on television. We know you have many friends, many people of the high places. We need you, *Señor*, to help us. It is short term. But you can take a message to the government from our people."

He paused and surveyed the group for effect. Jorge was scrutinizing his face, holding Marilyn's hand and at this he gave it a barely perceptible squeeze.

"What do you want me to do?"

"Go with us. Take us in your truck. Everyone here must swear to stay here for six hours. We will leave observers. No one can leave or communicate in any way with the village for six hours. Then open your doors and go about your business. Of course, if you report this to the police, it would be very dangerous for the *Señor*, for others too. But if you cooperate, it would be a great service to our cause, and you will all be safe."

"Can we discuss it?"

"Of course. Go into your room for ten minutes." He bowed, "We will stay here."

The two walked out of the room, leaving the terrified *mayordomos* and their children surrounded by armed men. Jorge quietly and precisely pushed the door closed while Marilyn perched on the edge of the bed, waiting. He approached her; their eyes were so full they could hardly hold them open. They gripped each other's hands and looked at each other for a long time without talking.

"I think I must go."

"I knew you were going to say that."

"It's the only thing to do. If I cooperate, I'll be back soon. Remember the artist in Bogotá they captured? It was just like this. He had to write down all their demands and complaints and present them to the government and on television. I'll be back, God willing."

"God. God." She clung to his hand.

"You remember I love you."

"Yes. You remember. Just like this," as they stood in embrace. There were scuffling noises and voices in the other room, signaling the end of their time.

"Here, then. Take your new book," Marilyn smiled and pressed the slim book into his hands. "You will be glad to have something to read." It was a copy of Fernando Gonzales, a local poet and philosopher, a friend.

The men surrounded Jorge. He walked with calm out to his truck. He did not look back.

"Remember *Señora* that the life of your husband depends on every one of you remaining inside the house for six hours. Then go about your life, but don't contact the police or it will not go well for you. You'll hear from us tomorrow afternoon at your phone in the village."

"You have my word." Her cheeks burned as she looked at him. He pulled the door closed and those inside could hear it being barricaded from the outside. The children looked up to the adults who breathed worried sighs, muttered prayers.

Marilyn made a sign for them to all sit very still as they heard the truck turn around in the drive way and start down the mountain.

"We must do exactly as they say."

She went into her room. She sat on the bed and looked out the window into the sky. She stayed there for several hours. A knock at the door roused her. It was Magdalena with a cup of coffee. She mumbled thanks but did not move. Shortly after, the sounds of the children crying while their mother tried to quiet them, made Marilyn stand, shake her head and walk into the kitchen.

"Let's make some food for the little ones so they won't cry or be afraid."

The two women began working together as they had so often. Marilyn talked to the little girls, coaxing a smile from them. When the meal was ready, she told the little girls to call their father and brother. Immediately, Libardo came into the kitchen, closing the door to his room behind him.

"José doesn't want any food."

"Well, that's not right. He must be hungry. It's because of me. I'll go back to my room. José!" she called him. As she turned to go, she noticed the dark face of the woman beside her. "What is it? I can see something is wrong." Then, seeing the worried faces around her, "Where is he? Where is José? Oh," she began to cry, keening their names, "How could he? How could you? Don't you remember what they said?" She called first on one and then on the other, bitter tears running down her face. They kept their eyes on the floor. Soon, Magdalena cried and all the children whimpered along. Libardo muttered prayers.

"Well, answer me!" she finally screamed.

Startled, Libardo answered, "He had to go to a school function."

"What? Is it possible? *Dios mío! Dios mío, Dios mío,*" again and again a prayer and a curse. "I don't believe it." She left the kitchen, blinded by her fear and anger.

At two o'clock in the afternoon, six hours and ten minutes since the old truck had gone down the mountain with Jorge and three strange men, she prepared to walk to her home in the old house where Jorge had been born. She spoke calmly to Magdalena and Libardo, determined to expect only the best. She swore them to secrecy a hundred times, then asked for the telephone. They both looked startled.

"It's in your room, I'm sure." Magdalena responded.

"No, we left it in the kitchen. I'm sure we left it there."

"José had it." One of the little girls piped up. Magdalena swung toward her, her hand out, but it was too late.

"It's not true, *Señora*. Why would the boy want the telephone? She's talking foolishness," and she turned and glared at the child.

Libardo spoke up. "The men, the men who were here," and he lowered his voice as though the sleeping dog and bleating goats could hear, and hearing tell, "They took it. They were using it. They must have people all around."

She began her walk down the mountainside with a heavy heart and a mind roaring with questions. She could think of nothing to do but pray. With each step she prayed and wondered and thought. After an hour the path began to be more heavily traveled and every person she saw, she examined. This, she thought, could be the observer. Even children who watched her curiously were suspect.

She entered the old farmhouse she had lived in for thirty years through the back door, went directly to the phone, but hung up as soon as she heard her son's voice. He was at home. He would be there with his wife. There was safety. Though she was exhausted from the walk and the upheaval of the morning, she prepared to walk to her son's house. Suddenly she could not trust the phone.

Soon enough she was at his house. His wife answered the door and the cello could be heard from the practice room in the back of the house. It sang out Bach as the two women stood without speaking, the younger watching nervously but unwilling to say anything. When they were all together and Marilyn was satisfied that there was no one to overhear, she told the story.

"Kidnapped! Not *Papá*!"

"Not exactly kidnapped. We think it's a political group. We think they just want your father to speak up for them. They knew about him. They knew he would be good for their cause." She could not keep the pride from her voice.

"And you believe them?"

When she did not answer, he looked at her face and saw how full of fear and horror it was.

"Yes." He stepped to her. "Of course, *Mamá*. There is nothing else to do for now."

The three of them went together to the old house. They sat silent as Hayden filled the air. Silently they huddled in the little room, drinking tea, starting at the telephone calls and knocks on the door. Over and over people called for Jorge. Over and over Marilyn practiced keeping her voice light, saying he had had to go on a trip, an emergency at one of the other centers for campesinos. That would keep them satisfied for a while.

The next day was a blur. The phone rang again and again, schools, centers, and friends. Late in the afternoon, Marilyn, despondent and tired, did not answer. She motioned her daughter-in-law to answer. There was no one on the line. Again. Again, the caller hung up. At the third ring, Marilyn rushed to it.

"*Señora* Marilyn." It was the voice she had feared and waited for. "Listen carefully. Go, with your son and no one else. Do not contact the police. We are close by and you can not fool us. Go with your son only to the telephone booth at the corner of Maturín and Maracaibo. Look under the shelf. *Ojo!*"

The coarse low voice spat out the word of caution. She was trembling when she hung up. "Come Diego", she panted. "We must go alone to this place. Something will happen there. Perhaps they will call! Maritza, please stay here. Don't say anything to anyone."

They went down through the village into the city; the intersection named was in a busy district full of the hundreds of workers waiting for busses, eating and visiting and talking on the telephones as they waited. Marilyn got in one line, her son in the other. There they waited holding back tears while those ahead of them made dates, checked appointments, flirted, argued. There were two booths, back to back. When the schoolgirl ahead of her hung up, Marilyn entered and pretended to call as she searched, as carefully as she could above and under the shelf. Nothing. Panic was in her eyes as she caught her son's eye. She moved into the next booth, cutting in ahead of him. She slid her hand under the shelf, rebounded as though burnt. Her hand had found a blob of gum. Its softness surprised and disgusted her but she put her hand underneath and there was a paper stuck to the shelf with the gum. She pulled it away and found herself holding a ticket for a parking garage on the other side of town, an hour's ride away.

Driving through the heavy traffic, mother and son broke tension by joking about the communication, by comparing it to spy movies, to James Bond. Finally, they pulled into the garage. Marilyn got out and offered the ticket to the man. He examined it, and her, closely, then gave her a bill for a thousand pesos.

"That's a lot for parking!"

"Oh, that's not just for parking. The *Señor* also gave the order to clean the truck, completely. Inside and out. It's like new."

She paid the money and walked back in the corner of the lot. Sure enough, Jorge's large battered old truck was cleaner than it had ever been. As she climbed behind the wheel, she squeezed back tears. She tried to remember what he had said about God. She clasped the parking garage receipt. June 5, it said. Cash on delivery.

\* \* \*

One month later she received a cassette of her husband's voice. He sounded tired but said he was well treated. He repeated his love for her and the children. The next day, a letter was delivered that demanded two million dollars U.S. within six weeks for his safe return.

Four weeks later, after raising only a small part of the money required, the family decide to involve the police. The police announce that all trails were cold and that it is too late for them to help. Perhaps private detectives, those who specialize in kidnapping. Perhaps public appeals. Private detectives are hired. A television program and on the same day a full page of the newspaper describes the simple life of Jorge Gomez, his family, his music, his dedication to the poor of Colombia.

\* \* \*

August 20. A phone call offers a two month extension but refuses to accept less than two million. A counter offer of $300,000 is made and refused.

September 30. A cassette arrives with Jorge's voice. He says he prays daily for his loved ones. Another deadline--November 15.

The letter that arrives November 14 indicates a willingness to negotiate. The kidnappers say they will be willing to accept the $300,000 U.S. if it is given in advance. Negotiations break down since neither side is willing to trust the other.

January 20. A letter arrives offering to tell the whereabouts of the body for fifty thousand dollars U.S.

\* \* \*

The family celebrated a memorial mass a week later. Hundreds and hundreds of mourners accompanied them in their sorrow.

# STORY 7

## Secrets

As soon as the Land Rover disappeared down the narrow dirt road, the old man walked into the white tiled kitchen. A small dark woman in a green uniform was pressing halves of oranges between the heels of her hands and divvying up the juice, a sip at a time, to the two little boys who waited, cups in hand, on each side of her. Every day began thus but this day the old man took the cigar out of his mouth and announced *el Doctor* gone, and the maid, the children and their mother all put down what they were doing. Excitement ran around the tile floor nipping at everyone's heels. Instead of washing clothes and chopping cane and bathing babies they went hunting for secret treasure.

The old man Miguel, the maid Elena, and the *gringa* with her three little boys who would not, who could not be left behind, gathered like mercury in the palm in the cleft in the mountain near the fence. The German Shepherd Golo went along; he stood and watched with the keenest of eyes, cocking his intelligent head this way and that.

The dog was not the only one who watched with a sharp nose for the unusual. The neighbor on the ridge, a *brujo*, a witch, also watched. You may believe that he did so just as the dog did with his own wide open eyes peering from the top of the ridge or you may believe that he watched them--as a *brujo* might--through the tiny black eyes of the buzzard who waggled his wrinkled grey head from top of the guava tree, a mere whistle away.

In any case, eyes were on them there as the old man took the pickaxe and the giant crow bar and the shovel to dig for the *guaca* the *gringa* had seen. Well, she had not exactly seen it; *guacas* are not so simple a matter as that. But she had seen something, and on one of her rides into the mountains she had heard gossip about the signs of *guacas*.

The *guaca*, like the *loteria*, offers piles of gold coin. Some *guacas* are from the Indians and involve wheelbarrows full of gold nose rings and life size gold frogs and other such treasures. Most *guacas* though date back to the time eighty years earlier when the government abolished gold coins. Rather than surrender their gold coins for paper money, many people buried them. The belief goes that these souls cannot rest until someone digs up the gold, releasing the treasure from the earth and freeing the souls to fly to heaven with the Blessed Mother and all the Saints. The souls give signs of their distress by haunting the spot; that is a *guaca*. Of course, modern, scientifically educated Colombians view all this as superstition and a disgraceful waste of time and energy.

This *guaca*, or at least the possibility of a *guaca*, was indeed taking a lot of time and energy. Digging a hole may seem a simple thing but not in the mountains, not in the Andes where rocks, stones, pebbles and depending on the *guaca*, perhaps even ghosts, conspire to keep things hidden within earth's safe bounds. It was such hard work and seemed so, so bizarre, that the *Gringa* had some misgivings.

"How will we know, Miguel, if this was a good person or not? I don't want to stir up anything bad."

"*Doña* Debbie! You're doing a great act of charity for the poor dead person who called you here to release his soul."

"*Sí, Doña* Debbie," Elena continued, "the poor soul can't rest while it's tied to this *guaca*. So we find it and the soul goes straight to heaven. Straight, straight." She moved her hands like arrows darting into the air.

"*Sí, Señora*, it's a good deed but if you want, to be safe we'll say some prayers too."

Then Elena ducked her head and screwed up her eyes tight and began to mumble the *Avemaria*, three *Aves* fast and they all chimed in on the *Dios-te-salve*, even the little boys. Not the baby of course who was trying with his chubby fingers to pry open the eyes of his mother. And Colombia being the place it is, you would see Martín, the *brujo*, also closing his eyes and crossing himself.

"What is a *guaca*, Mom?"

The oldest, a smart little boy about four, was tickled with the adventurous air of this day; he stood on the fringe of the adults while his little brother rolled like a puppy on the hillside and the dog wagged his tail and waited too for something to happen. The old man stood leaning on the heavy pick axe. He and Elena looked at the *gringa*.

"Where was it, *Doña* Debbie?"

"Was what, Mom?"

"What was it exactly you saw, *Doña* Debbie?"

"She already said she saw the candle flame."

"Did you hear something too?"

"Hush now, remember we can't tell anyone about this! And *niños*, listen. We're just here playing. It's nothing. Miguel is going to dig a hole but it's nothing, okay?"

"It's okay, Mom. We won't tell," the second little boy stopped tumbling long enough to say.

"But Mom, you still didn't tell me what a *guaca* is."

"It's a place. Is that right, Elena?"

"Ahh. *sí*. Place, a special place," she giggled.

"We are all looking for a place," the oldest child intoned, "in the ground."

"Be sure now you don't tell! I won't bring you with me any more if you do."

"I won't tell, Mom, I won't tell, Mom," and with one voice even the baby looked up with the most serious of eyes and they stopped their somersaulting and tumbling about on the grass to promise. The maid giggled again, recognizing, as did the mother, as did Miguel, as did even the buzzard in the tree, that this secret was doomed.

"Well," she said, "I think this is about right." She pointed down, her finger describing a sort of circle in a crevice in the ground. Miguel picked up the pick axe and began to swing it. Then he shoveled out the loose rock and the dirt into an ever-increasing pile on the ground. They all looked first at the hole that grew, then at the *gringa* who gazed into the stony depths of the hole. Soon enough the boys resumed their play but they too would pull back to watch.

"Do you see it yet, Mom?"

"What's you see Mom?" The three-year old would climb into her lap as she lounged on the grass smoking. He would nudge her for an answer, insisting.

"Nothing, nothing special. Hush," she made a great shushing at them although she knew it was too late.

"I don't see nothing, Mom."

"Anything."

"*Nada.*"

"Elena, *por favor*, take the boys back to the house to play and eat something."

There was a great outcry at this. All the boys began to wail and the expression on the maid's face showed her disappointment.

"There's probably nothing, you know," the *gringa* said coolly.

"*Sí, Señora*, probably nothing," Elena was bouncing the baby on her hip, "but I know what I know and I want to see."

"That's right, Mom, we know too and we'll be good; yes, we'll be good." And they all pouted, protested and promised in one breath.

"*Sí, Señora*," panted Miguel as he leaned on the six- foot steel crow bar trying to move a boulder much bigger than himself.

"It could be nothing," he said with a studied attempt at irony.

"Nothing what, Mom?"

"Yeah, Mom, nothing what?"

The one watching from the ridge would keep his doubts to himself. He saw through their protestations of nothing. *Nada* was something he did very well himself. Whether he was a *brujo* or not, he used it as a broom to clear the way for what he wanted. Everyone said he was a *brujo* and every one kept out of his way. Ismenia was the only person in the village who wasn't afraid of him--or, she would say, of the devil, as if the two were the same. Ismenia would swear that Martín threw a stick at her feet and it turned to a snake, hissed at her and when she grasped her scapulary of the Blessed Virgin and prayed for protection, the snake twisted away in the direction of Martín's house.

This had happened when she confronted him because the milk of her cow had dried up just like that without bad grass or frights or anything. She knew it was Martín with his red hair and the red eyes, the eyes of a red dog she would say and cross herself. She had other ways of knowing, secret ways too though she only hinted at these when someone like *Doña* Debbie argued that the red hair was not a true sign. At any rate Martín watched as the hole grew deeper and deeper.

"*Doña* Debbie. Is the hole in the right place?" Sweat ran in muddy streams down the cheeks of the old man, into his whiskers, and dripped in dark spots on his shirt.

"It seems right. It's hard to tell now."

"And say again what you saw--"

"Yes, Mom, tell me too what you saw!"

She lifted the little boy to her hip; he reached up and squeezed her face in his two dirty hands, forcing her eyes to meet his.

"You're not telling me stuff!"

"A candle."

"A candle!" The two little boys looked at her in indignation.

"Is that all?" Candles were everywhere.

"A candle!" muttered Miguel, grunting with new effort as he dug and scraped away at the hole that was now three or four foot deep.

"Are you sure, *Doña* Debbie?"

"*Sí*, Elena, and I heard a jangling noise too."

"*Ay, ay, ay*, Miguel. The spoons. That is always the surest sign. I knew a man who lived near my aunt on my father's side and he heard spoons inside a wall in his garden and began to dig and..."

"Hush Elena. Remember how many ears are listening."

"*Ay, sí*. Dig! Dig more, *Don* Miguel!" Elena rushed off to the house. Soon she returned with a large tray with glasses of lemonade and graham crackers. In the pocket of her apron was the baby's bottle at just the right temperature. Around her neck was the baby's blanket so he could sleep right there in the pasture. Miguel scrambled out of the hole to smoke one of his little black cigars and gulp down lemonade from the battered tin bowl that was his to drink from. The dog trotted off to the creek.

Soon it was noon and there was nothing to do but go back to the daily routine. Miguel had to catch the calves and close them up or there would be no milk in the morning. Elena went to wash the little jeans that now had grass stain in the knees and seats. The mother began to prepare the tubs with bath water. There in the sunny patio three large plastic tubs would be filled with warm water and she would scrub and shampoo the little boys. Golo would stretch there out of splashing distance, watching them. Everyone fell back into ordinary life.

It was late when the Land Rover rolled down the driveway and honked. The only one awake, the woman, went out to open the garage door and stand blinking in the headlights as her husband drove in. They kissed when he got out of the car and then she served his dinner and sat at the dining room table to watch him eat it.

"Anything new around here today?"

"No. No, nothing new."

"Did Miguel get anything done today?"

"Yes, as a matter of fact, he was pretty busy today."

"The boys?"

"Oh, they had fun playing in the pasture."

"Good. Remember that Ines and Maruja are arriving from Manizales tomorrow."

"Tomorrow?" There was some disappointment in her voice.

"I thought you would be glad to see them!"

"I am. I am. Do we leave early?"

"Yes. Everyone has to be ready to go when I leave in the morning."

The man was a little impatient. His wife often was bored on the *finca* alone. He couldn't understand her hesitation at this outing.

"You can do some shopping while you're there."

"It's fine. I'm looking forward to seeing the aunts."

The next morning very early the mother dressed herself and the little boys. She was polishing the baby's white shoes when Elena came through the door. She looked at the boys sitting in a row in their best clothes. They had been washed, dressed, combed, and placed in chairs to wait. They kicked their heels and poked at each other.

"Elena! We're going to see our grandmother Luisa and our aunts from Manizales! Mom's going to buy us something if we're good."

The mother rushed into the kitchen calling Elena.

"We have to go into town."

"*Sí, Señora*. Should I tell Miguel to continue or...."

The *gringa* studied the face beside her. She could hear her husband talking to Miguel, giving him his orders for the day and Miguel's steady "*Sí, Doctor, sí, Doctor.*"

"Okay, Deb. Let's go."

The little boys were running to the car before the words were out of his mouth. Elena grabbed the baby and carried him to deposit him in his mother's lap.

"*Adiós*, Elena. Do what seems most important."

The family returned after dark. Elena and Miguel and the dog were sitting in the doorway; they ran to open the garage door and Elena held out her arms to receive the sleeping baby. All the little ones were tucked in bed in their clothes, only shoes tumbled to the floor. There was a moment when Elena caught the lady's eye.

"We went on with the work today."

"Oh, good. And what?"

"Up to now, nothing. But, no matter. If you're sure, we'll keep going."

"I am sure. *Mañana. Mañana* we'll be here."

The next day they all spent several hours at the hole but there was less excitement. Now Miguel was lost from sight when he slid in to dig. Try as she would the *gringa* could not summon up that original flame or hear the metal jingling that had been the signs. The only thing she could hear clearly in her mind was her husband's outrage if he saw the now tremendous hole. Somehow it had all grown past her.

Saturday came and the whole family had to go to the city. Sofia was coming from Valle and Sola from Guarne and since these little boys were the only grandchildren and the *gringa* a much-loved member of the family, there was no staying away.

There was great excitement when the little boys went up the stairs of their Grandmother's house, rapping on the walls and calling out. All the aunts took turns during the day carrying even the biggest boy whose feet almost dragged on the floor. After the immense lunch with papaya and then clear broth and then roasted pork with raisins and wine sauce over the whitest fluffiest rice and Teresa's famous caramel cake, they all drowsed in the parlor, each of the aunts clutching a child whose face, flushed with sleep and food, rested on those maiden breasts. During that quiet time, the father slipped away.

"Where's my Daddy?" The oldest sat upright; he was always alert.

"He went back to the *finca*," the grandmother answered.

"What? Luisa, where did Francisco go?"

"He went back to the *finca* to meet with a tractor driver about your big garden."

The *gringa* couldn't hold back a yelp.

"I thought you wanted a big garden."

"I do. I do. I have always wanted a big garden just the way we have them in the states."

"Well, that's it. That's what he went to do. Don't tell him I told you. He wanted it to be a surprise."

The day went by with more eating and talking and reciting of the boys' virtues as they climbed from one lap to another: such dark eyes, straight white teeth, beautiful foreheads indicating great intellect, hair curling and fair. Finally the father returned, rushed and distracted. It took ten minutes to say goodbye with everyone giving everyone kisses. Finally they were on the road home.

"Crazy thing happened today."

"Yes? What was that?" She was glad for the dark and sleeping babies.

"Do you know the *loco* next door, the red haired man?"

"The *brujo*!"

"No! No! Don't say that, Deb! You know better."

"The one they call a *brujo*, Martín."

"Yes, Mar*tín*," and he gave it the Spanish pronunciation, drawing out the *teen* ending so that it seemed not even an English name. "I found him doing some crazy things there on the *finca*."

"What! Martín was on our land?" She was shocked that this might happen. Oh, she thought, it must be true. He is a *brujo*.

"Yes, you know that place where there's a big crevice down by the fence."

"Oh no! I mean, yes, I know the place. But what about Martin?"

"Well, I just noticed him running away in a suspicious way so I looked down by the fence and saw what he'd been up to and I really told him--"

"Please, honey, you know how dangerous--"

"Stop!" and then lowering his voice as all the children turned in their sleep, "talking such foolishness. You can't believe everything people say. You don't believe in witchcraft!"

"You're right of course but what about Martin?"

"You won't believe that crazy thing he did. Stupid."

"Stupid? I always thought he was pretty smart."

"No, no, no. *Es bruto*. You should have seen the hole he dug."

"He dug?"

"Yes. He denies it but who else could it be? I couldn't believe what a big hole there was there."

"Why would he dig a hole--there?"

"*Guaca*. That's all it could be. Somehow he got the idea there was a *guaca* there."

"Don't you believe in *guacas*, ever?"

"No, hell no!"

"Oh dear," she wailed, "I hate to have problems with the neighbors."

"You won't have any problem with him. He was mad. He was furious. He swore he hadn't done it, but I knew it had to be him. Miguel was hopping around, chewing on his cigar, scared to death."

"And Martín didn't give you any kind of look or sign--"

"Don't you start that stuff!"

"No. I just wondered."

"Anyway, it worked out just right. I had the tractor out there today. You have your big garden, as good as we can make it here with all the rocks. And while the tractor was here I had him fill in the hole and pile all the rocks from the garden on top of the place."

The headlights were turning on the bushes that grew up to the driveway. As she saw all the familiar features, she commented softly.

"Great idea, Honey."

"You don't seem very enthusiastic."

"I am. I really am. I guess I'm just tired."

Miguel and Elena were opening the garage door. They were serious as they held out their arms for the sleeping babies. Only the dog was happily cavorting among them.

The next morning the *gringa* got up and plodded out to the kitchen. Elena was washing dishes and Miguel sat on the old chair drinking coffee and smoking his cigar. The baby was in his high chair squashing bananas while the little boys waited, cups in hand, for their juice.

"Can we all go dig holes today, Mom?"

"No, *niño*," Miguel was serious.

"Tell me what happened."

"*El Doctor* yelled at Martín. I swear he gave him a black look–. How is he today? No twisted neck or bad eye or anything?"

"No, he's fine. Tell me just what happened."

"Be careful of everything," Elena said mournfully.

"Well, Ismenia says she saw Martín carry a big gunny sack into town yesterday."

"What! Before or after?"

"We don't know. Personally I think before. I think that's why he didn't do something terrible to the doctor. Also Martín gave me a very bad look today," and he crossed himself quickly.

"How can we ever find out?"

"There is no way we will ever know. Nobody will ever dig that hole again after *el Doctor* and the tractor got through. And who's going to ask Martín?"

Silence was the only answer.

"You see, he is a *brujo*. He got our treasure without ever digging for it."

So with the easy resignation of the very poor, Miguel and Elena gave up their chance at a *guaca*. As for the *gringa,* when she would meet the red-haired man on the road, she would remind herself that she too had red hair and return both his stare and his greeting.

# STORY 8

# The Specialists

Behind the row of royal palm trees, up the curving lane bordered with hibiscus and birds of paradise, is *El Campestre*, the Country Club of Medellín. Inside the sentinel post, a box executed in the style of the club itself, white with pink tile roof and black arabesques of grillwork, is an old man in a white uniform whose job it is to know every one of the more than three hundred members by sight. He must recognize them, along with their children and grandchildren, he must bend down, smiling and bowing, to look into the car and examine all who approach the gate. He waves the known in through the gates, but firmly and politely he straightens his back and waves away those he does not know. The unknown, the unrecognized may not enter through the gates, also in graceful wrought iron manned by a younger guard, uniformed and wearing a pistol in a holster. The armed guard is a sign of recent times. He waits for the older man, who first recognizes the car and then squints inside.

"*Buenos dias, Doña Mercedes.*" At his nod, the younger man swings the gate open.

"*Buenos dias*, Enrique. And my son, Carlos–? Has he been in today?"

The woman inside the Renault, sighs at his answer but then sees her friend easing her Mercedes Benz into a space. Her name is Mercedes and she would like to make just a little rhyme in her life that has lately been so out of tune, yes, she said joking so he would not know that it was important to her. "I Mercedes should drive a Mercedes, hah?" She didn't have too many jokes left, all her good humor swallowed up by worry about her son, their son, their only son. So, no Mercedes Benz for her although she could afford it. No, because of her husband's fears she must drive a tin can of a car.

She recalls the argument she has heard a hundred times from her husband's calm face. "Don't you feel anything?" She shouted about money and the car and about their son and her husband always slipped on a smooth mask. He put on that calm. But, she repeats her argument in a pretty voice there in the car as she parks. She wants to be reasonable, to show logic and restraint. "Thousands of Renaults are stolen because they are so common--so why not have the Mercedes, which is not much more likely to be stolen though it's worth twice as much, since it is harder to move once the robbers get it. So I might be safer with the elegant car." She ends with a dimpled smile into the rearview mirror. Safe!

Ah! She coughs out her exasperation. She unlocks the glove compartment and pretends to primp into the mirror as she surveys the area to see if any of the gardeners or guards are watching. Sniffs away a faint pinch of conscience as she takes a velvet pouch out of her purse. Her husband has forbidden her to wear her jewels in the city, but, as she struggles with the clasp of a heavy gold bracelet, she reasons, if I can't wear them at the club, then what's the use of having them?

She continues with rings, drawing on her diamond engagement ring and the huge emerald solitaire he had given her for their twentieth anniversary. Finally, she dangles large gold hoops in her ears before stepping out to meet her friend. They bend to touch their softly rouged cheeks; their long nails, soft red, shine as they sleek back any hair that might have become mussed during the greeting.

The two chat and smile as they lock the doors of their cars, check the handles all around and then catch the eye of the car watchman, this one armed with an old shotgun, who touches his hat and nods respectfully.

"Surviving, my dear Mercedes?"

"Of course, Marta, and you? and your family?"

"*Gracias a Dios*! Have you heard the latest about the kidnaping of the daughter of Olson?"

"Oh, don't tell me that! I can't bear to hear another thing!"

"God help us! The children. That's the worst. I can't bear to think of a woman, or a girl! Things are getting worse..."

"Remember last year we said things couldn't get any worse?"

"The Gomez are moving to Spain."

"Many families are going. I think about it but..."

"What does Manuel say?"

"He can't bear the thought. It makes us crazy to think that something would happen...but to think of leaving everything here..."

"At least as a medical doctor he could survive--and heart specialists even get rich!"

"Money isn't everything. I don't have to tell you that. That's why we're still here. We are *patriotas. T*hat seems like a sentimental thing to say," she continues somewhat defiantly as they stroll through the enormous wooden doors, nodding at the *maitre d'* in a tuxedo who bows them into the foyer "but we love Colombia and our life here and we're willing to fight for it. Miami...Barcelona. No. They're not for us."

As these two pass down the wide pleasant hall, their third friend, Olga comes breathlessly trotting in the door. She is always late, always breathless; she seems always about to come apart from perpetual motion and flighty good nature.

"*Buenas tardes, amigas!*" She bobs up to each. "I'm glad you didn't have to wait for me. I had..."

"Oh, no. For once we're all here at the same time," and they smiled at the *maitre d'* who motions them out through the French doors to the pool.

The three stroll to the table at the quiet end of the pool, where another woman waits.

Angela, the quiet one, rises and offers her cheek all around as the others begin to sit, scraping chairs, depositing purses. Angela opens her bag of heavy Spanish leather, and as she takes out her Marlboros, she lifts, with one manicured finger, a small shiny pistol. A quick excited intake of breath races around the table, followed by nervous laughter.

"Ooh, you sly one," Mercedes chortles," You finally did it!"

Angela smiles and tucks it back in her bag, and the bag behind her in the chair.

"Won't you be uncomfortable?" Olga inquires solicitously.

"Those of us who want to survive have to learn to live with some discomfort."

"Oh, can that be true? Can it?" Olga is at the edge of her chair, examining, it seems for the first time, this question that is settled and familiar to everyone.

"*Olguita*. Don't be such a child!"

Mercedes feels exhilarated and tense.

Angela glances at her and asks pointedly, "What's wrong with you? I know you and Manuel have your protection too--"

"Yes, my dear, we do. We must. We all must, so don't feel badly. It's the times that force us all to this. Who wouldn't turn back the clock, the calendar, to a time when all we had to carry in our bags was lipstick? You know everyone's doing it and it isn't a sin anyway. It's all in self defense. Or in defense of your child. Think about it Marta. What if it were your daughters?"

"I know. Don't talk to me. I know everything you say is true. We have discussed every detail of what we would do if it were Jaime--what if it were the girls?" and she shudders. She breaks off to light a cigarette and pull the double deck of playing cards from her purse. Pensively she shuffles while the other women watch her intently.

"You blame me." Angela whimpers. "I can tell you do. You think I don't care..." Angela's voice fades into large silent sobs.

Olga flutters her hands and chirps around the table. "Let's talk about the children, the family--how are the plans for your first communion, Marta? The twins will be beautiful, divinely beautiful, I know," and without pausing, "And your little Jorge Junior, Angela? Still bringing home top honors in his class? There's never any question about that."

Now she stops lamely in front of Mercedes, who blushes at the heavy silence. Everyone knows her son, a young man now, is always in trouble and has been kicked out of every high school in the city.

"I'm sorry, Mercedes. Tell us how your vacation plans are coming. What a wonderful trip: two weeks in Florida! Your first real vacation in years, am I right? And Carlos Manuel is in a new program...."

"Yes, the trip will be a dream. We both need a rest," the groan she punctuates her sentence with comes out stronger than she intends. "And yes, we are hopeful about Carlos Manuel. It's an illness, you see, and now we have this new doctor, specialized in New York...."

She squirms, remembering a frightening scene two days earlier when Carlos Manuel had demanded a large sum of money--and she, for the first time following the doctor's orders, had refused. Her son had stormed out of the house and she had not heard from him since. Still, the doctor assured her....

"I've heard of him. He's a wonder, an absolute wonder. No doubt, no doubt about it, he'll be able to help you all."

"And thank God you have a little *paseo*, a few weeks of travel and rest and shopping for the holidays...I envy you!"

"It's true. We really need a change. Manuel has a conference in Miami and then we'll go to Fort Lauderdale, and maybe, for fun up to Orlando."

Small sounds of delight travel around the table but stop at Angela who continues with a sad look.

"Well, " Marta remembers, "I don't blame you, Angie. I don't know what I would do, but Guillermo is prepared for anything--if the watchman and the gates and the alarms and the locks fail—then we, we.... God help us! I came to relax and play some cards. How about you? A hundred pesos a point, as usual?"

For the next several hours the four women concentrate, almost fiercely, on their game of canastas, on drinks brought almost unnoticed by boys in white uniforms. Without visible signal, but at five, the *maitre d'*, bowing, calls them to the tea table that has been set up for them. Marta totals scores over tea, small sandwiches, and fancy cakes.

"You're always lucky," Angela accuses Mercedes as she counts out colored bills of high denomination to her companion.

"Not always," the other protests as she too counts the bills and smooths them before tucking them into her bag.

"Well, I thank God my Ricardo asks no questions about my cards or my luck!" Olga makes everyone laugh as she pretends to cower.

Mercedes slips to the private telephone while Marta signs the bill. She calls her husband's office, packing her jewelry into her bag as she talks. Frowning, she joins the others.

"What has happened?"

"Oh, nothing serious, but Manuel had to fire his watchman at the office. He was drunk last night and they found him sound asleep." She is rushing through the door.

"What will you do?"

"I have to go home and send Libardo from the house to spend the night there. At least we can count on Libardo. Goodbye my dears!

"Until next week!"

The others walk out together into a brilliant but momentary sunset. No matter, they do not notice it as they unlock cars and carefully lock up again before driving out through the gate onto the crowded street.

Mercedes is rushing down the highway. She does not have air conditioning in her Renault and because of the dangers on the highway, she must keep all the windows up tight and locked. She reaches across and behind to check again all the doors. As she does this, she swerves out of her lane, narrowly missing a delivery boy on a bicycle. At red lights, she scans the crowds, and if she sees any of the young men of that particular type they all recognize as the *sicarios*, the paid killers, most of them desperate teen age boys, she revs the engine until her little car quivers. There are hundreds of stories of women stopped at lights with the window cracked just a bit for air and somehow they are stripped of jewelry or watch or even the car! Thank God she does not have anyone with her, as the latest gambit is for one man to level a pistol at the head of the passenger while the other presses his face to the driver's window. "Open! Open. You are lost if you don't!"

She begins to relax some as she turns into the quiet elegant residential district where their home is. They have almost half a block of marble facade and stylish wrought iron. Their garage has an electric opener but she presses the buzzer so that Libardo will come out and take her car down to the office where he will spend the night. In response to the buzzer, the old man looks out the tiny shuttered door in the heavy wooden front door. She sees him and gestures; she calls him to the car where she explains. He agrees, and as she hands him her car keys, she begins to breath more easily. Libardo drives slowly down the street and she goes up the stairs to the large outer foyer. Two women in pink uniforms stand in the door watching her approach.

"*Buenas tardes.* Has Carlos Manuel been in?"

"*No Señora.*" The woman's voice is flat. "*Nada.* Two calls for you. I wrote them down, on the paper just as you said. But nothing from Carlos Manuel."

"Oh, *gracias,* " she picks up the note and studying it hides her disappointment. "Just the two of us for dinner. I'm not sure what time *el doctor* will be here--Oh, Libardo won't be here for dinner. He has to stay at the office."

Mercedes goes to her room where she lies in the quiet dark, smoking.

On the other side of the city, up on the hills near the new clinic, in a building of medical offices, Dr. Manuel Soto sends his nurses home and settles in to read medical journals until Libardo arrives. Within minutes, he hears the outer door of the suite open.

"Libardo! *Entre!*"

But rather than Libardo, three young men slip through the door, one with a bizarre ski mask; the other two have stockings over their faces. Two are dressed in black, in the punk fashions of the city, the barrel of a gun appears from under a large jacket. The masked one has an ordinary grey sweat suit with a hood pulled forward.

"*Bueno,* Doctor Soto. We don't want any trouble but we heard you were taking a trip and had a little present for us from *Papá Noel.*" He pauses and giggles before shaking the gun and continuing, "Maybe you don't understand. We know about you, how you're a big rich specialist. We're specialists too." Again, he pauses. His companions do not speak, but the masked one begins to shift nervously. The speaker, the armed one, makes a sudden rushing movement at the desk.

Manuel Soto, medical doctor, heart specialist, is sunk in shock, wondering what to do now that it is happening, what he has always feared, and what he has said he would be ready for. Ready? No watchman. The Browning automatic pistol he had bought and forced himself and Mercedes to learn to use, at home, along with the money box, and just as the hoodlums said, a package of green bills. The old shotgun locked into the broom closet. He rouses himself as the speaker moves toward him.

"*Tranquilos, muchachos.*" His surgeon's nerves surface as he sees their nerves, feels the danger of underestimating them. In a calm voice, "I do have some money; money is nothing. Just relax. I'll give it to you. But it isn't here. It's at my home."

"Okay, Doctor" the young voice drawls the English *okay* as he jabs the air with the pistol, "Let's go to your house. Do you think it would be safe? We want you to be safe." He giggles. "All we want is a Christmas present. I'll ride with you in your car. My colleagues will meet us there."

"Meet us?"

"Sure. We know where you live. We know a lot about you."

Manuel put on his jacket, and moves through the suite of offices, ringed by the three, smelling their sweat and their tension. He is cool, suddenly marvelously cool. He feels in control, he feels he can use his wits to survive. He locks the doors, looks around the parking lot. At a distance, he sees the old man who guards the parking lot. He waves casually as he always does. He unlocks his Renault, another small grey car just like his wife's, and the young man pulls the large collar up to hide the stocking on his face, and then slides in the front seat. He stretches one arm across the top of the seat; the other extends the pistol to the doctor's ribs.

"What do you think Doctor? In your professional opinion, is this a good spot? or maybe a little higher?" Again he giggles, a high pitched snort.

"Just relax," the older man soothes him. "*Tranquilo.*"

He pulls out onto the street, watching in his rear view mirror the brown Landrover that follows. He sees out of the corner of his eye that the boy beside him has expensive American tennis shoes and a gold watch. *Increíble*, he marvels to himself. Incredible that this is happening to me. He thinks ahead, hoping that Mercedes will not break down, hoping, God please, that Carlos Manuel will not be there. He notices suddenly that the car is not behind him. He looks in the rear view mirror and brakes.

"*Está bien*, Doctor. I told you we know where you live. You just drive along home nice and smooth. They'll probably be there before you."

Within a short while, they are pulling into the street. Just as predicted, the Landrover is parked at the corner. The doctor has decided not to open the garage or to press the buzzer. He knows that his wife and the maids are there. As he pulls up, the two men stand at the door of their car and look around the deserted street before coming to wait for his car to pull up. They hunch their shoulders and crowd around him. From a distance, it would have seemed like a good natured family get-together going up the wide stairs and stepping into the recessed entrance way. He presses the doorbell. Mercedes opens the peephole, a tiny barred window within the door and sees his face, pale and trembling but calm.

"Manuel, *por Dios! Qué pasa?*"

"*Tranquila*, Mercedes. I am here. Listen carefully and calmly. It is important we do not make any mistakes."

She tiptoes, trying to see who is with him, sees bodies, forms, sees finally the gun.

"I am listening. Tell me what to do." She too is trembling but calm. Praying that no fool would come into this. Not the maids, not Carlos Manuel. God, please keep him away. She never thought she would pray that.

"Go to the safe in our room. Bring the box of dollars. I have agreed to give these--men--a gift."

"I will. I will. Just wait."

The little peep door slams shut, and the men wait, jockeying nervously in the space there, examining the brass doorbell, the heavy wooden door with the brass barred little peep door called the *postigo*.

There is only the sound of breathing. The doctor unclenches his hands, practicing slow even breaths.

Soon they hear steps and the *postigo* swings open.

"I have it here," Mercedes' voice trembles. "But... what shall we do? It's too big to fit through the *postigo*."

"*No hay problema*," Doctor Soto speaks very quietly. "Just open the door. They only want the money. They don't want to come in and pay us a visit."

There is the clank of the bolts being turned and the chain dropping off. Finally the large door swings open. She stands there, pale, clutching a metal box in both hands. She thrusts the box at her husband. As he reaches for it, she swings him and the box in an arc with one hand and lays into the trigger of the Browning with the other. Deafening noise, chips of marble, bits of flesh and blood fly around them.

The doctor stands amazed at what she has done and that they are still standing; he pries the gun out of her hand. Her eyes are closed; he can not bear to look at the bodies exploded in the blood, the flesh, no surgeon could ever repair. He puts his arms around her and turns away. He sees the maids' terrified faces in the back of the house.

"Call the police. Please."

Suddenly the street is full of people.

Neither of them speak. They hang on each other, oblivious to the voices and stares of neighbors and the maids. Within ten minutes the first police car pulls up. Three officers in khaki uniforms, with serious brown faces stride to the scene.

One officer asks questions, the second records his answers, the third examines the bodies.

The doctor answers in a monotone:

"Manuel Jose Soto Ruiz...Medical doctor...this is my house..."

There is an interruption as the third officer begins to unmask the men.

"Perhaps you can identify one of them? Yes, unlikely, but you understand, we must be sure."

He squeezes his wife's shoulder and they both turn to scan the first face, that of the armed man, the speaker, the joker.

"Never." He is quiet and sad as he sees the young face.

Mercedes shakes her head.

"No," again, the young pimpled face of a teenager.

The doctor closes his eyes and as he does he feels his wife's body slump in his arms. With a faint moan she is gone. He stumbles to catch her as he sees the face of the third man, the one with the ski mask who stayed in the background.

The officers stand amazed as the doctor slides to the ground, here he sits, cradling his wife and calling out to the handsome young face before him, "Carlos Manuel, Carlos Manuel, my son."

# STORY 9

# Matrimonio

The path is so steep and the air is so fine you must stop frequently in your climb. In one of your pauses for breath, you'll look back down at the valley and see Medellín sprawling below with the pollution from the factories creating a picturesque yellow haze. In another pause, you'll look up to see those who wait outside the tiny house perched high in the Colombian Andes.

Once you're almost to the top of the mountain, if you are going to Jose and Elena's house, turn onto a ledge and go down a narrow path with steps carved out of the red mud, right into the little house with red geraniums spilling over from the old coffee cans. A little boy will run out to catch the black and white dog barking there.

"Silver!" he says seriously, "stop! This is *Doña* Debbie!" He holds the dog in his arms and smiles at me.

"How do you know me?"

"We've been waiting for you to come. And anyway, I saw your picture many times. My name is Eduardo Morales Marín." He ventures a hand while hugging the now silent Silver in his arms.

Immediately after him, Elena rushes out the door, tears in her eyes, "*Doña* Debbie, *mi patrona*!" We both cry and stand close. She feels as small as a child within my arms. Her daughter Maria Elena went to the plaza to meet the bus I rode on, to escort me back up the mountain since her mother is no longer up to such coming and going. Now María Elena, the mother of Eduardo, follows me into the yard.

A crowd, all family gathered to welcome me, mills around the veranda: I am greeted by each. There are two other little boys, also claimed proudly by María Elena. They shake hands seriously and exchange glances. Perhaps they have practiced. Then I see Rafael and his wife Chita and their tall serious son. I recognize Alfonso who was in a factory accident and was left with a bad hand and arm and headaches that paralyze him. He never married. I move to the next group, Miriam with a new baby in her arms and a toddler in the arms of her oldest daughter, the oldest of the seven. Her husband Francisco, whom I taught to read and write on my porch twenty years earlier, has not arrived. Finally we all move to the veranda where José, since he cannot walk well, waits.

There in the big arm chair he is, still the man of the house though he is now very old. He is tiny, his narrow bridged brown nose jutting out over his shy smile, his straggly beard. He wears a dark grey wool *ruana*, white dress shirt and wool pants that brush the tops of his sandals. He is the picture of the typical Antioqueñan *campesino*, right up to his straw hat, broad brimmed and woven in dark and pale straw, on his head now even though technically we are in the house. Later, when I get out my camera, Elena will take his hat off, planting it on his knee; she will smooth his few remaining strands of hair and stand at attention by his side. If you see the picture you will understand some things words cannot tell about their devotion and humble dignity.

José has his cane between his legs, and thumps the floor with it, a happy punctuation to his greeting of me. The other arm chair is for me, visiting them after so many years.

I first came to this house fifteen years earlier, for the *matrimonio* of Maria Elena. The wedding party and the bride in a street length white satin dress with a garland of paper flowers around her dark hair had come walking up the very same trail. The groom had worn a new white shirt and a tie; he was shy and kind. The others, with the best clothes they had, came singing and drinking and shouting. Neighbors came out and accepted a drink and joked and congratulated them.

On horseback, later in the evening, we came. As the *patrones*, we were given the chairs, the same and only chairs and glasses of rum and plates of roast pig. We listened to the men who ordinarily milked our cows and weeded our garden play guitar and sing all the old sad songs of unrequited love, kicking up their feet and howling a falsetto at the moon.

In those days Elena's house was just begun; then the kitchen was just a hearth on the dirt floor, the dining room a bench against the wall, the sink, a leaking faucet outside the back door. Today there is electricity, two glass windows and tile floors that meet awkwardly the whitewashed walls. Today, unbelievably there is a toilet with running water. It is a proud moment for Elena when she tells the toddler to take me to the *baño*. She grasps my finger and wide-eyed leads me through the house, into the small room, floors and walls of cement, with a faucet sticking out of the wall several feet up for a shower, and a toilet next to which, in a large tin can, is a roll of blue paper. The sound of the flush brings a proud smile to everyone's face.

We have been reminiscing about the times past, looking at the photo album, seeing those wedding pictures and others, baptisms, serious little boys in white shirts holding large white candles tied with white bows.

"So, now I've seen the wedding pictures of all but Elena and José."

José, now in his late eighties and palsied, grins. His once demanding voice, now so slight even the toddler bends to hear, mumbles.

"What is it *Papá*?" demands Maria Elena in a loud voice. She, at thirty-one, is the baby of the family and the only daughter. She watches over her mother and father from her house, in progress just up the side of the mountain. She hates seeing her father fade away.

"Speak up *Papá* or we can't do a thing for you."

His hands begin to do their dance, a whisking motion that he will control by grasping his cane. Then, his eyes still intent on his wife he says in a surprisingly loud voice, "Bring my picture."

Elena, pulls her lip down to hide her laugh. All her adult life she has been missing most of her teeth, front and back, and she hides her laugh with her upper lip and her hands and a ducking of her shoulders that is her most common gesture.

"Oh no, José! Not that picture!"

"*Sí, Señora*! That's my picture and I want to show it to *Doña* Debbie!"

Everyone begins to laugh and José drums his cane on the earthen floor of the veranda and cackles without caring that his one tooth twinkles alone. Elena returns with an envelope, fat and of heavy paper. She opens it and takes out another envelope. José surveys the crowd, their anticipation with a smile, gesturing, "Go, go on." Out comes another envelope, this one is pink and the size of a valentine. Then comes a square wrapped in tin foil. With each unwrapping, the little boys on the railing clap.

"Now," Elena says, "I think this is it."

"No," José purses his lips at her, "you forget everything!"

Under the last bit of tissue paper there is a faded black and white photo, the size and quality of those made for identification papers. It shows a very serious young woman with a long nose and upper lip and shy dark eyes. Her lips are carefully closed. Everyone claps at this unveiling and at all the tiny papers and envelopes now on the table. Elena looks closely at it and covers her face.

José reaches out his hand, takes the picture and examines it proudly. "There she is. She gave me that thirty-fi-,fi-, thirty-si--"

"No, old man, be careful what you say! There stands Rafael and he's thirty-eight years old!"

"Anyway, she gave me this many years ago and that was our *compromiso*, our promise. Or that was hers. I had already made mine when I first saw her at *Doña* Dora's house and I looked at her and she was so timid," he closes his eyes and whispers, "and had such eyes--" he swivels his head around the group and then rolls his eyes.

The grown children are hooting encouragement to their father whose voice gets stronger and clearer with Elena's pleased embarrassment. The three little boys hop down from the railing to enter the circle and study their parents' faces. The youngest still holds his dog. They study the faces of the adults and laugh along. The little girl, a toddler of eighteen months pirouettes in the middle of the group clapping her hands. The grown-ups whose histories and wedding pictures have been shown tease their parents at the old man's show of enthusiasm.

Now Elena brings out other loved pictures, one of me with my five little children gathered around me, one of her other *patrona*, Doña Dora, whose place I took after Elena married and started to have her family. She brings out the wedding photo of this couple, a studio photo of a blonde young woman in a traditional satin gown and her husband in a morning coat and striped pants.

"This is the woman," Elena peers at the picture, "who gave us this land. When José and I got married, we didn't have anything. But José worked there as the *mayordomo* and I was taking care of the baby that was born just ten months after this picture. And *Doña* Dora was always trying to teach me to sew on the sewing machine until finally she gave me the sewing machine. Here, she said one day, you better take this with you for your wedding present."

José slaps his thigh and continues, "and I carried it home that night; it was electric, in its own box and heavy. I traded it for this little piece of land, right here, from old man *Don* Mateo who owned all the land on this side and needed a good present for his wife who was furious with him. It was my idea!" and he thumped the floor while we beamed at his foresight and *Doña* Dora's generosity.

"*Bendito sea Dios!*" Elena bubbled and we all chimed in our blessings on God.

"And you and *Don* Francisco and *Doña* Luisa who helped us build the house!"

"*Bendito sea Dios!*" We all repeat.

Soon the late afternoon wind began to blow. I stand and all around, eyes fill.

"Don't go so soon!"

"Don't take so long to come back!"

"Send us some pictures, and a letter too!"

"Yes, of course," I answer to everything.

They prepare to walk me down to the town to catch the bus home. Since each of the small families lives down the side of the mountain, we will walk together and I will visit each house. Everyone but José in his chair and Alfonso who still lives at home will go along.

It was a procession down the mountain with the little boys and Silver in the front. First, we went to Maria Elena's house where she showed me her refrigerator, shook my hand and then stayed to cook dinner for her husband. Her little boys begged to continue down to the village with me. We proceeded a few yards; then we stopped at Rafael's house so I could see his pig and his two dogs and say good bye.

Still we continued, Elena and I, the little boys and Silver, Miriam, her baby, the toddler and oldest daughter. They live lowest on the mountain in the largest and most ornate house. It has a life size statue of the *Virgen del Carmen* in the front yard with red rose bushes planted around it. Francisco has a good job with the *Empresas Publicas*. The little boys dash in the doorway and reappear sober faced in an instant.

"*Que pasa?*" Miriam pushes the baby over at Elena and rushes ahead; the teen aged daughter gives the little girl over to the largest of the three little boys to run behind her mother. We stand outside in the shade of the *Virgen del Carmen*, admiring the roses, talking to the babies, wondering.

I tell Elena how proud I am of her family who all have nice families and their very own houses. As I talk about how well their lives are going, with children all in school, the smiles around me get more and more strained. Voices come from within. Everyone is trying to pretend nothing is wrong.

"Please, Elena," I say, hoping she will hear me, "I need to hurry on. Please say goodbye to Miriam and thank her and I will just continue on by myself. You know I know the way."

"*Un minuto, Doña* Debbie, let's just find out..."

Miriam appears at the door. Her face is red and splotched, but she braves a smile and swings open the door.

"My house is humble," she begins as they have all begun, "but please come in and be at home here."

As we go up the steps, Elena passes the baby to Miriam and they excuse themselves, muttering pardons. I am left with the three little boys and Silver, again in Eduardo's lap. He says his dog was named for the famous movie star dog, Silver, and then the others tell me that they have heard tales of my good dog Golo, now ten years dead. I pass time by asking them to tell me the stories of the saints and virgins on the walls of this room. They speak up clearly and well, standing as at attention and reciting the history of the famous *Virgen de Chinquinquira*. They call her as everyone does, affectionately, *La Chinca*.

Soon the women come carrying trays of Coca-cola in glasses and plates of cookies. Another daughter, this one twelve or so, joins us, and we make a pretense at conversation but everyone is heavy with sorrow.

"Miriam," I say as carefully as I can, "I know you must take care of your family and I must get home. Your house and family are very special, I'm happy for you and for Francisco--give him my best since it doesn't seem--"

Miriam begins to cry, turning and sobbing silently into the patio while her daughters all look at the floor. Elena's wide eyes are dark.

"It is Francisco. He drinks. Did you know? Hmm," she murmurs at my response, and continues to hum dully for several minutes while looking out the door.

"Now we must wait for the big boys to get home and send them for him. He's passed out down on the street. We were trying to figure how to get you to the bus without seeing him."

I hug Miriam and Elena; we all cry for our own reasons.

"Despite everything, your life is good. Look at your children!"

"*Bendito sea Dios!*"

"*Bendito sea Dios.*"

We all ring like bells, or is it the evening mass in the square that sounds up into the evening sky? I leave them there by the rose bushes and the Virgin, crying and waving, while I hurry down the middle of the street, looking neither left nor right, until I reach the square.

# GLOSSARY

*abuelita, abuela; abuelo* grandmother, grandfather
*agradecido, agradecida* grateful
*ahora* now
*A la orden* May I help you
*algo* something, a snack in the afternoon
*Alto* Halt, stop
*Arreglo zapatos* I repair shoes
*arriero* one who guides pack animals
*Bendito sea Dios* Blessed be God
*boba, bobo* fool, retarded
*bruto, brutos* animal
*brujo* wizard, witch doctor
*cama de matrimonio* double bed
*Casa del Sacerdote* priest's house, rectory
*Cocacolos* teenagers
*con gana* with will, forcefully
*criatura* creature
*Dios te salve María* Hail Mary, full of grace
*desagradecido, desagradecidos* ungrateful
*Don, Doña* titles of respect
*es posible; no es posible* possible, not possible
*eso sí* this is it, just right
*excusado* toilet
*feliz, felices* happy
*finca* country house
*flota* old fashioned bus, long distance bus
*fogonero* stoker, driver's helper

***fonda*** inn
***Gracias a Dios*** Thank God
***maestro de obra*** craftsman, builder
***mago*** magician, wizard
***manicomio*** insane asylum
***manzanilla*** camomile
***maldito*** damned
***mayordomo*** a person in charge of a *finca*
***mediamañana*** midmorning snack
***mi amor*** my dear, my love
***mijito*** little baby, term of affection
***mierda*** shit
***misa de gallos*** midnight mass
***merienda*** before bed snack
***Mucho gusto*** Pleased to meet you
***muertos*** dead people
***nada*** nothing
***Niño Jesus*** baby Jesus
***negro mala clase*** low class man
***novio*** sweetheart, fiancé
***nunca*** never
***Palacio del Osterizer*** Palace of the Osterizer
***panela*** a cake of unrefined sugar
***pena, penas*** sorrows, heartaches, problems
***pesebre*** nativity crèche
***pío, pío, pío*** peep, a children's song
***pobre*** poor
***por Dios*** for God's sake
***plaza mercado*** outdoor market
***pueblo*** village
***puta*** whore
***Qué dolor!*** What pain!
***quinceañera*** fifteenth birthday, celebration
***Sagrado Corazon*** Sacred Heart of Jesus

*sala* living room,
*silleta* wooden frame for carrying things
*sinvergüenza* shameless, contemptible
*sirvan, no sirvan* it works, it will do; it doesn't work, it won't do
*soledad* solitude
*solomito* filet mignon of beef
*superiora* Mother Superior
*señora de casa* lady of the house
*tapia* mud and wattle
*tierra, tierras* earth, land, lands
*tinto* sweet black coffee, expresso
*tía, tías, tío, tíos* aunt, aunts, uncle, uncles
*tragos* early morning refreshment
*vamos* let's go
*visita* visit

www.ingramcontent.com/pod-product-compliance
Lightning Source LLC
LaVergne TN
LVHW091537060526
838200LV00036B/646